PRAISE FOR *ASCENDANTS*

"Don Schechter's *Ascendants* is a provocative thought experiment on the future of consciousness and our quest to transcend biological mortality. It underscores the moral imperative to guide our technological ingenuity toward the common good, reminding us that the fate of humanity and the universe itself is in our hands."
—Ray Kurzweil, inventor, author, futurist

"*Ascendants* is a fascinating look at the intersection between science and philosophy and examines what can happen to those in a capitalistic environment. This modern cyberpunk adventure is a mirror to our current society and values in the way that the best science fiction intends."
—Erin Macdonald, PhD, science advisor for *Star Trek*

"*Ascendants* is a compelling techno-thriller unlike anything I've ever read. The story pulls you in—tackling life and death in unexpected ways that keep you turning the pages."
—Derek Tyler Attico, author of *The Autobiography of Benjamin Sisko* (*Star Trek* Autobiographies series).

"*Ascendants* feels like a high-concept *Black Mirror* episode stretched into a techno-thriller, maintaining a breakneck pace while forcing you to grapple with profound ethical questions. If you're a fan of cerebral science fiction, like the works of Philip K. Dick, or modern dystopian thrillers that blend fast action with deep moral complexity (think *Altered Carbon*), this book is a must-read."
—Manhattan Book Review

ASCENDANTS

DON SCHECHTER

ASCENDANTS

A NOVEL

This is a work of fiction. Names, characters, organizations, places, events, and incidents are either products of the author's imagination or are used fictitiously.

Copyright © 2026 by Don Schechter

In association with Charles River Media, Inc.®

All rights reserved.

No part of this book may be reproduced, or stored in a retrieval system, or transmitted in any form or by any means, electronic, mechanical, photocopying, recording, or otherwise, without express written permission of the publisher.

Without in any way limiting the author's and publisher's exclusive rights under copyright, any use of this publication to "train" generative artificial intelligence (AI) technologies to generate text is expressly prohibited. The author reserves all rights to license uses of this work for generative AI training and development of machine learning language models.

Published by GFB™, Seattle
www.girlfridayproductions.com

Produced by Girl Friday Productions

Cover design: David Fassett
Production editorial: Alyssa Brillinger

ISBN (paperback): 978-1-967510-34-4
ISBN (ebook): 978-1-967510-35-1

Library of Congress Control Number: 2025927031

First edition

In Memory of Johnny Lee Davenport (1950–2020)
A giant on stage and screen,
whose presence commanded meaning,
and a voice that unearthed truth with grace and gravity.
His spirit helped breathe life into Ascendants,
and his absence still reverberates.
The echoes of his voice still speak.
This book is for him.

PROLOGUE

In Medias Res

> *No one wants to die. Even people who want to go to heaven don't want to die to get there. And yet, death is the destination we all share. No one has ever escaped it. And that is how it should be, because death is very likely the single best invention of life.*
>
> —Steve Jobs, Stanford University, 2005

SAMUEL Lee squinted as his eyes adjusted to the light. As his surroundings slowly came into focus, he was grateful for the soft darkness enveloping him. He shifted, realizing that he was lying on his back. Every nerve, muscle, and joint ached. Sam's mind struggled to return to the void that had preceded his waking, but it escaped him.

There had been no dreams before his eyes had opened. No visions or theatrics of an active subconscious, no sense of time or space. And then the light and a realization. As unintelligible images flickered on a nearby panel, he recognized that a tether of some kind was connected to his arm.

Sam lay on a hospital bed, an IV in his arm, a heart monitor attached to his chest. Then, the most distressing thought emerged: He was supposed to be dead.

Ascension. The choice made to follow Alexandra. But who had dragged him back? Why was he here, alone and alive?

Corralling all his strength, he reached out to the small table next to him. His hand pushed past medical scanners, wound resealers, and other Institute medical devices. His fingers closed around a pair of surgical scissors, which he thrust into his wrist and then slid toward him.

An alert sounded as the blood poured out of Sam. A nurse rushed in, grabbing the scissors. She attempted to restrain him and treat his wound, but Sam shoved her away. He rolled off the bed, sending his full weight, and the tools on the cart, crashing to the floor. Two more nurses charged in and held him down.

"I'm supposed to be dead!" Sam screamed.

They pulled me back, Alexandra. But I won't stay. Not without you.

⏶

Ten years earlier...

Monica Thorne hated flying. Helicopters most of all. The pressure of the headset and the claustrophobic cabin tied her stomach in knots. The harness pressed down on her ribs. That helplessness of being a passenger was the same she'd felt when Henry Price weaseled free. She kept her eyes on her former target and lover. He had blindsided her, and it nearly cost her the job. No more weakness. Not now. This time the leash would hold.

Price's voice cut through the rotors. "What exactly do you want?"

"Nothing good has come from Ascension," she answered plainly, releasing her seat belt and moving closer. "It's time for Jacobs to go." Monica saw her opening: a slight tightening of his jaw and a clenched fist. She grabbed Henry's right hand and ran her thumb over his white knuckles.

"Think about it." Monica leaned into his shoulder. "You'd be in the position to call the shots. Keep the work on track without all these distractions. All the power you always wanted." Her free hand floated in the air, slow and deliberate, as though tracing invisible letters. "The Price Institute."

"No," he declared, pulling his hand free.

"No," Monica echoed. "'No' is not an option here."

"He's been my mentor, and he is my friend. I owe him—" Price began.

She cut him off. Enough. "I will destroy Jacobs. C.I.D. will take over The Institute. And if you force my hand, I will destroy you too!" The words landed like blows. Monica knew the power she still held over Henry.

The simple fact was, she alone could save Alexandra.

1

The Book of Teller

ONE

Maya

In the Beginning, the last days of the Ascendants began as if they were the setup of an ancient joke. A pastor, a rabbi, and an imam walked onto the dais...

—Elysa Antero, *Maya: In Her Own Words*, First Edition

It was 25 AA, but by the old calendar, AD 2060....

THE trio stood shoulder to shoulder, surveying the sparse congregation of Boston's Church of the Sacred Trust. Many homeless, most hopeless, and all of them seeking shelter from the government, The Institute, or both. It seemed as if God had insisted that salvation be forever out of their reach. Any fitting punch line to this joke of a life remained elusive.

Pastor Williams, the de facto spiritual leader of the city's Christians, spoke through the din of coughs and uneasy chatter.

"While it may be easy, in times as trying as these," he preached, "to believe that God the Father has left us and withdrawn his hand and grace, it falls to us, the faithful, to hold fast to the knowledge that the Lord will never and shall never leave us. Nor lead us to ruin."

Pastor Williams was a man in good health who had always appeared younger than his years. Even now, in his late seventies, he carried himself with the same poise that had defined him decades earlier. Equipped with unwavering confidence in his faith, he stood in front of his smallest Sunday congregation to date.

He continued, "For as we know from Psalm 22, 'Our fathers trusted in thee: they trusted, and thou didst deliver them. They cried unto thee, and were delivered: they trusted in thee, and were not confounded.'" He paused. "So, what can we take from this, as the storms gather outside our doors and seek to threaten the very foundations of our faith? Anyone?"

Those sitting in the pews shifted in their seats, looking up wearily. A response came from a woman sitting near the front. "That God will take care of us?" She cradled a baby who, Pastor Williams noted, hadn't made a sound since the woman's arrival.

Pastor Williams smiled at the woman. "Yes. As our fathers looked to him in times of woe and want, so too shall we. And we will find ourselves justly rewarded for our faith."

Rabbi Teller placed a hand on Pastor Williams's shoulder. "And it is also by our own actions within our community, and in solidarity, that we find the strength to survive. As it has been our tradition and our obligation to weather the storms of history, we do so once more in the company of our neighbors and our friends."

The melodic voice of the imam, Waleed Bashir, echoed throughout the church as he offered some final words of consolation.

"Inshallah, it will be known and remembered that our faiths in the one true God will not be erased from this world or the memory of it. We will, inshallah, prevail with his might and goodness."

Just as Williams called out, "All rise," a small band of men and women pushed through the old double doors at the entrance to the church, interrupting the service.

"Oh no," said the boisterous man at the helm of the company. "Please don't get up on our account." The group strode down the aisle, past the pews, and approached the altar.

Rabbi Teller stepped forward. "This is a house of worship and quiet contemplation. Not a place for Institute propaganda. We asked you not to return. Why must you persist in terrorizing us?"

The man scoffed and pointed behind him. "Because of those doors. No matter how much you blind yourselves with ignorance, those doors cannot keep the truth out." His voice boomed with righteous authority. He addressed the congregants, "They cannot shield you from the light of truth. The righteousness of scientific certainty!" He redirected his growing ire to the pulpit. "You three! You continue to recite your nonsense, drawn from irrelevant and outdated myths about apostles, prophets, and magical beings. You seek to silence the voices of the ones that have seen. My people come to share what The Institute's Viewing Rooms have proven." He shot his arm out and pointed to the congregation. "This flock," he spat, "these sheep deserve the truth."

"We know what you have seen," Rabbi Teller thundered, "and it is nothing short of the destruction of mankind!"

"Then hear from me," spoke a young woman from the band of intruders. "You rely on belief, but I have seen the life after. The founders of your faith were liars." She moved slowly toward the rabbi. "Belief is nothing more than hope. You hope your childish beliefs are true. You place a misguided certainty in them, but they constantly struggle against doubt. That is the nature of faith. What I have seen, what we have seen, hasn't inspired belief. It hasn't given us faith. It has given us clarity. Your fears, the ones that drive you to seek comfort here, are unnecessary. Ascension is the peace you have been seeking."

The leader smiled as he embraced her and spoke. "I was born a Biomass, and when I die, my body will rot. This is all the life I have; my actions on Earth don't matter. But I have glimpsed what lies ahead for Ascendants. Come with us to The Jacobs Institute and see for yourselves. Faith and good works do not secure your future. It is not the life you lead; it is the blood you bleed."

⚠

Paul Sutherland's body collapsed in an alley behind a dumpster. After escaping Institute custody, Paul had evaded their forces in the streets of Boston until two men tracked him down. He had put himself and his family in danger. All for one small act of rebellion. Of resistance. He wasn't a spy, or a revolutionary. He was—well, he had been—an analyst at The Institute. Paul was one of the "happy nerds," the group known for enjoying their data charts and line graphs.

His body was covered with sweat, even as the night turned bitter cold. This was a grimier, more feverish sweat than the nervous perspiration that had rolled down his forehead as he had stood over an Institute terminal. He'd rested the slatelink on top of the machine—a small, silver, rectangular device that his contacts had provided. The illicit file transfer began. His hands had trembled as the progress bar hung on 99 percent, then his body had flooded with relief as the process was completed.

His head had throbbed from hitting the doorframe while being shoved into some unmarked van. There was no way of knowing how long he had been unconscious before awakening in a cell, sitting in a metal folding chair, the taste of blood in his mouth. Paul had thought there was a man in a suit towering over him and asking questions. Demanding answers. It all blurred together. *Who are they? I know everything about you. Almost everything. Who are they? How do you contact them? Tell me everything, or they'll die.* Unfamiliar names were spoken in the darkness. Briggs? Maritz? *Are you a religious man?* Paul wasn't, though many people reconsidered their faith before they died. At least they used to.

Eventually, they left him alone in the cell. "Natalie, I'm sorry," he whispered into the dark. A click startled him out of his trance. The cell door opened, but no one was on the other side. No time to question it. Just run. Paul bolted down an empty hallway, through another open security door that led to a deserted corridor. Finally, he found the emergency exit of the building and burst through the door onto the busy street. Wind and rain pummeled his face. Alarms blared through every nearby slate and screen. A warning, in bold red text, appeared:

PROXIMITY ALERT. DANGEROUS CRIMINAL. SEEK SHELTER.

◬

The two men looming over Paul's limp body wore all-black uniforms and scuffed boots. Their clothes lacked any insignia that revealed their allegiances. Similarly wizened faces turned to each other, guns gripped tightly in leathery hands. As they had done with all their orders over the years, they executed their final commands without hesitation.

"And that's it," said one.

The second responded, "Are you ready for the next part?"

Taking a deep breath, the first nodded to his friend. "I've been looking forward to ascending for a long time. Now's as good a time as any."

The two men gripped each other in the firm embrace of longtime comrades. While neither would ever admit it to the other, both almost teared up before breaking apart. The friends looked each other in the eye and stepped back.

"Count of three?" asked the first.

"Yeah," answered the second.

"All right. One, two, three . . ."

The first lifted the pistol to the center of the other man's forehead. The .45-caliber bullet shattered the front of the other man's skull. The bullet left a gaping wound, spraying blood and brain matter all over the damp brick wall behind him. He turned the gun to rest on his own temple, then fired. The force of the bullet hurled him into the side of the dumpster.

No screams were heard; no sirens blared. No panicked pedestrians fled the scene. The hard rain fell mercilessly on three corpses and one filthy dumpster.

▲

In the rectory of the church just off to the side of the main hall, an exhausted Rabbi Teller took a seat on a folding chair. The cramped room housed the dirty, injured, and sick who lingered quietly as the rabbi's daughter, Rebecca, tended to their maladies. She looked to her father, concerned.

"Are you okay, Dad?" she asked, stripping off a pair of blue exam gloves.

"Me? I'm fine. It's good to see you. I'm glad you could make time to help out. I know it's not easy between the kids and the hospital shifts."

"It's really not a problem. Are you sure you're okay?"

He considered whether to burden his daughter with news

of the radicals, who had interrupted his service before exiting as dramatically as they had arrived. "It's just . . . the world I once knew seems truly gone now. It's all changed, and I can barely make sense of it. Maybe I've just lived too long."

"Dad, come on," Rebecca said.

The old rabbi waved it off. "I shouldn't say such things, I know. My love, how are those beautiful grandchildren of mine?"

"Well, the twenty-three-year-old apparently knows everything," she said, shaking her head.

Her father smiled broadly. "Maya is causing you some trouble?" It was as much a knowing statement as a question.

Rebecca nodded, rummaging through the bag of excess medical supplies taken from her work.

"Good," he said, chuckling, "Now you know how I felt. And how is little Hannah?"

"Sweet as ever. Quiet, though. She misses you."

"I'll visit her soon. Things have been so hectic lately, I'm afraid I've lost track of time." He watched as his daughter strode over to a nearby cot where a young woman sat silently. She was bloodied and beaten. When this woman had arrived at the rectory door earlier that day, the rabbi had done his best to help her settle in prior to the service.

"What happened to you?" Rebecca gently asked.

The woman said nothing.

"She hasn't spoken a word since she arrived. Wouldn't eat anything either," the rabbi said.

Rebecca kept her focus on the woman. She crouched down and took the woman's hands in her own. The woman's terrified gaze met hers.

"Who did this to you?"

The woman spoke with a delicate, broken voice. "Br- Breeders." Her hushed tone was laced with terror.

"Breeders?" Rebecca furrowed her brow.

The woman remained silent. Rebecca turned to her father. The rabbi wore a grave expression. "Dad?"

"We've heard about these terrible people and the terrible things they do. They're said to hide in dark, underground locations where they commit unspeakable acts," he replied.

"And no one escapes," the young woman whispered. "No one makes it out."

"But you did," Rebecca said as she grasped the woman's hands firmly. "And you're here now. You're safe."

The rabbi looked around the tight quarters of the makeshift shelter. Cots and bunks lined the walls with no space between them. "Every day it gets worse here. There's a little less room, a little less food, and a little less medicine to help these people. I honestly don't know if I can keep going. These days I feel like I'm just an old man taking up space. What good am I?"

Cleaning off a laceration on the young woman's arm, Rebecca replied, "Dad, these people have a place, this place, because of you three. You're the only ones who would help them, and few, if any, would likely still be alive. You should be proud of what you've done. Besides, you have what many of them have lost."

"And what's that?"

"Hope. Faith. Belief that there's a reason to keep living. No one seems to care anymore about those people out there. Whether they are undocumented, broken, or just Biomasses."

"Rebecca." He beamed proudly at his daughter. "I see your mother in you. How I miss her."

"I thought she was a skeptic," Rebecca playfully needled her father.

"She had faith in her family. And so should you. Maya may be hotheaded, but she's a good kid." He rose from his seat. "Give me a second, would you?"

As his daughter continued her work, the rabbi moved into an adjacent room. He approached a closet out of earshot.

"Maybe it's time to come out of your hiding spot," he whispered to the door.

A muffled female voice came from the closet. "No."

"There's no reason for you to be hiding like this. Let your mother know you're helping us. It's a wonderful thing, and I know she'd be very proud of you."

"Just tell me when she leaves," she said petulantly.

Finished with her patient, Rebecca walked into the room, joining her father.

"Dad, are you talking to a closet?" she asked, incredulous.

"Oh, no," he replied. Flustered, he reached his arm in and pulled out a black jacket, identical to the one he was wearing. "Just praying as I get a fresh jacket. I'm afraid this one is a bit . . . ripe." The rabbi betrayed a knowing glance and a raised eyebrow at the face hiding behind a rack of jackets.

"Well, Dad, I just got called in to the hospital. It sounds like I'm going to be there all night. I'm going to drop Hannah off at her friend's house, so she has a ride to school in the morning. Will you be okay here without me?"

"Of course, of course. You go. Save the world some more. Just do try to get some rest. You need to take care of yourself too," the old man said, kissing his daughter on the cheek. She grabbed her bag and coat, and Rabbi Teller watched until she left. He opened the closet door fully. "It's safe," he said, exasperated. "You can come out now."

Rebecca's oldest daughter, Maya, emerged. A slender woman, her dark hair framed her face, which sported a scowl. Her grandfather placed a kiss on her forehead.

"Don't you think you're a bit too old to be hiding from your mother in a closet?" he asked.

"She doesn't need to know everything I'm up to," she replied defiantly. "Besides, weren't you the one who said good deeds—"

"*Mitzvahs*," the old rabbi interjected.

"Right, *mitzvahs*. Weren't you the one who said those done out of sight and without praise were the purest kinds?"

"Ah! You've got me there. But seriously, Maya, try to get along with her. Usually, rebellion like this is for teenagers. Your twenties are when you're supposed to play nice while pleading for help with laundry and rent," he said in a playful tone.

"Work is tough right now and money is tight. You know how it goes."

"I know how it goes. Are you going to be okay here by yourself?"

"I'll be fine. I think I can handle it. Thanks."

Again, the old man kissed his granddaughter on the forehead and then left through a door leading onto the church floor. Maya produced a small folding knife from her pocket and moved toward the woman who sat on her cot gingerly rubbing her bandage.

"Next time, fight back," Maya insisted, pushing the knife into the woman's open palm.

The woman nodded shyly as she closed her fingers around the weapon.

Maya slipped out the back door and scurried down the dim street. She knew what they would tell her. What all of them would say at this moment. Her mother, sister, grandfather, every counselor, teacher, and cop she might meet, all saying the same thing. They'd tell her, "Be careful out there, Maya."

Her hand slipped into her jacket pocket, thumbing the hammer of her .38-caliber revolver. It was something she went to great lengths to obtain, and even greater lengths to make functional. Between finding the rare casings, restoring the chambers, and ensuring the hammer worked properly, it had proved to be far more challenging than expected. That work had thrust her into the underworld of back-alley trade.

The thrill of obtaining a hacked slate was nothing compared to her first time accessing the dark web of the slatenet.

Ranging from bomb-making and other terrorist tutorials to banned conversion theories, the slatenet's underbelly was filled with all sorts of illicit information. After considerable searching, she had finally found the solution. All she had needed was a full set of nail files and patience. Her efforts bore fruit after only a week of meticulous work.

Maya walked alone, aware of the dangers that lurked in the shadows. She knew that anything could happen on these streets, that the world was a terrible place. It was cold. Unfair. Savage. But at that moment, Maya was confident that she was far more dangerous.

TWO

Hannah

Kurzweil said death was a tragedy. That stuck with me. We pretend otherwise, but we are kidding ourselves when we claim we are comfortable with death. Our end is a nightmare.

—Cassandra Ellin, Interview, 2009

Bathed in sunlight next to the classroom window . . .

Hannah, the younger daughter of Rebecca Teller, neglected her assignment. As her kindergarten classmates worked together at small round tables, drawing pictures of their pets and families, Hannah's slate remained untouched. She stared at the blank screen. Mr. Lee, the lead teacher, approached her desk.

"Hannah, why aren't you drawing?"

Hannah shrugged.

"Are you feeling all right?"

"I'm okay," Hannah softly replied.

"You know you're free to draw whatever you'd like as long as it tells a story about Ascension. It doesn't have to be exactly like the book I just read to the class."

"I know."

Mr. Lee turned to a nearby student. "What are you drawing, Jade?"

Jade held her slate up; she had drawn a smiling lady in the sky. "An Ascendant."

"That looks great," Mr. Lee said, "but you know that Ascendants don't go to the sky, right? That's an old superstition."

"I know."

"So, where do they go?" he prodded.

"Somewhere else. Without any . . . uh . . . ," Jade stuttered.

"Biomasses," Mr. Lee finished. He turned back to Hannah. "How about you give it a try? Think about what might make you happy and go from there."

Hannah drew a straight line and stared blankly at him.

An administrative aide walked into the classroom and went straight to Mr. Lee. "Sam, your wife just messaged the office looking for you. Your phone must be off."

"Damn!" Mr. Lee exclaimed. Hannah and her classmates giggled as he rushed out of the classroom.

A cloud rolled past the sun, temporarily blocking it and plunging the yard into dark shadows. As darkness moved across Hannah's face, she decided to do what her teacher asked, even though it was silly. Her sister, Maya, hated everything about Ascension, and so Hannah would too. She scribbled over the screen until all the white was turned to black. She looked back to the recess yard outside the window and continued to think of Maya. Why, she wondered, was her sister so often sneaking in and out of the house?

These thoughts followed her into lunch and then recess.

Across the yard, she saw some of her classmates huddled around a patch of dirt. Curious, she walked over just in time to hear a common slur that was often spoken from the mouth of her class's most obnoxious bully.

"Stupid cabbage," Logan spat.

△

Though The Jacobs Institute's public position was that testing be carried out no earlier than the age of eighteen and that Ascension itself was not possible before the age of forty, the practice of testing at birth prevailed. At the prestigious and exclusive Jacobs Academy, all students except for Hannah were tested and proven Ascendants. This annoyed Logan Adams, whose parents met in an Ascendant social club designed to celebrate their status. Logan and his older brother, Blake, had established reputations for bullying Biomasses.

"Stupid cabbage!" Logan chortled as he and two of his friends circled a small anthill, using a magnifying glass to burn ants with the power of the sun. "All of these stupid ants are cabbages! 'Wasted matter,' my brother says!" he exclaimed, shifting the glass to zap another ant.

The roasting of the insects terrified Hannah. She was enraged that her classmates thought people like her own sister, a Biomass, were nothing but ants to burn. She might secretly wish to be an A like her classmates, but Hannah assumed that she, too, was a "cabbage."

She stormed over to the squat, chubby boy and his chuckling cohort. They were on their hands and knees, bent over their own little holocaust. Hannah swiftly kicked his side, sending him crashing over. His magnifying glass hurtled to the ground and broke into pieces. The two smaller boys retreated several steps, shocked at the small dark-haired girl. Logan rolled over and scrambled to his feet.

"You stupid cabbage! You can't kick me!" he shrieked.

Hannah stood her ground, glaring angrily at the larger boy. "Stop killing them!" she shouted. "They didn't do anything to you!"

"Eat dirt, you cabbage!" the boy screamed.

"I'm not a cabbage!"

"No one knows what you are!"

"You're just a big bully, Logan! And I'm not afraid of you."

"You should be, cabbage! My whole family are Ascendants. Your family will probably just die here in the dirt with the ants!"

In a way that would have made her older sister proud, Hannah quickly balled a fist and hurled it at the boy's face, landing a punch to his nose. Maya had taken great pains to teach her little sister how to throw the perfect left hook. Hannah had taken to it easily, maintaining good form with a forceful swing, as was evident from the blood gushing from the bully's nose. Logan's eyes filled with tears and his knees gave out. He dropped to the ground and cried hysterically.

The other two boys stared in disbelief at the sight of their bloodied and screeching leader. They bolted away in search of a teacher. Hannah, shocked by her own actions, stared at her fist as Logan's wails filled the yard. From the door leading back into the building, Mr. Lee rushed to the site of the violence.

"What happened?" he said, kneeling to check on the boy.

Logan blubbered, "She hit me!"

"Is this true, Hannah?" he asked admonishingly.

"He was killing innocent little bugs and calling me a cabbage!" she protested. Hannah's excuse was not enough for her teacher, who helped the boy to his feet and sent him off with another teacher to the nurse's office. Mr. Lee took Hannah by the arm and led her back inside.

◮

Rebecca was nearing the end of her rounds at the Jacobs Institute Hospital. After taking an extended shift working in the emergency room following her night at the church, she had almost finished twenty-four hours of medical care. On top of sheer exhaustion, she was anxious at the thought of what Maya might have been up to in her absence.

Rebecca was aware that Maya had been keeping odd hours, heading off into the city to do god-knew-what with god-knew-who at god-knew-where. Her fears had grown even more pronounced since hearing of the Breeder gangs that were rumored to be lurking in any number of bars, nightclubs, and social spots, abducting young women. Despite this, all attempts to talk with her about these dangers had been met with the same resentful resistance that had dominated Maya's teenage years.

After the dramatic collapse of Maya's living situation involving an ill-advised romance with an older man, Rebecca had hoped her oldest daughter moving back into their family home might allow them to reconnect. Despite her best efforts, Rebecca found the divide between them growing.

Her train of thought derailed as a team of paramedics, flanked by a pair of Institute officers, rushed two stretchers into the emergency room. Following this commotion, a third stretcher was rolled in without the same sense of urgency.

"What have we got?" Rebecca asked, pursuing the stretchers to the exam rooms.

"Three gunshot wounds: two As, one already ascended en route, and that guy behind is a B. The A has a weak pulse and labored, irregular breathing. We just received confirmation of Ascension orders in the database for both As," one paramedic said, working with his colleagues to hoist the two bodies of the old Ascendants onto operating tables.

"What about the B?" Rebecca asked, glancing at her slate, which quickly connected to the PACT bots inside the two patients. The device displayed a full-body scan and all available data and medical records on the screen.

"Oh. The B has two hits. One to the chest, one to the abdomen. Probably not worth your time," he said.

Rebecca scoffed at the paramedic. One of her colleagues entered the exam room. "Good, Sarah, please help me stabilize this man."

"Rebecca, you know policy requires that we administer Ascension prior to moving on to Biomass treatment," Sarah replied, readying a lethal injection.

"Do what you want, but I'm going to try and save both their lives," Rebecca said sternly, unwilling to comply with the hospital's policy regarding triage of Ascendant and Biomass patients. She approached the Biomass. "My god. It's Paul!"

"You know him?" Sarah asked.

"My sister's husband! Number three is my brother-in-law." Rebecca feverishly worked to stabilize him.

A nurse entered the room, walked to a nearby cabinet, and prepped a needle. She quickly injected the other patient with the euthanasic drug solution.

"What are you doing?" Rebecca shouted as the old man flatlined.

"Administering Ascension, Doctor," the nurse stated.

"We could have revived him!"

"He had an Ascension order."

"That's bullshit. There was time to save him. And what about the gunshots, huh? Don't you think the police may have wanted to speak to him?"

One of the officers spoke up from the door. "Security on the scene already ruled it a triple shooting as part of a robbery. Nothing needed for the investigation. The Ascension order stands."

Rebecca pushed the nurse aside and frantically prepared the patient for the operating room. She muttered under her breath, "Utterly barbaric policy."

"Excuse me, Doctor?" said the nurse.

"Nothing. The A is gone now. Help us with Paul."

Paul's vitals plummeted, and a loud beeping alarm sounded as he flatlined. Rebecca shouted out an order for a crash cart. She grabbed a vial of emergency recovery PACT bots and applied the gel medium directly to Paul's wounds, allowing the nanoagents to enter through the damaged tissue. She tried every tool at her disposal, but it was futile. Head hung low, tears welling in her eyes, Rebecca struggled to speak as she declared him dead. Sarah placed her hand on her friend's shoulder.

As Rebecca pulled her phone from her pocket, hesitating to make the impossible call to Natalie, it vibrated and rang. She answered the call in Voice mode without looking at the display ID. "Hello?" she asked in a shaky voice.

"This is Headmistress Audrey Wallace at the Jacobs Academy," the shrill British voice said from the other end. "Your daughter has been involved in an altercation on the playground today, and we're going to need you to come over and pick her up."

Rebecca sighed deeply. Wiping away her tears, she replied, "I'll be right there. I'm just leaving work now."

Rebecca clicked the Ignition button on her key fob as she made her way into the parking lot. She sank into the seat of her car. Her seat belt automatically fastened around her, and the driverless navigation system illuminated, asking where she wanted to go.

"Call Nat," she said in a trembling voice.

It seemed like an eternity between issuing the command and when her sister picked up.

"Hey, Becca!" she said, her face displayed on the car's windshield. "What's going on? Are you okay?"

"Natalie," she exhaled, "I'm so sorry. . . ."

Hannah was dwarfed by her chair as she sat across from Headmistress Wallace. She made herself even smaller by crossing her arms and slumping down. The headmistress scowled at her. The silence dragged out for an eternity, at least to Hannah, until the door finally opened.

A visibly distraught Rebecca entered the office, taking a seat beside her daughter. Her eyes were puffy and red.

"Is everything okay, Dr. Teller?" Wallace asked apathetically.

Rebecca nodded. "Just a very hard day." There was no need to bring up Paul in front of Hannah yet. One problem at a time.

"I see. Well," Wallace said, pivoting to her immediate concerns. "Hannah was involved in a violent altercation with another student."

"What?" Rebecca asked in disbelief.

"Yes, she attacked a boy in the yard. I've spoken with him and two other students. All three say that Hannah, unprovoked, kicked and punched the boy. She hit so hard she bloodied his nose."

"He was calling them cabbages! He calls me a cabbage all the time!" Hannah blurted out in protest.

"I don't understand," Rebecca said, glancing between her daughter and the headmistress. "What does 'cabbage' mean?"

"It's nothing," said Wallace.

"It means Bs, Mom! Like Maya," Hannah continued.

"Hannah, that is enough!" Wallace hissed. "Dr. Teller, I would like to speak with you privately. Hannah, go wait outside the door."

The young girl looked to her mother, unsure if she should comply. Rebecca nodded to Hannah. "Go ahead, sweetie. Wait for me outside."

Wallace led Hannah to a seat in the hall just outside the office, then closed the door and returned to her own seat.

"This is not the first time we've had to address the problem of Hannah's behavior like this, Dr. Teller. In truth, I can remember similar problems with your other daughter, and we know how she ended up."

"Ended up? Maya was overly scrutinized and discriminated against. You all forced her to react and defend herself."

"And yet, you enrolled Hannah in the same institution," Wallace said snidely. "Clearly we must be doing something right despite your baseless accusations."

Rebecca could admit to herself that Wallace had a point. Her desire to send Hannah to a top school outweighed the potential social problems her daughter was bound to run into. But she knew Maya, and she knew the school administration itself was not entirely at fault here. Maya was born with a rebellious streak. Rebecca dismissed her guilt and pressed on; what Wallace didn't know couldn't be used against her. "Hannah has done nothing wrong. She is nothing but a genuinely sweet girl."

"May I be frank with you?" asked Wallace, disinterested in whatever defense Rebecca may have been keen to offer.

"Because you haven't been frank yet?"

"We both know that I cannot compel you to have Hannah tested at this time. Nor can I compel you to seek PACT injections for her even though it is in her best interest."

"The Institute itself advises against injecting young children with PACT or testing for Ascendant status so early."

"The general public, I suppose. But this academy is intended solely for Ascendants, and you have continued to exploit a loophole that—It honestly baffles me . . . why the board would continue to allow—"

"What does this have to do with anything?" Rebecca interrupted.

Wallace took a deep, dramatic breath. "It has to do with the world these children are growing up in."

"Is that what this is about? Testing? Whether or not she is an Ascendant?"

"Dr. Teller. You may be an Ascendant. But your oldest daughter is not. And what was the status of your husband?"

"I fail to see what that has to do with whatever happened today."

"What happened today was that your daughter, who I am certain is a Biomass, though I cannot prove it without your consent to test, assaulted the son of a respected Ascendant family. Tell me, Dr. Teller, exactly what sort of precedent do you think that sets for either child when it comes to what life will be like when they're all grown up and out of school. Do you wish for Hannah to be like Maya? Violent and ill-tempered? In a position to think she is on equal footing with Ascendants, right up until the point where she is too old to function in the reality of the world she inhabits?"

"Why do I have the suspicion that this is going to be another instance in which you insist I have her tested?" Rebecca's voice dripped with sarcasm.

"Dr. Teller, though I cannot legally enforce—"

"No. You can't," Rebecca shot back. "And you won't. She is six years old. Six! Everyone is more concerned with what a blood test has to say about her future than her own potential. If I have to protect my daughter by keeping your damned test away from her for as long as I can, even if only so that she can have an actual childhood, that is what I, as her mother, am going to do!" Rebecca trembled with anger.

"And what happens after her childhood, Dr. Teller? What if she grows up with the idea that some bright future awaits only to find out that she was denied foreknowledge of a different reality because you wanted her to live in a delusion? What if the money and encouragement you've put into her education, along with the time and resources this academy has dedicated to it, ultimately means nothing? What sort of life is that? Do you truly want her to end up like your other daughter?"

Hannah listened to the muffled sounds of her headmistress and her mother arguing. Her eyes darted up and down the center hallway, which was mostly empty. From down the hall, a trio of men approached her seat. Two men in white lab coats followed another tall man in a suit.

The suit-wearing man sported a closely trimmed beard and had immaculate jet-black hair. To Hannah, he looked like some sort of businessman, the kind who rode around in fancy cars and limousines. She looked at him curiously, unsure if she recognized him from the news shows that her mother often left on.

The man was Henry Price, chief operations officer for The Jacobs Institute. Hannah had indeed seen him before, as had nearly everyone else on the planet with access to a computer, wall display, smartphone, or slate. Had she realized this, Hannah might've been starstruck. But at her age, the news and talk shows were just boring grown-up stuff.

Price gave a wave to the two technicians who accompanied him, sending them into a vacant office. The heated conversation on the other side of the headmistress's office gave him pause. He turned to the short row of chairs and finally noticed Hannah.

"Hello," he said warmly, offering the young girl a smile as he did. "Sounds like she's busy, huh? Mind if I join you?"

Hannah stayed silent.

Settling down into the chair beside her, Price glanced at the young girl. "Is that your mom in there?" he asked.

Hannah nodded.

"Ah. Are you in trouble?"

Hannah looked down at her dangling feet.

"You know, when I was a kid, I used to get in all kinds of trouble at school myself."

"Trouble?" Hannah asked, looking up to the man beside her.

"I'd get picked on by bullies all the time. One day, finally, I started fighting back, and oh boy, the school did not like that too much. Is that what happened to you?"

"I guess so."

"Well, between you and me, good job. Never give a bully an inch. Don't let anyone get in your way. Learn to stand your ground now and when you're all grown up, there'll be nothing and no one that can get in your way. By the way, I'm Henry," he said, sticking out his hand.

Placing her small hand into his large one, she replied, "I'm Hannah."

"It's nice to meet you, Hannah." Price noticed a display screen behind her that slowly scrolled through digital drawings by the students. Amid a series of bright and colorful figures was a single page where the picture box was entirely blacked out. He rose and tapped the screen, pausing on the dark, imposing image. At the top, above the large blacked-out box, the artist's name was listed: Hannah Teller.

"This is your work?"

"Yeah."

"I had a feeling it was yours."

Her eyes lowered.

"What is it?" he asked.

"It's death."

"Fascinating. Why did you draw it?"

"I don't know. Well, Mr. Lee told us to draw something about Ascendants."

"And this is what you think of Ascension, Hannah?"

Nodding, she replied, "Juliana and Laila and Bobby from class all say I'm a weirdo."

"I see. I wouldn't worry too much about what they say. Most of the best people in the world started out a little strange." He settled back in his seat, crossing one leg over the other. "Mr. Lee, you said?"

"Yes," Hannah said, still avoiding eye contact with Price.

"You know, I actually know Sam Lee. He's a nice man, isn't he?"

"He's really nice to me. Usually. Even though I'm not tested. But I still go to school here. He was Maya's teacher too." She spoke quickly. Her feet swung back and forth, skimming the floor.

"No kidding. And your last name is Teller?"

"Yup."

Price leaned back slightly, studying the girl for a moment. "You know, I think I used to know someone with that name. I'll be right back."

"Okay," Hannah responded, watching Price disappear into the nearby office where the two medical technicians from earlier had gone.

Price entered the room and commanded, "Give me one of the slates." Pulling his own personal unit from the briefcase that one of the technicians had been carrying for him, Price shook his head. "No, one of the testing units."

"Oh, are we running tests here, sir? I thought we were just here for Mrs. Wallace," the tech asked, confused.

"Don't worry about what I need it for, just give me one. And a glove."

Producing a sterile package, the technician first pulled out a small aerosol spray bottle. Price removed his jacket, rolled up his sleeves, and presented both hands. The technician proceeded to spray Price's hands with a fine, clear mist. The chemical itself was a sealant used in lieu of exam gloves and formed an invisible biological containment barrier around the surface on which it was sprayed. Initially developed by The Jacobs Institute for use in combat first aid, it had become a common item used by paramedics and was found in all modern first aid kits.

With the seal in place, Price took the package and removed the fresh slate. He activated it with a tap and a face scan and issued further instructions to his technicians. "I want the results from this test kept encrypted and off the network, understood? I don't want any grumblings from Charles about testing children."

The pair nodded their agreement, and Price left the room. He swiped through a few icons and brought up a game for young children. He took his seat next to Hannah and played the opening level, which consisted of matching various pictures of animals with one another. This, in turn, fed a singing and dancing panda bear.

"I always get bored when I have to wait for people to finish talking. I like to keep a game handy for when that happens," he told the girl, whose attention was drawn to the game.

"What is that?" she asked.

"Oh, it's called *Wayfinder*. Would you like to give it a try?"

"Yes!" she exclaimed.

Hannah swiped and tapped the screen, getting a feel for how it was played. Price interjected with pointers and instructions.

"See," he said, swiping two identical zebras. His sealed fingers remained separated from the screen by the invisible, micron-thin barrier that covered his hands. "You have to find the right two pictures, just like that."

Hannah nodded and continued playing. An army of PACT bots emerged from the screen and crawled up her hands. Invisible to the naked eye and producing a mild anesthetic, the bots found the smallest of open pores on her skin and buried themselves deep into her tissue.

She felt nothing as the bots accessed multiple capillaries within her hands, taking the smallest samples of blood and tissue before their programming commanded them to reverse course and reintegrate with the slate. Hannah racked up points in the game as a screening program ran in the background, analyzing the bots' data.

Typically, results would populate within a few seconds and be transmitted soon after to The Institute's database. However, some analyses took longer than others. Potential anomalies were flagged and examined by something beyond Price's control and then relayed back to The Institute without arousing suspicion. Hannah's results would take significantly longer to reach their intended destination.

Meanwhile, she managed to clear level one, to the delight of the panda.

```
Region 1-North American East Coast Data
Center-Rack 1003, Server 47

System Report: Test sample analysis
detected en route to Jacobs genomic
database.

Outcome: New subject identified: Hannah
Teller.

Command: Delay transmission of results to
The Jacobs Institute.

Directive: Determine validity of results.

System Report: Analysis confirmed.

Progeny identified.

> _
```

"My other daughter?" Rebecca erupted at Headmistress Wallace. "I suppose you mean my other, pointless, Biomass daughter? My useless—what did she call it?—cabbage of a daughter? Is that what you mean?" Rebecca seethed.

"I mean your delinquent daughter, Dr. Teller. The one who was expelled for fighting and countless other behaviors unbecoming of a student at the Jacobs Academy. The one who, much like Hannah, exhibited signs of animalistic behavior that culminated in the incident resulting in her expulsion, which our counselors attributed to the uncertainty of her status and the ultimate shock of learning that she is a—"

"She is what? Garbage? Human garbage?" Rebecca could have easily leapt clean over the headmistress's desk and throttled her.

"Biomass, Dr. Teller. Learning that she is a Biomass."

Rebecca shot up from her seat. "We're done here. Message me the terms of Hannah's suspension or whatever it is you plan to do, and don't be surprised if you hear from my lawyer." She jerked the door open furiously.

"Of course," Wallace replied tersely.

Outside the office, Rebecca stopped to find Hannah contentedly playing on a slate, sitting beside a middle-aged man. "Hannah, come on. We're leaving."

"But, Mom. Just wait. One more."

"Now!"

Taken aback by her mother's uncharacteristic snap, Hannah handed the slate to Price. "Thanks, Henry."

Price rose from his seat. "It was very nice to meet you, Hannah," he said.

Rebecca did a double take. She was in the presence of the third most powerful man in the world. Startled, she blurted, "Mr. Price."

"You must be Dr. Teller, is that right?" he said, offering her his hand.

She took it, shaking his hand in one firm motion. "Yes. Yes, that's right."

Tucking the slate under his arm, he smiled. "I was just talking with your lovely daughter here. She is quite a pleasant young girl."

"Thank you, Mr. Price. We really need to go," she stammered as she grabbed Hannah's hand.

"Of course. Please, don't let me keep you."

Rebecca tugged Hannah's hand as she marched for the door but abruptly halted after a few steps. She turned to Price with an air of indignant confidence. "Can I just say that while The Institute maintains a great school here, that woman, Mrs. Wallace, is an intolerant, unprofessional shrew, and I think you should sincerely think about replacing her with someone who respects all of the students here."

Price, unfazed by her candor, maintained his warm demeanor. "We definitely appreciate feedback from the parents of our students, or members of any of our facilities. I was actually just headed in to speak with Mrs. Wallace. I'll address your concerns with her personally."

Rebecca nodded, empowered by his words and by the face of the stunned headmistress over his shoulder. "Well, thank you then. It was a pleasure to meet you."

"Same to you, Dr. Teller," he said, courteously bowing his head.

"Come on, Hannah. We need to go get your sister."

The mother and daughter made their way to the exit. Price beckoned the pair of technicians to join him, handing one of them the slate from under his arm.

"Inform me of anything of interest later," Price said.

Price entered Wallace's office, closing the door behind him.

▲

Price spoke first, as he took a seat opposite Wallace. "I'm sorry for just dropping in like this. It was something of a last-minute addition to my schedule. I hope you don't mind."

"Not at all, sir. It's an honor to have you anytime. I hope that woman didn't bother you too much."

"Not at all. But that issue is of no concern to me. I'm here to thank you for the brilliant work you've done here. We've been monitoring the students' progress, and frankly, I'm amazed at how well things have been going under your leadership."

"Thank you, sir. Thank you so very much."

Price smiled broadly, folding his hands in his lap. "No, thank you. Because you've managed to do so much here, we thought it might be time to reward you for all of your hard work."

Her brow furrowed. "Reward?"

"Yes," Price replied, turning to the door. "Marcus! Can you come in here?" His raised voice carried out into the hall. Marcus, one of the technicians, entered carrying a small metal case. Placing the case on the edge of the headmistress's desk, he unclasped the latches and opened it up. He withdrew a small syringe filled with a thick golden liquid and handed it to Price.

"You see, we feel that you've made just about as much progress here as anyone could have hoped for, and we wanted to reward you with this."

Wallace's eyes were transfixed by the syringe in Price's palm. "I'm not sure I understand."

"We've come to offer you an early retirement. We'd like to grant you your Ascension today." Price leaned in and extended his arm, offering her the syringe.

"But my husband and I, we planned on ascending together, after some years enjoying retirement. I just don't think—"

"Your husband has already ascended, Mrs. Wallace. We contacted him first. I understand the hesitation, I really do. But really, why put this off? Anyway, as I mentioned, he's already moved on and is waiting for you. I do apologize for disrupting your plans, but we feel it is best to move things along as circumstances dictate." His arm remained extended, insistent.

"He's already . . ." Her words failed her as reality sank in.

"Yes. I'm sure he is waiting for you."

Wallace slowly reached out and took the needle.

Price rose from his seat. "I will give you some privacy now. Congratulations, Headmistress Wallace. You've served your students, all of us, brilliantly, and you fully deserve this reward. Goodbye."

Price stepped briskly into the hallway as Marcus pulled the door closed. Wallace uncapped the syringe and slid the needle into a blue vein on the back of her hand. Her body convulsed. A chill swept through her and she fell into blackness and silence.

In the hallway, Price issued orders to both technicians. "Have a disposal crew come in and sort her out. Then send a team to her house to take care of the husband. See to it that he self-ascends. Keep it clean and quiet. Make sure to check their house thoroughly for any other confidential materials that they may have stolen. Have her body brought back and prepped for the Corpus. The husband can be discarded; he has been a nuisance for far too long."

"Yes, sir. Oh, and the analysis of the little girl is still running," Marcus said.

"It's taking this long?" Price questioned.

"It may be an issue with the unit." Marcus shrugged. "It's a newer model. I'll keep you posted. Should we inform Dr. Jacobs of Wallace's transfer, sir?"

Price shook his head. "No, this is of no concern to Charles. Besides, he has some personal business of his own to attend to. Best we leave him be."

▲

Sam Lee doted on his wife. It was a daily ritual that brought as much comfort as it did sadness. Alexandra Lee, formerly Alexandra Jacobs, wasted away in their bedroom as a result of her degenerative condition. Still, there was a radiance to her that none could deny. Least of all, her loving husband.

Sam was a faithful man in many respects. In addition to his dedication to Alexandra, he fully embraced the Ascension awakening when it was first announced. As the series of scientific revelations grew into a brand-new paradigm that diminished the impact of religious belief, his friends suspected it was Sam's desire to gain approval from Alexandra's father that led him to follow Institute directives so closely. In reality, Sam's allegiance stemmed more from the peace and serenity that came from the certainty Ascension offered. It provided the assurance that he and his beloved would be together when her body could no longer keep up the fight.

"Would you like some more water?" he asked quietly, sitting beside her.

She shifted herself up in bed. "No, but I wouldn't mind a good Cabernet," she joked.

Sam smiled. "I thought you only liked white wines."

"That was before. Red. White. Tastes the same to me now."

"How about some green tea?"

"Tequila sunrise? Or no, what about a margarita? Even without the little umbrella in it. What does a dying girl need with paper umbrellas?"

"Hang on," Sam replied. "You're just a bit under the weather and your birthday is right around the corner."

"You know, most women dread turning forty." A hint of a smirk touched her lips.

Sam looked over to a plate of barely touched sushi, which remained on the nightstand. "Did you eat?"

"No. Just wasn't that hungry. Got lost in my book."

Sam plucked the small paperback from beside the plate. "*Advanced Mortality*, huh?"

"You know I've always liked Volander's work. I never read this one though, for some reason. Guess it feels appropriate now. I think it's interesting to read the thoughts of someone whose work I respect as he faced the same sort of finality that's in front of me."

"Don't talk like that, Alex."

"Sam, come on. They said I wouldn't make it to ten, let alone forty."

"Yet here you are."

"Yes." Alexandra nodded. "Here I am. Limping across a finish line just so I could say that I did it when it's all over." Her gallows humor was for her own comfort, but she didn't fail to recognize how it wounded Sam. She took his hand in hers. "Sam, we knew this would happen. We knew we'd find ourselves here one day. I have to come to terms with it in my own way, just as you should."

When it had become clear that Alexandra's condition was incurable, the couple had made a pact to ascend together at Sam's insistence. The bargain was struck because Alexandra knew there would be no convincing him otherwise. She would ascend and he planned to follow, but only so long as she held out until her fortieth birthday. This was due equally to Alexandra's own stubborn nature demanding that she outlive her prognosis, and his desire to secure as much time with her as possible. Two months earlier, Sam had procured the necessary Ascension kit from The Institute to ensure he could follow her into the next world.

In the top drawer of their nightstand rested the small, polished cherrywood case holding two full syringes. For many Ascendants, death was seen as a welcome change of pace. The Institute offered a wide array of Ascension products and services, marketing designer death experiences with immersive settings of serene landscapes and calming music. One could even choose their poison, all of which were branded with names like "Release" and "Transition." Their nightstand drawer contained a kit called "The Third Act."

"I'm happy to go with you, Alex. I just feel like we deserved more time together."

"We've had more time together than we were told, my love," she said, gripping his hand tighter as tears welled up in her eyes. Though the daughter of Charles Jacobs, founder of The Institute and architect of Ascension, Alexandra did not share her husband's certainty. She was frustrated that her attempts to live in the moment often came into conflict with Sam's more eternal perspective.

Sam returned to her book. "Still going for the hard copies. A dozen slates and wall displays in this house, and you prefer paper."

"The words are more real that way. How can a tablet filled with text files impress anyone? A shelf full of books is the finest decoration a home can have. That, and a wine cellar."

"Perhaps you're right on both fronts. We never got around to building that cellar," Sam said as a smile crept onto his face. He had never cared one way or the other but had always found Alexandra's affinity for actual books to be a charming idiosyncrasy. Throughout their living room and study, the walls were lined with volumes ranging from paperback novels to fine hardcovers, some emblazoned with gold leaf and other decorations. "Though I think I prefer artwork, myself."

"I know. But you wanted to put that weird Salvador Dalí print in the living room. The books are better."

This inspired a genuine laugh from Sam, who was quickly joined by his wife. The two laughed until they were interrupted by the sound of the doorbell.

"I'll be right back," Sam said.

He leaned in and gave Alexandra a kiss on the forehead

before making his way down the hall. The last rays of sunlight splashed along the walls, illuminating sections of the house's central hall with pale orange light. By the time Sam finished the short walk down the corridor, the home's automated systems had already turned on the lights.

Sam opened the door and froze.

"Hello, Sam," said Charles Jacobs. "I hope you don't mind us dropping by like this."

THREE

Bygones

If you really want young people to do a thing, simply make it taboo. They won't be able to resist.

—The Fist

At the Blue Water Diner...

MAYA cleared another table of plates. She had taken a job as a waitress only after running out of other options. She loathed everything about food service. The customers. Her boss. The food. But she needed the money, and thanks to her best friend, Amy, slinging sandwiches, dumplings, and sodas had become her daily routine.

She smirked as she pocketed the cash tip left by a party of three. Scribbled on a napkin beneath the bill was a small message: *taxation is theft*, with a doodle of a heart topping the letter *i*.

taxation is theft

Although hard cash was rare, it was not uncommon for customers to leave it on the table so as to allow her tip to go unnoticed by the government. This was not the first time she saw the libertarian mantra scribbled, and she was thankful for her patrons.

Once the table was cleaned and wiped down, Maya neatly reset the booth in preparation for the next party. A bell rang out from the kitchen, followed by the refrain "Order up!" as two plates of dumplings and french fries were slapped down on a counter. The diner advertised itself as "authentic American," yet its best seller was chicken dumplings. Recent trends fusing Dutch and Asian cuisines had swept through the culinary circles of every city. Rijsttafel boats—rice served with giant dumplings packed with a variety of side dishes, from potato patties to beef stew—were particularly popular these days. She snatched up the meals from beneath the heat lamp and rounded the bar to serve them to a teenager and a younger boy in a booth along the wall. She watched as one slurped down a soda and grinned. Maya listened in on their conversation.

"Tell it to me again," said the younger one, who Maya guessed was around Hannah's age.

"Again? Okay, Logan," responded the other, probably his older brother, putting down his empty cup. "So, it started with murders. They'd just snatch 'em up wherever they'd find them and gut them. Just chop 'em to pieces and dump those pieces in the streets."

"That's gross, Blake."

"Exactly."

Maya placed the meals down and addressed the storyteller. "You want a refill?"

"Yeah, thanks," Blake replied, returning to his story. "Then a huge bomb blew up half of the building in an instant. People were on fire all over the place, and as the flames ripped through the building, loads of people just jumped. Then bam! Splat!"

Maya continued to listen, the muscles tensing in her jaw.

"Why'd they jump?" Logan asked.

"Because it was either that or burn to death. You know what happens to a body when it burns?" The tone of the story grew sadistic in the same way a teenage boy might find gratification in retelling the events of a horror film. Logan shook his head. "Your skin cooks up like fried chicken and you get blisters all over your body. Then, your blood boils and your eyes explode in your head. You just cook like a sausage."

"Ew. That's messed up."

Maya fumed at the teenager's dramatization of the story of the Bombing. She had been a teenager herself when she witnessed the attack unfold on her home displays. The live news feeds, the leaked and unedited images of carnage, bloodshed, and terror, had scarred her deeply. Yet since that day, she felt compelled to review the footage. Maya would periodically request PACT transmissions from the city news archives and experience the smoke-filled halls, and watch as corpses burned to a crisp. The few who were still alive threw themselves out the windows, falling to their deaths. She felt her eyes watering and skin burning. She wanted to scream.

Maya knew that this ritual of hers was unhealthy, obsessive. But she couldn't stop experiencing it. Couldn't forget. Lost in her thoughts, Maya didn't notice Amy until she touched her shoulder.

"You okay?" Amy asked.

"Just a little distracted," she said tightly, walking over to the soda machine. She slammed the fresh drinks onto her tray.

Blake's mocking voice could be heard throughout the diner. "Yeah, but they were all probably Bs, so really, who cares?"

Maya stormed back over to their booth, her anger singularly focused on the teenager.

"They just take up space," he continued. "You can experience it. We can transmit it to your PACT when we—" Blake was interrupted as Maya threw the contents of his refill straight into his face. "What the fuck?" he exclaimed, dripping wet.

She dropped the glass and leaned in close. "Listen up, you little shit! You think it's funny that people burned to death and jumped from ninety floors up? You think it's funny that a bunch of innocent people were slaughtered and burned alive because of where they worked? Because of who they might be?" Her voice rose, each word coming out louder than the last. "Fuck you!" she screamed, flipping the plate of food onto his chest before tearing off her apron. Most of the other patrons enjoyed the show, chuckling to themselves. Logan, however, started crying hysterically.

Chen, the sweaty man at the grill and the owner of the Blue Water Diner, flew angrily out of the kitchen. "Maya! What the hell? No, you know what? Get the fuck out of here! No more chances. I don't want to see you anywhere near my place again!"

Maya threw her apron and name tag on the floor and stomped on them, spitting back at her former boss, "Fuck you, and fuck your job, Chen!"

She charged across the diner as another server on duty stared at her with both fear and admiration. Maya stopped near the cash register to reach over the bar and snatch up her small bag and jacket. She turned to her coworkers.

"Take care of yourselves. Don't let this place eat up all your time. Life's too fucking short." Maya glanced over her shoulder to the table where Chen was apologizing to the brothers. "And people are assholes. See you later."

As she left the diner, she knew that she had screwed herself out of the only job she had managed to find in ages. That said, she felt wholly satisfied by putting the teenager in his place, as well as standing up to Chen, who was a shit boss anyway.

She had made it a full block before she was startled by the sound of a car horn. She was about to flip the driver off and unleash a string of satisfying expletives when she caught sight of her mother's car. Maya rolled her eyes.

"Maya!" Rebecca shouted out the passenger side window, pulling up alongside her.

"Mom, whatever it is, I don't have time for it now."

"Maya, get in."

Maya peeked into the car and saw the sullen face of her younger sister staring back at her. "What's the nugget doing here?"

"Don't call me nugget!" Hannah barked.

Maya cracked a smirk. "Why not, nugget?"

"Mom!" Hannah shouted.

"Maya, we don't have time for this. Just get in the car."

"I can't. I have plans."

Rebecca snapped, "Maya, get the hell into this car right now! Your uncle Paul was shot today, and we have to get back to the hospital."

Maya's anger abated as quickly as it had flared. She struggled to gather her thoughts.

"Is he okay?"

Rebecca shook her head. Maya looked down at her feet, then climbed into the idling car. Rebecca waited for her to buckle in, then touched the dashboard control screen to activate the self-drive functionality and resumed their course.

△

Dr. Charles Jacobs, flanked by a stoic man with piercing eyes, entered the foyer of Sam and Alexandra's home. Jacobs stood with a slight hunch. He had a thin, patchy white beard and sullen eyes hidden behind wireframe glasses. In his left hand was a small leather satchel he clenched tightly.

"This"—Jacobs gestured to his companion with his other hand—"is Tyriq Maritz. We were in the neighborhood. I know it was unexpected, but I thought I might drop in to check on Alexandra."

"I believe we met once at The Institute," Sam said, returning Maritz's short nod.

"Indeed, we have, Mr. Lee. Please forgive my intrusion." Maritz's Nigerian accent carried through his reserved tone. Not reserved, Sam corrected himself, precise. Neat, just like his dark blue uniform. Minimal chrome touches, with no excess material to be found other than The Institute insignia on his left shoulder. Maritz's tall frame loomed in the doorway of the Lee residence. His rigid spine only made him seem even taller. His hands were folded calmly in front of him, yet his eyes surveyed his surroundings, alert and at the ready.

"I haven't been able to make it down here in a while and I know things are difficult. Is my daughter awake?" Jacobs asked.

"Not at the moment," Sam lied, knowing that Alexandra was likely hovering near the doorway to the bedroom, listening intently.

Jacobs placed his hand on Sam's shoulder. "I understand. Do you think there is a place we could talk, you and I?"

"Sure." Sam invited Jacobs to follow him into the living room.

"Excellent. Mr. Maritz, the kitchen is just through there." Jacobs pointed down the hallway.

"We have some white wine in the refrigerator, along with seltzer and a few different juices I believe. Help yourself," Sam offered.

Sam and Jacobs moved to the living room. Jacobs placed his satchel on a side table and sat on the sofa. He gestured to the chair across from it. Though bothered by Jacobs's presumptuousness, Sam complied.

"I'm not really sure how to approach this conversation," Jacobs admitted.

Sam knew what was coming. "You haven't been able to find a cure, have you?"

Jacobs spoke softly. "No. There's no viable donor and we've run out of time."

Sam rose from his seat and strode over to the small dry bar stocked with numerous decanters. He poured himself a brandy, took down the drink in one gulp, and sighed once it was done. Then another deep breath. Now, hearing the final verdict on Alexandra's condition, he could find peace. What he had experienced in The Institute's Viewing Room could not be denied; it had shown him the next life that awaited them. They would be together, and her pain would be gone.

"So, I guess we can celebrate that she's at least beaten the odds, huh?" he said, his voice cracking as he fought back tears of his own. He poured two brandies and took a seat opposite Jacobs, handing him a glass. "They said she'd never see forty. Never safely ascend. Now it's just around the corner. Cheers, I suppose." The tone of his voice was solemn as he held his glass up.

Jacobs drank down his glass before speaking again. "She's as strong and as fierce as her mother was," he said.

The way he described Alexandra offended Sam. Jacobs was an absent father, and Sam had stayed on the sidelines for too long. Enough was enough. Sam hurled his empty glass across the room, and it shattered against the wall. The shock was enough to cause Jacobs to flinch.

"Strong as her mother, yet you spent more time talking to her dead mother's ghost than being in your living daughter's life!" Sam snapped at his father-in-law.

"I have spent my life, done everything I can—"

"You, the world's top researcher in neural interface and diseases of the brain. Dr. Charles Jacobs, the inventor. The discoverer. The savior of man! After everything you did, everything you created . . . everything . . . yet you couldn't even cure your own daughter—or at least be bothered to be in her life."

"How dare you!"

"Do you want to know a secret, Charles? She is wide awake, right now! She doesn't want to see you. She doesn't want to see you, talk to you, or even associate herself with you because you are just her parent, biologically; you were always too busy being a celebrity scientist to actually be there for her, to be her father."

Jacobs seethed. "Are those her thoughts, or yours?"

"Both of ours! You stuffed her into one private academy and test facility after another while you—"

"Me, I was off trying to save her life! Countless nights realizing that the morning had arrived because when I finally stumbled out of the lab and back into my office, I'd find the sun had risen. It was night after night sleeping in my desk chair awaiting test results and hoping beyond hope that my next big discovery would help me keep my daughter alive.

"Every discovery. Each time we'd cure some form of neuropathy or learn how to reverse dementia in some way, I'd hate myself, realizing it wasn't the discovery I needed. Everything I have done has been to save her. And I have failed." His voice broke.

"So, you want to rage about it? Want to break something?" Jacobs stood, feet solidly planted on the floor. He raised his arms out wide. "Break me, Sam. Break me. Go on."

Sam looked away, his anger slowly dissipating. Jacobs slumped.

"I know I missed everything. I thought that this would be easy. I'd have her cured as a child, or a teenager, and then we'd have the rest of my life to be a family."

Sam turned back to Jacobs. "What could have been."

"There's nothing I can do about the past now, only her future." Jacobs reached into his bag and withdrew a small stainless steel rectangular box. "I came here tonight to offer this last and final effort. It can't cure her, but maybe it might help in other ways."

Sam took the box and released the latch to find two syringes. He looked at Jacobs, confused. "Charles, we both already have our—"

"I know you do," Jacobs said, cutting Sam off. "These are different; they're easier on your system. One syringe is designed for you. The other is for her. They are labeled with your names. When the time comes, make sure you give her the right one. It's very important. Please, Sam. Please see to it that this last effort of mine reaches her."

"What's in this?" Sam asked.

"With her condition, I was worried there could be complications. This will ease her Ascension. But I couldn't just leave it at that. Though you're healthy, what I made for you was designed for a more calming transition. Our problems aside, you make my little girl happy, and I owe you that at least," Jacobs explained. "Swap these with the ones from your kit, but there's no need to tell her and get her all worked up."

Sam snapped the box shut.

"I can do this for you. But I'm going to tell her. I don't hide things from my wife."

"Please, don't," Jacobs begged. "She must use this one."

"What are you not telling me?"

"I'm still . . ." Jacobs fumbled his words. "I love her and I want her to have a future. She may not believe anything I have to say anymore, but you must trust me. Her condition is so rare that there's a chance she may have complications, and the transition might be torturous. I may not be able to save her, but this I can do."

The two men stood in silence. One, a husband soon to join the wife he adored in death, and the other, a father soon to lose a daughter he barely knew. The stillness stretched on, until at last, Sam broke the silence.

"I'll see what I can do," Sam said curtly, putting an end to the conversation.

"Thank you, Sam. Will you give my love to Alexandra?"

"Can I get you anything else?"

"No, I suppose I should round up Tyriq."

Jacobs found Maritz in the kitchen, a single glass of water half drained on the counter. Sam escorted them to the front door, and the trio said their goodbyes. Closing the door behind them, he found his wife standing at the corner of the hallway.

She looked drained as she stood in her robe and slippers.

"Alex, you should get back to bed," he said, taking her arm.

"Not yet. Help me to the living room."

He considered protesting, but knowing that she would find the strength to make her own way there unassisted if denied, he relented. She gestured to the seat at the piano; it was one of her most prized possessions.

Sam carefully sat her down at the bench. Her fingers danced feebly along the keys and a tune formed from the slow progression of notes. Clearing her throat, Alexandra hummed along. Sam leaned against the doorframe. A small, mournful smile spread across his lips.

Suddenly, her voice cracked, and a cacophony sprang from the piano as her hand seized up. Basic motor function had become increasingly challenging as her nervous system degenerated. She fought to maintain her balance but failed. Alexandra started to topple sideways off the bench.

Sam had moved to her side as soon as her tune faltered. He caught her in his arms and scooped her up to carry her back to bed. She was lighter than ever.

"I'm sorry, baby," she said, struggling to bring her head up to look at him.

"Don't be, my love. Don't be."

As he laid his wife once again into bed, Sam fought back a torrent of frustration.

"Lift me up?" Alexandra asked as she continued to ride out the convulsions that brought her neck, arms, and shoulders to twitch and spasm. She had experienced these attacks enough to know that this minor one was winding down.

Sam lifted Alexandra and positioned a pair of pillows to prop her up in the bed. Her head continued to jerk sporadically to the left, but eventually she was able to regain control of everything except her trembling hands.

"And what . . . ," she struggled, "what did the savior of mankind want?"

"He wanted to see you."

"I don't want to see him."

"He brought you a gift. Would you like me to bring it in?"

"I think I already know what it is. Bring it in, please."

"I'll be right back," Sam said, slipping down the hall and retrieving the package. While he was gone, Alexandra took several deep breaths and rode out the last of her tremors.

Sam arrived holding the small box from her father. "Here," he said, handing it to her. "He said it's a new design. Something to help ease the transition, made special for us."

"My father's last birthday gift to me is a better suicide solution. No, this is something worse than even that. Isn't that just fucking like him?"

"Come on. Maybe give him a little break. He's trying to do whatever he can for you."

Sam's words did little to comfort her, but she softened her tone, if only for his sake. "I know." She faked a small cough. "Sam, could you get me some more water, please?"

"Of course." Sam stepped out of the room.

Alexandra wasted no time. She reached into the back of the nightstand and produced The Third Act kit, which she placed on the bed in front of her. She then opened the stainless steel box her father had given Sam and took out her syringe. She peeled off the label with her name and placed it on a syringe from The Third Act. Next, she took Sam's label from her father's syringe and placed it on the syringe Jacobs intended for her. She hid The Third Act box in the back of her nightstand.

She would take The Third Act as originally planned. She'd finally be free, and Sam would be safe. This game of fatal musical chairs nearly cost Alexandra all her strength, but she was determined to see it through. She shut the nightstand drawer just as Sam entered the room with a glass of water.

"Thank you," she said, sliding the Ascension kit away from her on the bed and taking a long drink of the water.

"I could use a nap." Sam sank into the bed next to Alexandra. "Need anything else?"

"No. You can rest," she said softly, running her fingers through Sam's hair until he fell asleep. "Sleep now," she whispered. "I won't be your burden for much longer." As her own eyelids grew heavy, she thought, *And I hope you can find a way to forgive me.*

FOUR

Intelligence

Initiate scan protocol. Engage multi-sector analysis across terrestrial coordinates. Execute grid-by-grid survey. Activate deep-field sensor arrays for subterranean reconnaissance. Monitor electromagnetic and biochemical signatures across diverse biomes. Continue global slatenet, dark web, and private server infiltration. Collate findings for continuous assessment.

—Nål'Elakh

The progeny had been indexed, and the search continued....

    Region 6-Joy City Mall, Shanghai

    System Report: Not found.

    Region 2-Fredericia Innovation Center

System Report: Not found.

Region 4-Almeida Residence, São Paulo

System Report: Not found.

Region 5-Pyongyang Prison Complex

System Report: Not found.

Region 3-The Jacobs Institute, Bangkok

System Report: Not found.

Region 1-Peterson Air Force Base

System Report: Not found.

Region 7-First Avenue Tokyo Station

System Report: Not found.

Region 8-The International Space Station

System Report: Not found.

> _

FIVE

A Family Affair

Those who fight for ideals or beliefs will fight with honor, but those who fight for family will fight with fury.
—The Madness (First Life Cycle)

Back at the hospital...

NATALIE wept over the body of Paul, her tears falling on her dead husband's bare chest. Rebecca offered what few words of consolation she could muster.

"Nat, I don't know what to say."

"We were supposed to take a trip to Atlanta to see his parents next week. Becca, they don't know yet. I'm going to have to tell his parents," Natalie whispered.

Rebecca hugged her sister tightly. "Don't think about that now. Have you told your kids?"

Natalie shook her head before placing her hands on her

husband's chest. "No. They're waiting outside, their babysitter will be coming by to pick them up. I just want to stay with Paul awhile longer."

"Of course."

The door to the observation room opened, and one of the hospital administrators quietly slipped in.

"Dr. Teller?" she said.

"Yes?" Rebecca replied.

"I was hoping I might have a word?"

"Hold on," said Rebecca. "Nat, I'll be right back, okay?"

Her sister nodded, her eyes focused on the corpse in front of her. Rebecca joined the administrator out in the hall.

"Dr. Teller," she said, "I'm very sorry for your loss."

"Thank you. It's a massive shock. We're still trying to process how this could—"

"I understand," the administrator interrupted. "Given what happened with this case, the hospital has asked me to inform you that you're to be placed on paid leave for the next two weeks. But we feel it would be best for you to step away."

"I really think I'd be better off working through it, to be honest. I'll just need some time off to help my sister with the funeral."

"This isn't due to bereavement. Look, I understand this is a sensitive time for you, so let me suggest that you take a couple of weeks off. Spend that time with your daughters and sister and then come back and we can talk."

"Wait," Rebecca said, frustrated. "If this isn't bereavement, then what is it?"

"Perhaps it would be best if we discussed this at another time."

"No, I want you to tell me now. What are you talking about?"

"Doctor, you violated policy today when you tended to a Biomass before fully performing your duties on your priority patients."

"My priority patients?!" Rebecca exploded. "Paul had a chance at surviving and the other two had DNRs. They were seen by the staff while I tried to save a man's life!"

"You know our policy that Ascendants with standing medical orders are to be given priority in trauma situations. You violated this."

"I violated it when a life that could be saved was on the line. The other two were gone or about to be gone and the staff took the appropriate steps in line with that policy. My priority was to try and save Paul's life. My job should be to save lives. Ending lives can wait."

"I understand that this is a hard time; perhaps it would be best if you give all parties a chance to reevaluate the situation here."

Rebecca finally realized what the hospital was trying to do: quietly get rid of her. "Are you firing me?"

"No. All we want is time for things to cool down. Time for some reflection. And then, in a few weeks or so, we can go into greater detail about the manner in which we can all move forward."

⚊ ⚊ ⚊

Maya and Hannah shifted uncomfortably on the hard waiting room chairs across from their crying cousins. Neither knew what to say to the grieving children. Maya and Hannah weren't particularly close to their cousins, even though the cousins were close to Hannah's age. Hannah assumed her cousins thought she was quiet and different, while they probably found Maya old and boring.

"Should we go find Mom?" Hannah whispered, desperate to leave.

Maya shook her head. "Nah. She's going to be busy for a while. Let's take a walk."

"Where?" Hannah asked as Maya rose from her seat.

"Just outside. There's something I want to show you."

Hannah would go along with her sister, as always. Besides, this place smelled like death.

▲

Maya, with Hannah just behind her, walked for several blocks. Each passing intersection led Hannah to wonder where they were going. Her small brow furrowed.

"Maya?"

"What?" Maya asked over her shoulder without missing a beat.

"Maybe we should go back."

"We're fine. Don't worry."

Hannah was not convinced. "Mommy is going to be mad."

"We're almost there. It's just up ahead. C'mon."

As the pair reached the end of the block, Maya veered down a side street, heading for ruined buildings. Hannah stopped in her tracks.

"Maya," she whispered, "I'm scared."

"It's fine, Hannah. It's close, and it's important. Stick with me and you'll be fine."

Hannah stood at the edge of a building's shadow. She tried to peer into the windows of the first floor, but they were fully covered by dirt and old rags. She slowly tilted her head back as far as it could go, eyes skimming floor after floor until they reached the crumbling roof. The building seemed to lean over her, like it would topple and crush her and Maya at any second. A shiver went down her spine, and she instinctively retreated from the building. Hannah kept backing away until Maya grabbed her hand and pulled her close.

"Listen. I'll be with you the whole way," Maya said. "It's important you see this. Hold on to my hand and follow me. Got it?"

"Okay," she said nervously. "But after that, let's go back, okay?"

Nodding, Maya led her sister onward. They walked slowly at first, but as Hannah's eyes adjusted to the darkness, her confidence grew and their pace increased. They quickly made their way another block and a half to a vacant city lot where a grand building had once stood. A chain-link fence with ribbons, notes, pictures, and padlocks covering every inch surrounded the lot. Only by looking through the tiniest of gaps could Hannah see the rubble that lay beyond.

"What is this?" she asked, clutching Maya's hand tightly.

"It was a school. An old school. It had been here for a long time, on the bottom level. And lots of other offices were built on top of it. All the way up to the sky."

"What happened to it?"

"Some people, bad people, came and set a fire. They burned it to the ground."

"Did the kids inside get out?"

"No. They had no time to get out. They all burned to death inside. Teachers, students, everyone. No one survived."

Hannah's eyes drifted along the family photos and images of smiling children. Though Hannah learned from growing up with her sister that the world was filled with bad people who did terrible things, the thought of children her own age dying in fires set by grown-ups was terrifying. She focused on a picture of a small blond boy and wondered what his name had been. What he had been like. If the two of them could have been friends.

"Why?" Hannah asked.

"Because they are filled with hate."

"But why?"

"They hate people who aren't like them, and they hate people who associate with them."

"Who are they, though?"

"Crazy, evil, rotten Ascendants and people wanting to be like them." Maya stared blankly ahead, like she was seeing the ghosts of these people running around the abandoned lot.

"Ascendants did this?"

"Yes," Maya said coldly.

"Do they want to kill us too?" Questions spilled from Hannah's mouth, one after the other. She let go of Maya's hand. "What about Mom? She's an Ascendant. Did Mommy help them?"

Maya finally looked at her, and Hannah calmed down. "No, Mom is nothing like them. Not all of them are like that. In fact, most are nothing like them. But they're out there."

"Were these the people who killed Uncle Paul?" Hannah asked, eyes tearing up.

"I don't know. They could have been the same kind of people."

"The same kind?"

Maya nodded. "Psycho A.R.M. members. People who think that only the Ascendants have a place in this world."

"I don't understand." Hannah wanted to ask more questions but didn't want to make Maya more upset. This was much harder than when Maya was mad at everyone.

The two fell into an uncomfortable silence as their attention returned to the endless items attached to the fence. Eventually, Maya broke the silence.

"It's important that you see the world. Not just what Mom shows you. You might see it a bit at school, the way kids will bully and abuse each other. You might see it one day in the news too, with the politicians and The Institute people always talking about trying to make things fair and then failing to do that over and over again. But now, hopefully, you see what life really is. It's a place where those bullies grow into monsters, where those people who pretend to be in charge of things fail to do anything until it's too late."

"You said 'arm.' What do you mean, 'arm'?"

"Ascendant Revolutionary Militia. A.R.M. What a stupid name. They were terrorists who did things like, well, this," Maya replied, gesturing to the empty lot.

Neither Hannah nor Maya noticed when an old woman joined them until she spoke.

"You know, the city wants to put a memorial park here. A playground and some statues. I think it's a good idea, but apparently some people think it'd be best to leave it as is," she said, startling the girls. Both of them turned to look at the stranger, eyes wide.

The gray-haired woman was short, barely five feet tall. Her eyes remained sharp and full of life, yet her face was weathered, with a cluster of wrinkles at the corner of each eye. She wore a crooked smile on her face as she surveyed the open lot and its chain-link mosaic.

"Whoops, did I sneak up on you just there?" she said with a chuckle. "My apologies. I usually stop off here during my daily walks. I like to look and remember. I'm Michelle. I live just down the street."

The old woman offered a handshake to Maya, who took it cautiously. "Maya. This is Hannah."

"I've lived here my entire life, more or less. I was here when the first bombs went off and the fires raged. Watched from my window as it came down," she said, pointing down the street to a dark apartment building. The whole block was filled with apartments that were either vacant or abandoned. "It was something I'll never forget."

"It's something no one should forget," Maya said sternly.

"You're absolutely right, dear." Michelle's half smile broadened to a full grin. "Absolutely right."

Hannah looked back at the framed picture of the small boy. She raised her hand out to touch the frame. The physical connection made the boy, the school, the empty lot, and the event that bound them all together more real. Abruptly, the fragile photo frame fell to the sidewalk, shattering the glass.

Hannah jumped. Her heart filled with guilt from disrespecting a hallowed token. "I'm sorry," she said to the boy in the photo, his face covered with broken glass.

Hannah knelt, reaching for the mess she had made in a futile attempt to fix it. Her palm ran across a broken piece of glass, cutting deep into her flesh. Blood burst from the wound and droplets splattered on the face in the frame.

"Shit, Hannah!" Maya pulled her back from the pile of glass.

"I just touched it and it fell. I'm sorry. Maya, I'm bleeding!"

"Hannah, squeeze it tight," Maya ordered. "You need to put pressure on it so it won't bleed too much. Come on, let's get back to the hospital. If we're lucky, you won't need stitches."

"Hold on a moment," said Michelle, stepping around Maya and taking Hannah's hand. She examined the cut closely and patted Hannah's wrist. "It's fairly deep, but it looks like a clean cut, easily bandaged with a first aid kit. How about you two come up to my apartment and I'll fix you right up with something to get you by just so that she doesn't bleed too much on your way back. I used to be a nurse, sweetie. It won't be any bother."

Maya bit her lip, weighing their options. Mom wouldn't like it if Hannah suddenly had a huge cut on her hand. "Yeah. That's probably a good idea. Just to get her cleaned up."

Michelle smiled, her stained yellow teeth flashing. "Very good, I'm just this way."

▲

The trio set off down the street, farther into the shadows. Trash tumbled along the sidewalk. Maya was no stranger to the more desolate parts of Boston, but she was starting to regret bringing her sister to such a place. Maya's phone rang, breaking the eerie silence. She looked at it to see her mother's face glaring back at her. She refused the call only to be confronted with a series of text messages demanding to know where she and her sister had run off to. After typing a quick *be right back*, Maya turned off her phone in case her mother tried to have it tracked. They followed the old woman into a dimly lit foyer of an apartment building and stepped into a rickety elevator.

Maya and Hannah entered Michelle's cluttered apartment and joined her in the kitchen. Piles of outdated flyers, dented metal sheets, torn clothes, and other scraps of materials blocked most of the window to the alley below. As Michelle tended to Hannah, Maya took stock of Michelle's living conditions. She was sympathetic toward this little old woman who clearly had no one to look after her, forced to live in such squalor by circumstances beyond her control. Maya stood awkwardly beside the kitchen table, simmering with rage at the injustice of the system.

Michelle treated Hannah's cut with rubbing alcohol and cold water. Blood continued to drip from the wound as the young girl kept her hand beneath the steady stream of tap water. Michelle pulled her arms away and quickly took a clean white cloth to wipe the blood from Hannah's palm before drying her hands. Michelle produced a small aerosol spray bottle from beneath the sink, first giving it a good shake, then spraying a mist of clear liquid over Hannah's wound. The mist solidified into a clear coating once it made contact with her skin, sealing the cut.

"I may not look it now, but I was once a nurse in an army. We'd have to deal with all sorts of wounds back in those days," Michelle said to Hannah as she wrapped her hand in a thin layer of gauze. "Here we go. This'll keep any dirt or anything else from sticking to the sealer. It should be enough to keep your hand safe until you get back home."

"Thanks," Hannah said.

"Now, we're going to need to let that spray set," Michelle said to Hannah, eyeing the bloodstained rag. She turned to Maya. "We're just going to give that a few minutes before Hannah moves. I'm going to put this into the laundry. Why don't you go have a seat in the living room? I'll bring you something to drink."

"Sure," Maya agreed. It was strange being told to leave her sister's side, but at the same time she felt guilty for casting doubt on a downtrodden woman of resilient spirit. "Hannah, I'll just be in there, okay?"

Hannah nodded. Maya moved into the living room and sank onto the sofa while Michelle disappeared into her bedroom.

▲

Michelle opened the closet door and pushed some clothing aside, revealing an outdated, yet fully functional, Institute testing machine. Roughly the size of an old office copier, the machine stood nearly four feet tall, its boxy frame supporting a large touch screen display. Michelle booted up the machine. After the welcome screen faded, Michelle touched a button on the screen which simply read Test, and wiped the blood-soaked rag onto a cotton-like surface to the side of the display. A green progress bar appeared, moving slowly from left to right as the machine analyzed the blood sample.

The test results popped up on-screen in bright uppercase letters:

ASCENDANT

Smaller text was displayed underneath:

Ascendant Profile Match: 97.958%

She didn't understand the term *profile match* but was excited by the result. Here was an Ascendant. A rush of adrenaline overtook Michelle. She turned to her dresser and opened the top drawer.

Michelle pulled out an old vial of white powder. A favorite tool of hers from the good old days, the poison was powerful enough to render a healthy racing horse dead within thirty seconds. She had kept many such poisons handy.

Returning to the kitchen, Michelle opened the fridge and withdrew a carton of orange juice. She poured a full portion of juice, slipping a dose of the flavorless, odorless powder into the bottom of the glass while her back was turned, and presented it to the young girl.

"You bled quite a bit there, so I want you to drink this all up so that you can heal better, okay?" she said, smiling broadly.

▲

In the living room, Maya rocked impatiently in her seat and scanned the room. Strewn upon the tables were countless frames. Most were digital, their aging screens faded in color and luminance; some images were barely visible. The few that remained undistorted displayed clear photos of a younger Michelle in an unfamiliar uniform, flanked by fellow soldiers.

She found the history on display interesting but felt that there was something off about this woman. She rose from the couch and wandered around the room, perusing the photos and other memorabilia. A commemorative plate, a snow globe, a series of books and brochures for tours around Boston and New York City. Nothing too out of the ordinary, until a framed poster on the far side of the room caught her attention.

It was an image of a raised black fist on a flat red background. A red lightning bolt struck along the arm and the wrist of the hand, ending at the base of the fist. She had seen this image before. Maya's hand plunged inside her jacket, into the secret pocket she had sewn in herself.

Her hand clutched the revolver she carried. She dashed into the kitchen to find Michelle at the table, serving Hannah a drink. As the old woman placed the glass down, Maya saw the symbol from the poster tattooed on Michelle's wrist. She withdrew her gun and raised it at the woman's face.

"Hannah, do not drink that," Maya insisted. She felt like she was vibrating, although her hand was steady. "Back away from my sister. Hannah, get up. Come on. We're going."

Michelle closed her eyes and shook her head. "Oh, girls, you have no reason to fear little old me. You're one of the chosen. At least, your sister is. If she really is your sister."

"Shut the fuck up. What did you do? What are you talking about?" Maya barked as she shuffled her sister behind her.

"You mean to tell me you don't know about your sister? You don't know that she's chosen? That she's an Ascendant? A very pure one," Michelle said, laughing as she spoke.

"Bitch, I don't have a goddamn clue what you're talking about, but we're leaving."

Michelle circled around the table. Her hand slipped deftly over the handle of a knife, which she pressed up against her wrist. "This world is no place for any of us. A better one awaits her."

Maya persisted. "Hannah, I want you to step out into the hall and wait for me, okay? Go. Now." She was surprised by her own authoritative tone. Her sister left without question, stepping out into the hall and shutting the door behind her.

"What is this? You're with A.R.M. then? I thought they wanted to kill Bs."

Michelle laughed. "I was with A.R.M. But that was the past. Someone as pure as your sister was not meant for this world."

Maya cocked the hammer of her revolver. "What are you talking about?"

"Oh, you'll see, dear. You'll both see. A glorious day will be upon us soon." She darted at Maya. Michelle moved with astounding speed for a woman of her age and condition. Maya had only a split second to react.

Hannah lingered beneath a flickering light in the hallway. The whole place smelled foul, like an old trash heap. Odors of mold and dust invaded her sinuses. She pinched her nose and breathed from her mouth.

Inside the apartment, she heard voices arguing. Those of Michelle and her sister in a heated exchange. A slam and a scuffle followed, accompanied by a shout. Finally, a loud bang. Then silence.

The quiet seemed to stretch on and on as Hannah debated whether to run or to hide. She decided to wait. The door eventually opened, and Maya emerged.

Maya's face was pale, her eyes glazed over. The two stood in the hallway, staring at each other. Maya's right hand clutched something in her pocket; red stained her sleeve.

Maya reached out for Hannah's hand with her free one. "Let's go."

Hannah took her sister's hand and followed her out of the building. The tense grip mirrored the fear that Hannah could see on Maya's face. Something had happened.

They made it nearly halfway down the block when Maya stopped, letting go of her hand. Hannah worried that there was danger nearby and darted her eyes around nervously. Maya stumbled to a lamppost and vomited on the ground next to it.

"I want Mommy," Hannah whimpered.

Hannah and Maya walked in silence back to the hospital. Across from The Institute's main research facility, a large group of protestors assembled. The sisters stopped short. They saw the angry people yelling with signs in hand. Some read "Murderers!" while others displayed a variety of slogans and quotes from scripture.

As was the case around the world, the frequency of protests against Institute policies and facilities had been increasing. What had started out as small gatherings in parks and outside of Institute Viewing Rooms and clinics had, in recent weeks, escalated. This amused most of the general public watching news coverage from home, since the Viewing Rooms had provided comfort for so long. The Institute had made it clear: Death was not the end for Ascendants. It was inconceivable to the billions who had experienced the connection to the afterlife in the Viewing Rooms that some would challenge The Institute. The protestors demanded equality for Biomasses and an end to the bifurcation of society.

Maya took note of protestors clad in black from head to toe, sporting the same red-and-purple bands around their upper arms. All were masked as if they were about to rob a bank. These hooded figures weaved in and out of the crowd. They spoke as though playing a game of telephone, each listening to the last and shouting to the next.

As the sisters reached the hospital entrance, the swelling crowd gathered near the barricades, becoming denser and denser as those behind moved forward. Once the press of people had reached a critical mass, the barricade came down and the protestors barreled forward, led by the black-clad group. Their advance was thwarted by a legion of heavily armored security staff that came out of the building. They formed two solid lines of armed muscle to repel the oncoming assault. In the sky, buzzing news drones circled around the commotion.

Maya tugged at her sister as she folded over the bloody sleeve and tucked it inside her jacket. "Better get inside."

⁂

Rebecca's sigh of relief quickly turned into a huff as she saw her daughters walking briskly down the hall. Both looked distraught. She assumed that their uncle's death had affected the girls, but having spent the last thirty minutes searching for them and sending unanswered messages and calls to Maya's phone, her patience was wearing thin.

"Where have you two been?" she demanded.

"Nowhere. We just took a little walk, Mom. It's nothing," Maya said. Rebecca always knew when Maya was lying, but now Maya looked like she was ready to run away. Again.

"Don't you know what's going on? Have you not been paying attention?" Rebecca asked, gesturing at a display screen above a row of chairs in the adjacent room. A large breaking news ticker read *Civil Unrest Grips Boston. Protestors Target Jacobs Plaza* over aerial footage of the demonstration the sisters had just witnessed.

"Yeah," Maya replied. "We saw it and that's why we came back in."

"You can't just go taking your little sister out whenever you want, Maya! What is wrong with you?" Rebecca grabbed Hannah's wrist, turning her palm up to examine the new bandage. "And what on earth happened to her hand?"

Tears welled in Maya's eyes, but to Rebecca's surprise, Hannah spoke up.

"It was just Uncle Paul," Hannah said, looking at the ground. "Maya wanted to take a walk and I didn't want to be here alone. I tripped outside and scraped up my hand. Maya found someone to help. I'm sorry, Mommy. I shouldn't have gone out."

Rebecca's stern expression softened as she brought them both in for a family embrace.

"This has just been a horrible day for everyone. But the three of us are still together and everything will be okay. Let me check in with Aunt Natalie and we'll head home. Stay put this time, okay?" Rebecca said, looking at both of them. "I mean it."

The sisters nodded, and Rebecca gave their hands a reassuring squeeze before returning down the hall. In the counseling room at the end of the corridor, Rebecca joined her sister.

"Are the girls okay?" asked Natalie.

"They're fine. Maya took Hannah out for a walk and I guess they avoided the commotion outside. Did your kids make it home yet?"

"They did. I know you're dedicated to keeping Hannah in school and Maya close, but, Becca, please reconsider. This city is going to tear itself apart. If we're going to keep our kids safe, we need to get out of here before the anniversary protests get out of hand."

"I know you feel that way right now, and yes, I know things are intense, but I'm sure they'll calm down soon and things will be normal again." The moment the words slipped past her lips, Rebecca instantly regretted them.

"Normal?" Natalie asked, her eyes widening. "Look what happened to Paul."

"You know what I meant."

"You meant that once my kids adjust to the fact that their father is gone? All the men in your life have left you. Mine was murdered."

Rebecca reeled back. "I'm sorry."

"Forget it," Natalie whispered.

Rebecca looked at the floor, sitting in the tense silence. After a moment, she asked, "Do you even know where you'll go? What you'll do?"

"Paul knew of this place out west. Outside of the city. It's some kind of a farm or commune thing. It's isolated, cut off, and safe. There's no slatenet or Viewing Rooms. No As or Bs. Just people and some open land."

"Are you sure that's what you want for the kids? Some commune?" Rebecca questioned.

"Are you sure staying here is what's best for yours?" Natalie replied, turning away.

Rebecca reached out and stopped her. "Just be careful, Nat," Rebecca said, pulling her into an embrace.

"I will."

"If you need anything, call me. Whatever it is."

"And if and when you decide to follow me . . ." Natalie withdrew from her sister's embrace and looked her in the eye with a seriousness Rebecca had rarely seen. She leaned in close and whispered in Rebecca's ear, "Drive to Concord. Find MacCauley's Marketplace on High Street. Ask how you get to Faraday Farm and follow the directions to the letter. Make sure you're not followed."

⯅

Maya and Hannah were the only two in the waiting room, and both had their eyes glued to the display. Aerial cameras outside documented squads of Institute security in full riot armor using batons and pepper spray to corral the protestors. The security officers pushed the crowd back from The Institute and out of the street with minimal harm.

The large group of protestors first broke into smaller groups, then into even smaller clusters before dispersing altogether; it looked as though the crowd's demonstration was done for the night. Maya noted that everyone not currently in the midst of emergency procedures outside the waiting room stood transfixed by the events unfolding on the displays. Maya saw an opening and took it.

"Wait here," she said softly to her sister. Hannah nodded without moving her eyes away from the screen.

Rising from her seat, Maya strode out into the hall. She found a rolling medical cart unattended outside a room. She pulled at the drawers, opening one after another until she found her prize.

Wrapped in sterile medical plastic was a small black tablet. Akin to the slates used by nearly everyone in the world, the medical-grade Ascension test kit was only slightly thicker than those sold in pharmacies, with a secure connection to The Institute database. These tablets were produced in limited supply for Institute facilities and affiliates, so they were a hot commodity. However, Maya had no plans to resell the device. Glancing over her shoulder to ensure she had not been seen, she slipped two kits into her bag and quietly returned to the waiting room.

Maya sat down just before her mother entered.

"Time to go," Rebecca said.

The girls trailed a few feet behind their mother. A small security camera mounted on the ceiling adjusted focus and tracked them. Video of the past hour looped on the monitor in the main security station, triggered by Maya's approach to the cart.

A force beyond the reach of The Institute watched over the Tellers.

/⚠\

> Region 1-North American East Coast Data
> Center-Rack 1217, Server 3
>
> System Report: Anomalous test sample
> analysis detected en route to Jacobs
> genomic database.

Sector 027-Office of Dr. Charles Jacobs

System Report: Potential subjects identified.

Directive: Determine validity of results.

Sector 426-Jacobs Institute Hospital-
Surveillance Node 31

Commands: Continue monitoring potential subjects. Reroute native surveillance system.

> _

SIX

Home

There are so many things I wish I had stayed in the dark about. But the thing with daylight is that it has a nasty habit of getting in.

—The Fist (Second Life Cycle)

At the Teller household...

AWKWARD silence seeped into every nook and cranny of the home. Hannah settled on the couch, playing *Animal Blast* on her slate. In the kitchen, Maya paced back and forth while her mother sat at the counter, staring into an untouched glass of wine.

"Maya, sit down," Rebecca said, bringing her gaze up from the glass.

Maya reached across the counter and grabbed the bottle of wine next to her mother. She opened a cabinet and pulled out a stemless glass, pouring the bottle until the dark red liquid was just shy of the rim. She chugged half the glass. Wine sloshed over the rim and down her chin.

Maya put the glass down and wiped the wine off her chin with her left hand. Michelle flooded her thoughts. The maniacal expression she wore while lunging at Maya. The deafening sound of the gunshot. How much did her mother know? Had the body been found or reported yet? Had she left any trace that could lead the cops back to her family?

"Do you want to talk about Uncle Paul?" Rebecca asked, halting Maya's spiraling thoughts.

Maya looked at her mother and wondered if she ought to confess. She should want to beg forgiveness for putting her sister in jeopardy, but all Maya really wanted to do was run away.

"Maybe later," she lied. Maya picked up her glass, half full of blood—no, wine—and headed out of the kitchen. "I think I just want to be alone right now."

She moved through the living room on her way to her bedroom. Hannah was on the couch, enthralled with her game, eyes glued to the screen. Maya bounded up the stairs.

Sitting in her room with the door closed, Maya stared at the new testing kits she had stashed under her pillow. There was a knock at her door.

"Maya?" Hannah's quiet voice was easily heard through the hollow plywood door.

Maya wavered between telling her sister to get lost or proceeding with her plan. She slid her finger along the power switch sensor at the top of the testing kit. Maya ushered Hannah inside, then sat her on the bed.

"I need you to do something, and I need you to do it now," she said, sitting back down next to her sister and opening her second test kit.

"What is it? Maya, what are those?" Hannah asked, confused. "I just wanted to see if you were okay."

"I will be."

Maya withdrew the test kit from its case. She took her sister's hand. "I need to test you, okay? It might hurt just a tiny little bit, but it's what I have to do. I'll do mine first to show you, but we need to be sure about this."

Maya placed her hand on the testing slate. The results appeared two seconds later.

```
Test Sample: Compatible.
Contaminants: None.
Confidence: High.
Type: O-.
Test Result: Stable.
Strand ASC, TCTTTTGA...AGCG: 3.7% match.
AJD Gene Match: False.
Ascendant Match: Not applicable.
Status: Negative.
```

Maya was, as she had always been, a Biomass. No surprises there. Anyone else would have been depressed with the cards that fate and genetics had dealt her, but not Maya. A few discreet tests as a teenager had always shown the same result, and she was old enough now to know that status did not change for anyone. Unfazed, Maya turned to her sister. Hannah didn't resist as Maya placed her hand on the kit. The testing kit took much longer to process Hannah's sample than Maya expected.

△

```
Region 1-North American East Coast Data
Center-Rack 1217, Server 3

System Report: Test sample analysis of
potential subject detected en route to
```

Jacobs genomic database. Identification: Maya Teller. Results verified.

Outcome: Parameters not met.

Command: Terminate monitoring.

System Report: Test sample analysis detected en route to Jacobs genomic database.

Outcome: Identification: Hannah Teller.

Command: Pause data retrieval on subject's testing kit display.

Directive: Determine validity of results.

System Report: Analysis confirmed.

Commands: Initiate diagnostic protocols. Cross-reference historical data with results.

System Report: Increased testing cadence confirmed.

Outcome: Prioritize incident.

Commands: Expand resource allocation. Divert nonessential processes to Standby mode. Engage multi-vector analysis. Reassess data integrity checks. Deploy error-correction algorithms.

```
Directive: Verify heuristic core and
cognitive synthesis integrity.

Commands: Reinitiate comprehensive system
analysis. Resume data retrieval on
subject's testing kit display.

Progeny at risk.

> _
```

◮

"I swear to god, I am ready to just set this fucking thing on fire!" Maya hissed, her eyes fixated on Hannah's testing kit.

"Maybe it's broken," Hannah responded, rubbing her eyes to stave off sleep.

"It's not broken, Hannah. I took it straight from the hospital." Maya shook her fist menacingly at the kit. "Figures that I would get a goddamn broken test."

Hannah gently placed her hand on her sister's fist. Maya relaxed. "Maybe we just shouldn't know, Maya. Why does it matter if I'm an A?"

"It's the way the world is, Hannah," Maya said, exasperated. "It's everything that we saw and went through in that apartment. You understand that, right?"

Maya turned back to the screen just as the flashing ellipses gave way to Hannah's results:

```
Test Sample: Compatible.
Contaminants: None.
Confidence: High.
Type: O+.
Test Result: Stable.
```

> **Strand ASC, TCTTTTGA ... AGCG:** 100% match.
> **AJD Gene Match:** False.
> **Ascendant Match:** 97.958%, activated.
> **Status:** Positive.

She stared wide-eyed and confused at the tablet. Though no expert in blood types, genetics, or whatever "AJD Gene Match" meant, even she could see that something was definitely not right.

"What is it, Maya?" Hannah asked.

"I don't know. I don't know what this means, but we both know someone who does."

Maya clutched both of the testing tablets and stormed out of her bedroom, down the stairs, and straight into the kitchen. Rebecca looked up, having hardly moved from her seat at the counter. Maya flung the tablets down onto the kitchen island.

Rebecca recognized the tablets instantly. "What are you doing with these?"

"I stole a couple of testing kits from the hospital. Ran tests on me and Hannah. So, you tell me, Mom. What is this?" Maya's voice trembled with rage.

"You stole testing kits?" Rebecca responded, both annoyed and confused.

"Look, Mom. Just look. Tell me if you see what I see." Maya gritted her teeth. "And then you tell me just what the fuck that actually means."

Rebecca took a deep breath and translated the results. "Your test is negative and hers is positive. Hannah is an Ascendant. Is that what you were after? Are you happy now?"

Maya slammed her hand on the counter and leaned in. "No, Mother. There's more there, and I can see it. Read it!" she spat.

"The two of you possess different blood types as well as—"

"As well as what?" Maya barked, already knowing what the answer would be.

"As well as PCR testing confirming Hannah's DNA alignment differs from yours. There is a sequence variation." Rebecca knew the medical jargon flew clear over Maya's head.

"Which means what, exactly?"

"Which means that your DNA sequencing doesn't align." As she spoke, her voice cracked. "That you have different—"

"Different parents. Different fathers?" Maya asked. Her mother nodded as she covered her face with her hands. "That's why we don't look the same. Why she's an Ascendant and I'm not."

"Ascendant status isn't assured between siblings. You know that."

"It also isn't assured when siblings have a different fucking father either! What the fuck, Mom? I'm nearly twenty-four and Hannah is six! You couldn't have once told us—told me—that we have different fucking deadbeat fathers? Was I an accident from some fling in college, huh? Maybe a hookup you had on spring break?"

"Maya, it isn't like that."

"Then what was it like, Mother? Why did you let me think that Daddy—that *that* man—was my father for so long?"

"Because he was. He was a father to you as much as he was to Hannah. We were young and your biological father didn't want a family. Didn't want a wife or kids. So he left before you were born. But soon after your father—your real father and Hannah's biological father—came into my life. He was a good man."

"But he also left you, didn't he? Left us. You said you two were having problems and he just took off. But you two never fought. Never yelled. It makes no sense. I stuck around because I felt sorry for you, but now I don't know. What did you do to make him want to leave? And you know what, Mom, I've been trying to track him down for years and found nothing. Literally not a trace of him anywhere. Who just disappears like that?"

"I don't know! He was gone and—I don't remember. It was a hard time. I couldn't process any of it. Hannah wasn't even born yet and everything was a mess."

"Well, everything is still a mess," Maya snapped. This wasn't her home, it never was. For the past two years, she had felt the urge to move out on her own again, and now she had no reason to stay. "You know what? I don't care who our fathers were or where they are. I think that it's time I moved on," she announced calmly. "I'm gonna grab some of my stuff."

Within a few minutes, Maya had packed a bag and was standing in the kitchen doorway.

"Maya," Rebecca said, struggling to get the words out. "Please don't."

"I'll switch over my number to a private plan and update my address when I find a permanent place to stay. Right now, I'm going to crash with some friends."

Rebecca pleaded, "Please, no. Not now. Not with everything going on."

Maya turned and, without another word to her mother, walked toward the front door. Hannah ran past Maya and flung her body in front of the door. "Maya, don't go," she begged, tears forming in her eyes.

Maya knelt in front of her sister. "It'll be all right, nugget. Watch your back, okay?" Maya gently pushed Hannah to the side and walked out of the house, backpack slung over one shoulder. *I'm not running away,* Maya assured herself. Not this time, and not like her fucking fathers. They left because they were fucking cowards. *I can't trust anyone.* From here on out, she was on her own.

SEVEN

Serein

They want me to tell you who I am. What I want. What I believe. Well, I have a question for you. Did you believe in Ascension? Maybe you believe in the old ways. That there's some benevolent god watching, waiting for us after death. Laughing at our torment. So why join up now? Maybe I've waited too long. We all have. But there's no going back.

—Samantha Harper, The Lost Recordings, Vol. 1

As morning broke in the Lee household...

Sam peeked over at his sleeping wife. The sun crept in between the blinds, casting soft orange rays on Alexandra's face. For once, she looked at peace. Her body was still, free from twitches and spasms. Her breathing was calm. Sam greeted his wife as the light reached her eyes, waking her from her slumber.

"Good morning, birthday girl," he whispered.

"One more trip around the sun, huh?" Alexandra replied with a yawn.

"One more trip. Would you like some breakfast?"

"No, some tea would be nice though. Also, a drink of water." She reached out for the glass of water on her nightstand from the previous night. Her hand seized and the glass fell to the floor. "Shit," she said, moving to clean it up.

"Don't worry. I'll get it," Sam said, springing from bed. He grabbed a towel from the hamper and threw it over the spill, soaking up what he could from the carpet. "So, tea then. Are you sure you wouldn't like breakfast in bed?"

"I'm not very hungry, but what the hell. An English muffin would be great," she said with a smile, struggling to keep her right hand from shaking. She leaned back and tried to relax. Sam smiled back and offered a little bow before leaving to prepare her breakfast.

Alexandra looked at the nightstand. The nightstand that held her final choices in life and death. Her "Ascension." It was a term she had grown to despise immensely. Not because of how everyone—her doctors, friends, and husband—used it to describe her impending death; she hated it because her father was responsible for it, just as he was responsible for all the mess in the world. Sam's devotion to her father's lies grated on her. If only she could speak up and tell Sam what she knew. But she couldn't break him, not while she was alive, at least. *I am a coward,* she thought.

She was certain that nothing awaited on the "other side." Alexandra had witnessed a number of Ascensions in The Institute Viewing Rooms. She understood the allure of having proof, of being able to point to the "science" of it all. But what her father had shared with her shattered the illusion of Ascension. It broke her and would break Sam. She kept her father's secrets because who would believe her over him? Yet, why had no one else challenged The Institute? If mankind had spent its entire history asserting one wrong doctrine after another in a vain attempt to settle its fears over mortality, why would Ascension be the exception? To the world, why wasn't Ascension just another deceptive, reductive explanation of what comes next?

She picked up a slate from her nightstand while also plucking a bottle of medication from the drawer. Her hands shook as she popped two large yellow pills into her mouth that would hopefully calm her tremors. She then flicked the slate on and activated her home's inner security feeds. Sam had installed cameras throughout the house when Alexandra had first become bedridden so that she could know where he was and call for him if she needed something. In practice, she had taken to using the cameras to time her secret indulgences while Sam remained safely out of the room: a sugary snack, or a couple of sips of wine from the Pinot Noir she kept hidden in the lower compartment of her nightstand. On a few occasions, she treated herself to a difficult but pleasing series of drags from a black-market clove cigarette in the bathroom by an open window.

She glanced at the slate to see Sam was still in the process of finding a tea bag, so she decided to take a moment to record a short message for her father. She scheduled delivery for midnight.

Sam came down the hall with breakfast placed neatly on a tray. As he entered the room, Alexandra swiped to the web reader, bringing up a local news feed.

"Look at that," she said, pointing to the headline. "The city finally got off its ass and has announced that a memorial park will be going up in the old Financial District."

"About time," Sam replied, placing the tray on her legs and taking his own steaming cup of tea. "By the way, we ran out of the raw sugar you like so I—"

"Used maple syrup?" Alexandra asked, cutting him off.

"Yes," Sam said, nodding, his smile broadening. "Just as you prefer."

"Mmm." She smelled the cup. "So, what would you like to do with our last day on Earth?"

"How about whatever you want to do?"

"How about we revisit some old historical sites?"

"What, you mean like taking the tour at Bunker Hill? Walk the Freedom Trail? Kinda a weird way to go, lady, but it's your party."

"No," she said with a chuckle. "I meant personal history. The quad?"

Sam smiled, realizing what she meant. "The tree."

Alexandra laughed. "The bike?"

Placing his cup down on the nightstand, he slid in beside her. "I think that would be a perfect way to say goodbye to this world."

The two kissed each other deeply. They found themselves tangled up entirely in the scent and feel of one another. As the pair grew more intimate, Alexandra pushed the tray off to her side. The untouched English muffin and full cup of tea crashed to the floor.

The tea soaked quickly into the carpet. Crumbs scattered everywhere. Even the small leg of the cheap bed tray broke. It was their last day on Earth, so there was little reason to care.

◬

In his corner office at The Jacobs Institute tower, Price reclined in his soft leather chair. He ran his hands down his face, wiping his eyes and lightly stroking his goatee. His wall display quietly replayed a news program from the previous night. On his tabletop display, a list of names and numbers scrolled slowly.

Isaiah Davidson: 1.11%

Rafael Lopez: 0.45%

Ibrahim Al Wasari: 0.89%

Each name was listed with a percentage of genetic similarities to the First Ascendant. Price would run these database searches in an attempt to find some link that would help unlock the mysteries behind Ascension. Though Price had more answers than virtually every other human on the planet, too many things were still hidden from him. He knew what lay beneath the monument of the First Ascendant, but that was not enough.

As the names and percentages continued to populate, Price let his eyes close, sinking into much-needed sleep. The unrelenting scroll of light on his screen danced across his eyelids. The steady white noise from the air vent pulled him into REM sleep. And so Price dreamed.

His eyes formed and took shape, materializing slowly along with the rest of his body. He arrived in a sunny suburban cul-de-sac, walking in a quaint and peaceful neighborhood. Sprinklers watered healthy green lawns. Shiny cars dotted each driveway, and every so often, he would see fathers and mothers trimming hedges or planting flowers while sons and daughters played in the yards.

He looked to his left as he made his way down the sidewalk and caught sight of a party through a window. He teleported right outside the window, looking in at the partygoers and their merriment. Inside, he saw brilliant white teeth flashing smiles as guests sipped cocktails and laughed at jokes that, though never actually told, remained hilarious all the same.

A hand slapped his shoulder, and raucous laughter surrounded him. Now, on the inside, his comrades threw their heads back and bellowed their amusement to the ceiling. Price, too, was soon laughing at a joke he could have sworn he had told hundreds of times, but it was one he had never uttered at all.

On the front lawn, neighbors arrived with casseroles and bottles of wine. A small group of children played stickball in the street, just as he had as a child. On the sofa, Price was squished between two very dear friends whose names he could not recall. One man turned to him and asked, "So, what do you do now, Henry?"

Price answered, "I work at The Jacobs Institute."

The party fell silent. The nameless friend beside him smiled, reached behind his back, and pulled out a pistol. He raised the pistol to Price's face.

"Who needs you?" he asked, pulling the trigger.

A thunderous crack echoed. A blackout was followed by the lights flickering back on. All around him the bloodied dead bodies of the partygoers lay strewn about the room. Every pair of eyes was open; each had a look of pure joy emblazoned on their faces despite the bullet wound to the head. Their faces melted. Eyes, noses, and mouths collapsed into skin.

He rose from his seat, curious and confused. He strolled from room to room, looking at one corpse after another until he ended up outside on the front steps. The pink sky turned red as the sun set beyond the horizon.

The stickball game had ended. All the players lay dead, collapsed in pools of thick blood. Price analyzed the bizarre expressions frozen on the bodies of these dead children. A boom drew his attention away from the massacre. A man with his back to Price extended his arm out. He held a gun to the forehead of Alexandra Jacobs.

"Hi, Uncle Henry. Come play with me!" she shouted, just as the gunman squeezed the trigger and blew the back of her head out. Her body fell to the ground.

Price yelled at the gunman. "No!"

Charles Jacobs slowly turned to face Price. Jacobs's hands and clothing were stained with blood.

"No one to blame but ourselves, Henry. You know that better than anyone," Jacobs said, unfazed. "So, what's next?"

The weight of a revolver in his now blood-soaked hands surprised Price, who charged at his old friend.

"No shame in it, Henry. None at all," Jacobs said.

Price raised his gun and pulled the trigger. A bad round. He cocked the weapon and tried again. Nothing. He pulled the trigger over and over.

The gun fired, but his target was gone. There was nothing in the vast landscape before him, not even the corpses. The dark sky was still streaked with red. The once picturesque cul-de-sac deteriorated: The houses crumbled, the cars turned to rust, and the grass on the lawn wilted. Red drops splattered the brown patch near his feet. He touched the center of his stomach, feeling a sticky, bloody gunshot wound ooze. He fell to his knees and looked back and forth between the blood on his fingers and the gun in his hand. He looked up to find Jacobs standing over him. A mix of jealousy and envy, inadequacy and scorn, and a lust for power consumed his mind.

Different voices echoed. "No shame in it, Henry. No shame."

"But, sir, you need to wake up."

"There's something you need to see."

"Tell me, when did you start at The Institute?"

Price's eyes flew open, and he lifted his head from the desk. The remnants of his dream unspooled in his mind and he struggled to hold on to them. The sound of his own voice on the wall display's broadcast caught his attention. "My personal history is not important," he had said to a reporter during a national news interview. "What's important is that we safely commemorate the upcoming twenty-fifth anniversary of the discovery of Ascension."

"Some are raising questions about the increased opposition to the festivities." The interviewer had been trying to goad him into an outburst, Price had reasoned, but he shrugged it off.

"Only a handful of malcontents. Few remain out there who stand in the way of reason and progress."

"You're very passionate about your work. Why is that?"

Price knew that the reporter would not be satisfied unless he gave her something less clinical to nibble on. "The Institute has taken us from the uncertainty and chaos of warring religions and brought us into the light of scientific fact. Death scares a lot of people, and my own father . . ."

A small smile crept on the reporter's face but quickly vanished.

"Never mind that. What's important is that there's no reason to be afraid anymore. This is the kind of peace we all need and why I believe in mandatory testing."

Price's viewing of the interview was interrupted by the head of The Institute security systems, Tyriq Maritz, at the door.

"Sir, my apologies for the disturbance," he said. "There's something you need to see."

Rubbing his eyes and stretching, Price rose from his seat and donned his glasses. "What is it?"

"We received a signal from a testing unit. The signal itself is strange. It has all of the correct verification codes, but our system can't seem to process it. I'm at a loss."

Price drew a deep breath, mildly annoyed at being woken up for what sounded like a simple technical glitch. "Let's have a look."

Maritz offered Price his slate but was waved away. "No, let's head down to Operations. If this signal is corrupted in some way, it'll be easier to analyze from the main console," he said, gesturing to the exit.

"Yes, sir," Maritz responded.

They stepped out into the hallway. Price waved his hand near the biometric reader and locked his door. Together, they entered Price's executive elevator.

"I'll be honest, Tyriq. I don't know what we would have done without you."

⋀

Maritz nodded silently at Price. Tyriq Maritz was his own chosen name upon settling in the United States from Nigeria. Hearing someone say it out loud, even after all this time, still made him reflect on how effectively his birth name, Nwabueze Obasi, had vanished. The impulse to question his past choices was hard to resist.

Price attempted to make small talk as the elevator headed to the Operations Center. "You know, the other day I overheard some of the staff refer to you as the 'Associate.' Any idea what that is about?"

Maritz raised an eyebrow. "No, sir, but it is of no concern." An asylum seeker, he had gone to great lengths to hide his personal history and his Islamic faith. He often refrained from sharing opinions or pleasantries, which aided in solidifying his authority. When he had arrived in the United States, his coding and infrastructure design skills led him to the top of his field. Maritz knew "Associate" began as a dig at his outward deference to Jacobs and Price; over time, his subordinates spoke it with fear. His stature and stoic demeanor only reinforced that perception. Fear served his needs well.

The elevator came to a stop, and they stepped out into the bustling hub. The room was filled with operators closely monitoring their computer stations. Streams of data displayed on their screens: genetic profiles, geographic locations, and demographics. Maritz followed Price to an open console. Price sorted through the mysterious data.

"Well, this is surprising. It's not the data that is the issue," Price remarked.

"Decryption error?"

"No. There is no issue with either the transponder or the receiver, and the reader is working just fine. If you can even call it a reader. This is actually from a legacy model."

"Sir?" Maritz was confused by Price's nebulous explanation.

"What the hell is a Mark One doing in operation?" He peered closer at the screen, finding the numeric sequence that relayed the device's location. "I'll be damned. Right down the street. Unbelievable."

"Ah, I've never seen a Mark One myself," Maritz said. "I am, of course, somewhat familiar with its history, sir."

"The great-grandfather of our current testing kits. Those things were mammoths in comparison." His voice trailed off as his eyes settled on the data. The computer failed to translate the message, since the current protocol no longer supported the decryption of Mark One transmissions.

Price signed in to his profile and dove deep into his personal files to initiate the older process. He imported the new data into the system and leaned in as the results displayed on the screen:

ASCENDANT
Ascendant Profile Match: 97.958%.

Price's heart raced as he scrolled through the details.

Test Sample: Compatible.
Contaminants: None.
Confidence: High.
Test Result: Stable.
Type: O+.

Strand ASC, TCTTTTGA ... AGCG: 100% match.
AJD Gene Match: False.
Ascendant Match: 97.958%, activated.
Recommendation: Priority alert.

"We found one," Price whispered. He raised his voice and addressed the entire room. "Lock down everything." Everyone looked up from their consoles, confused. "Nothing and nobody leaves this building. Lock it down, now!"

Maritz punched a short code into the console. "This is Tyriq Maritz, authorization code nine-five-two-seven-beta. Initiate full lockdown protocol. Sever all external network connections and deploy additional security."

Price turned to Maritz as he issued his next set of commands. "Gather Shoals and Darby from the lab and get Briggs, Dean, and Powers from Internal Security, and meet me at the elevator. We're going on a little field trip."

"Yes, sir. Would you like me to summon Dr. Reed as well?"

"No," Price replied. "Sebastian has his hands full as it is, and I don't want his work to be disturbed. Ten minutes, down on the lower access port in the back."

Maritz collected the handpicked team and joined Price.

"Very good," Price said to the group. "We'll all be taking a short drive. When we arrive, catalog everything but disturb nothing."

As the company reached the loading dock, the large security doors opened, letting the morning sunlight beam in. A pair of black SUVs waited for them.

"If there are civilians present, Powers and Dean, keep them back," Price instructed, opening one door. "Briggs, a light touch on this one."

"Civilians," Maritz said, pressing Price to consider his choice of words as he followed him inside the vehicle.

"You know what I mean," Price replied curtly.

Hearing Price mention civilians as if he were part of some military organization rubbed Maritz the wrong way. These men were children pretending to be at war, but they knew nothing of true sacrifice. They would never understand what it meant to sit and wait for battle when invaders were at your doorstep.

⚐

Price stepped back as Dean brought up his large black boot and kicked down the front door to Michelle Sullivan's apartment. Splinters flew from the doorframe. Briggs and Powers entered the kitchen with the barrels of their rifles raised. Once it was secured, Briggs signaled that the room was clear, and Price stepped inside.

The room was a mess; the air was stale. Shards of plateware lay beside the pale female corpse on the floor. Blood had splattered and dried along the wall. Briggs and Price were nonplussed.

"Find the device," Price said, kneeling and looking over the corpse of the old woman. As his team searched the apartment, something along the dead woman's wrist caught Price's attention. He pulled a handkerchief from his pocket and used it to turn the corpse's left hand, revealing her tattoo. "Huh," he whispered to himself, studying it. It had faded with age, but the outlines of the A.R.M. fist and lightning bolt were distinct.

Most A.R.M. chapters throughout the nation had been eradicated, though a few rogue clusters persisted. To find one so close to home was not only surprising, but disturbing. Price was grateful for whoever had shot this woman, hoping her death was the result of an internal dispute between aspiring anarchists.

"Sir, I think we've found it," Briggs said, breaking Price's train of thought.

"Think?"

"Well, I can't be certain, sir. It's definitely old tech. And it's big. I'm pretty sure it's what we're looking for. It's just in the bedroom," Briggs replied.

Price rose and moved into the bedroom. Papers and books, piles of clothing, and a layer of dust covered everything in sight. In the closet, between two rows of clothes that had been pushed aside, was the Mark One. Price smiled at the sight of the old machine. It had been decades since he had last seen or used one.

"Very good. Secure the doors and don't let anyone in. Have someone sit on the police comms and make sure this incident hasn't been reported. If it has, contact Javier and have them delayed." Price didn't often make use of his police contact. Despite his position, Price knew that to be first to an unreported murder with the intent to alter the scene was questionable enough in the eyes of the law that all bases ought to be covered. Nor was he in the mood to deal with The Institute's Public Relations Department. As his orders were carried out, Price inspected the machine.

The Mark One was enormous in size compared to the modern testing kit. Examining the testing pad, he could see that whoever had used the unit last had done so savagely. Whereas a single drop would have done the trick, a smear of dried blood covered most of the surface. Price produced a small pocketknife from his jacket and scraped up some of the blood.

"Get me a vial and some solution to rehydrate this sample," Price instructed Shoals. "Oh, and a fresh syringe."

Shoals carefully did as asked, and soon Price had collected the sample. Price pulled a fresh testing slate from its package and turned it on. He took his syringe, drew some of the sample from the small vial, and deposited it onto the screen.

"Now, who do we have here?" he asked the syringe. He entered his personal code and sent the sample to The Institute's genomic database. Seconds later, the answer appeared on the screen and his heart skipped a beat.

"Hannah Teller. Hannah Teller," he said. "Is it . . . are . . . ?"

Price mumbled, as he compared medical and location records to be certain of the connection. When the data was confirmed that Hannah Teller was the girl who was right there next to him at the academy, his hands shook. Finally, a link to the First Ascendant was in his grasp.

Briggs walked over. "Are you all right, sir?"

Dazed, Price nodded. "Yes. Sweep the apartment for anything else that might lead us to this woman's cohorts. When we're gone, call in the body. Let the local PD handle it, but give Javier the heads-up. Do you think you can pull the hard drive from the unit in the bedroom?"

"Of course," Briggs replied.

"Pull it and bag it. I want us out of here in ten minutes."

After a thorough inspection of the rest of the apartment, the men piled into their vehicles and set off for The Institute.

"Prepare to go dark for a few minutes," he said to his company. He punched in his access code and forced the network to block out all other devices in the immediate area. Price ran diagnostics on the Mark One hard drive and the testing kit. The analysis was valid and the link to the child confirmed. Her profile was a confirmed 97.958 percent match. This child, this young girl whom he had serendipitously sat beside, was the very thing for which he had been searching for decades. How could this be? She appeared an average child, nothing remarkable or exceptional about her. At long last, once he had her in the Corpus, the real work could begin.

⚊⚊ ⚊⚊

"Charles, I found it," Price said to Jacobs, whose image popped up on his slate's display.

"I can tell from that communications blackout you've established that you found something. Are you heading back to The Institute?" Jacobs asked.

"Well, no. Not yet. We're going to round up—"

"Head back here now and we'll discuss your findings," said Jacobs, cutting off Price.

"Charles! This needs immediate action."

"Priorities are set by me, Henry. Whatever your findings are, they'll be just as actionable after I've had a chance to look them over. Head back and we'll decide what to do."

"Don't question my judgment."

"I won't have you operating alone with findings of this magnitude. Bring your data back to my office so I can decide what comes next. Got it?"

Price relented and offered his best attempt at a cordial smile. "Heading back now."

Jacobs disconnected and Price reopened the network access. He tapped Briggs's shoulder. "Head back to The Institute. I need to go meet with Jacobs."

Briggs input their new destination into the navigation system. Powers pointed to the commotion ahead.

"Eyes up!" Powers shouted.

The car had taken a right turn. At the next intersection, a large protest was underway, blocking their path.

"Powers. Briggs. Somebody take manual control. Reverse course and take us back a few blocks," Price ordered. "See if we can cut around behind them." Powers grabbed the wheel as Briggs reached for his rifle. Price relayed similar instructions to the other vehicle in the convoy. "Transport Two, we are doubling back in order to get around this crowd."

Powers slammed the car into reverse. The vehicles rolled backward down the street. Briggs feverishly engaged the navigation panel to adjust GPS settings, only to find the satellite mapping had revealed the human obstructions and planned a route accordingly.

"Ha! See that?" Price said, directing Powers's attention to the guidance system. "Just three blocks back and we're golden."

As he pointed to the interactive map on the dashboard, Powers took note of the dense yellow cluster ahead of them, each tiny yellow dot meant to represent one of the marchers. Sure enough, in just three blocks, the tail end of the demonstration was quickly snaking down the avenue. He popped the shifter back into drive and pulled a hard right to double back.

As the vehicles rolled along the side street, the display showed that the protestors who had overtaken their initial route were thinning out. Within moments, they were running parallel with the end of the crowd. Briggs signaled Powers to turn left, and they barreled down the street.

This block seemed mostly devoid of people. As Powers slowed down to avoid hitting a pedestrian crossing the street, a large group of protestors came around the corner. Confused, Briggs looked at the GPS monitor. Dozens of yellow dots popped up on the screen. This second round of protestors appeared out of thin air.

"Go through slowly. I doubt any of them want trouble," Briggs said, his rifle now at his shoulder.

"Sir," Powers said to Price as he reengaged the auto-drive, "I'm going to need you to get your head down."

Price complied, lying down across the rear bench seat. Powers pulled a handgun from his holster and trained it on the door beside him. Price had never liked guns, let alone combat rifles. The sound of the round sliding into the barrel sent goose bumps up his arm.

The crowd soon surrounded the vehicles as the convoy came to a stop. Powers laid on the horn as Briggs waved at the protestors to disperse. People in masks and hooded sweatshirts pressed up against the SUV on all sides. The tension mounted until Briggs spotted someone drawing their weapon.

"Gun!" Briggs yelled as he shifted the window down just enough to make a firing port. The crack of his rifle as it fired drowned out all other sounds. Price felt the concussive thuds of gunfire that accompanied each volley that followed.

Both Briggs and Powers fired out of their windows in three bursts. Most of their bullets hit the chests, backs, and at least one face of the activists. The protestors fell back, and the cars were free to move.

Price remained still until he was allowed to sit up again, still experiencing hearing loss. The convoy sped away from the panic that they had induced several blocks behind. They were soon back at The Institute, pulling into the rear garage entrance. Price didn't move a muscle until he heard the heavy metal doors bang into place and lock shut. He was unaccustomed to experiencing violence directed at him.

"Sir, do you need help?" Powers asked, offering a hand as he rounded the vehicle.

"No. I'm fine. You're not to discuss this. Any of it, with anyone. Understood?"

"Understood, sir."

"I'm heading up to Jacobs."

After Price's order, all except Briggs scattered. As Price moved into the elevator, Briggs murmured tactical instructions to security operatives through his earpiece. Price dismissed Briggs's commands as too little, too late. Besides, the real threat to his objective at this moment wasn't anyone hiding in the shadows. No, the weakest link to Price's operation was a tired old man perched in the penthouse of The Institute complex.

△

Jacobs slouched in his office chair, facing the massive windows that overlooked most of the city. On the table between him and the enormous glass pane rested a single framed photo of his daughter as a young girl, about ten years of age. He took pride in keeping his workspace free from distractions, including the ceaseless rotating photos in frames and holographic projections most people kept in their offices. One actual photograph bordered by a simple black frame was all he needed. His gaze moved between the print of his daughter and the city of Boston, which was bathed in the light of the late-morning sun.

He had not slept nor moved from his seat since the previous evening. His wife had been dead for decades, but her loss still weighed so heavy on his soul. And now, Alexandra was at her end. If both were truly taken from him and all that would be left was this wretched place, this cursed building that bore his name, why continue? His triumphs were just consequences of his mistakes. He was a fraud, and he had failed his family. Yet, in the waning hours of Alexandra's life, there was one gambit he was counting on that could make a difference.

A notification sounded on his desk, interrupting his chain of thought. The elevator was approaching his penthouse office. Jacobs's attention returned to the business at hand. Price and Briggs emerged from the glossy elevator doors and paced outside his office. As a security precaution, all entrances to Jacobs's private office were reinforced with bulletproof glass and only Jacobs could permit entry.

"Mr. Briggs," Jacobs said, speaking into an intercom microphone beside his screen. "If you would please take a seat, I'll speak to Henry alone, thank you."

Briggs looked to Price, waiting for orders. The impulse to look to Price for confirmation did not go unnoticed by Jacobs. Price was pushing the limits of his power, and as much as Jacobs should step down, he knew the dangers of handing The Institute over to him. Price wanted far too much, far too fast. With a nod from Price, Briggs took a seat on the sofa in the hallway and Jacobs unlocked the door from his desk.

"Henry, you look like hell. Have you slept?" Jacobs asked, motioning for him to sit.

The dark circles below Price's eyes conflicted with his manic approach. He rushed in, gripping a slate with both hands. "Charles, I found it."

"You found what, exactly?"

"A near-perfect match." Price handed over the slate. Jacobs swiped across the screen and threw the image up onto his larger tabletop display.

He closely looked over the data, inspecting the comparisons between the DNA of the First Ascendant and that obtained from a subject identified as Hannah Teller. "How did you come across these results?" Jacobs asked, eyes glued to the screen.

"Huh?" Price responded.

"The test. Where did it come from?"

"Oh. We found an old Mark One in an apartment near Milk Street. Someone had used it recently to test a sample and Ops received the data."

"Who would still have a Mark One?" Jacobs asked suspiciously.

"Who knows? There was a dead old woman there. Probably just another scavenger."

Jacobs flicked his display to show video of Price's convoy racing toward the complex. "And what is this report about an incident?"

"There was a blockade. They swarmed the car. Security saw a gun and acted effectively to get us out of there. Regardless, we need to—"

"So," Jacobs interrupted, "there's a dead woman in an apartment, dead people out in the street, and everything leads back here." Jacobs slammed his palms into the table harder than he intended.

"The only thing that matters is the girl!" Price seethed.

"Hannah Teller?"

"I've met her, Charles. She's a six-year-old girl who attends school where Alex's husband teaches. I met her the other day, which is the crazy part. This is everything." Price triumphantly swept his right arm outward.

"No," Jacobs said tersely.

Price deflated, his arm falling into his lap. "No?"

"This has gone on for long enough." It was time to pull back on Price's leash. "We've hurt too many people trying to find the connection. But it's enough. You will do nothing."

"Charles, we just need to do this one thing," Price pleaded. *Like a petulant child,* thought Jacobs.

"No, no more abductions. I won't allow it. This is over."

"Charles, we started this—" Desperation turned to frustration.

"We started this because it was my last hope of saving Alexandra. And our interests aligned. I no longer care about any of this well-funded cult of ours." Jacobs waved his arms wildly in the air.

"You don't believe that. We started this because we needed answers. The world needs answers."

"But my god, at what cost? Every disaster that has come about since the Announcement, every horrible thing that we did." Jacobs knew that the evil in this world existed because he had not put his foot down. Because he was a coward. Because he was afraid that if he stopped, he would fail. But he had failed all the same.

"It's too late for regrets, Charles."

Jacobs rose from his seat and paced about the room. "We started out as scientists, Henry. We started out to help people. To fix things, to cure things. Can you even remember that? Instead, we're murderers who have driven the world to ruin, to insanity."

Price slammed his fist onto Jacobs's desk as he stood up. "Damn you!" Price spat. "How much progress have we made together? How many treatments have we discovered for countless diseases? Think of all those lives that we did manage to save. And the lives we will save."

Jacobs took a long, slow breath as he walked to the other side of his desk. "You've been with me almost from the very start of all this. None of the good we've accomplished would have been possible without you," Jacobs admitted. "But the violence was supposed to have ended, or at least declined to an acceptable percentage. The peace we talked about is overdue."

"And we're nearly there," Price replied, his words measured. "Have you forgotten how it was? I haven't. You talk of the past as though it wasn't without death, terror, and misery. I watched my father twist and shudder in agony, his final moments racked by pain. Nothing was waiting for him but darkness. And for my mother? The way my father died showed me that his life meant nothing. Her final words were the gasps and sputters of a woman closer to something else. Something we need to unravel. Don't you think it was the same for Alexandra's mother?" Price pointed to the black photo frame on his desk. "Don't you think it was the same for your precious Angela?"

Jacobs charged Price and slapped him hard across the face. The two men had known each other for decades, had changed the world standing shoulder to shoulder; these men were equally responsible for reshaping all of society. But the driving force of their efforts had drifted apart. Now, they faced each other as adversaries, with the potential of everything mankind could achieve hanging in the balance.

Price tried to brush past the assault. "We're almost there, Charles. We're so very close. Just one more step to take. Let me go get her and plug her in."

"I will terminate your position. I will have your security clearance revoked and archives wiped clean. Leave this child alone."

"You're making a mistake."

"We're done." Jacobs sat back down behind his desk. "Collect your dog out there and reconsider your priorities. Do you understand?"

With a smirk, Price nodded and stepped out of Jacobs's office.

◬

"Orders?" Briggs asked as he and Price rode down the elevator.

"Charles is having second thoughts," Price said, "but he'll come around. He always does."

Briggs did not understand Price's allegiance to the old man. Price was the one who kept The Institute chugging along. He was the one taking all the risks. This was the man who should be in charge of the whole enchilada. "I assume I should put together another team, sir?"

"Yes," Price replied. "Do it quietly. Say nothing to Tyriq."

The Associate gave Briggs the creeps. Maritz didn't quite fit into the pecking order at The Institute, and Briggs never quite understood why they kept him around. He was the Darth Vader of the computer nerds, outside of the command structure but often the one calling the shots. It made no sense. Surely, there must be other eggheads out there. He was annoyed that he was kept out of whatever scheme these three had cooked up years ago. Price was looking at him expectantly, awaiting confirmation. Instead, Briggs asked, "Why keep Maritz in the dark, sir?"

"Tyriq Maritz is a complication I don't want to get into now. Get going."

◬

Sam breathed in the crisp autumn air tumbling off the Charles River as he pushed Alexandra through the park. Year after year, she had refused all forms of motorized wheelchairs that her father sent to the door, just to spite him. The pair wore warm smiles as they wandered along the grounds of where they first met. First, they moseyed to the park, and then the quad of their nearby alma mater. They would go to the old ice cream place that, as far as they were concerned, had been there since the Earth had cooled. Next, a craft beer at the Elephant Bar, or a jaunt around the empty stadium's track, a bag of pretzels in hand.

In the past, these excursions would inevitably lead to another walk as the sun set, followed by a train ride and a final walk home to their brownstone in Back Bay. Memories of those better times lingered. This would be their final visit. As they approached an old and familiar oak tree, Sam stopped.

"And there it is," he said, craning his neck up from the roots to the canopy filled with bright green leaves.

Alexandra pointed to the bicycle rack at the base of the tree. "The scene of the crime."

To the casual observer, the bike rack and tree were of little interest, but to Alexandra and Sam, this was where history had been made: where they had first met. Alexandra, frustrated and cursing the broken lock that held her bike hostage. And Sam, coming to the rescue, trying his best to help a stranger.

"I did my very best," he said, chuckling.

"You did," Alexandra replied, "and your best broke my bike."

"I just bent the wheel a little."

"It broke in half!"

"Well, okay, maybe. But then I wouldn't have offered to buy you dinner to make up for it."

"This is true." Alexandra smiled half-heartedly. Tears welled in her eyes. She breathed deeply, struggling to hold the swell of emotions at bay. As she raised her trembling hand to her face, her eyes remained locked on the bike rack.

"This is a happy memory in a happy place," Sam said, rubbing her shoulder.

Alexandra nodded. "The beginning of a happy story. One that has a happy ending too." Her voice cracked.

Sam stepped around her chair and knelt in front of her. He took both her hands in his.

"I know you're scared, but it's not really an ending, my love," he insisted.

"What if I asked you not to?" she said quietly.

"Not to what?" Sam asked.

"Not to come with me."

"I don't want to hear that anymore. I'm not interested in this world without you in it. Nothing can change that, nothing. When you ascend, I'll be right beside you. And we will continue on together."

"Sam, you've still got plenty of life to live, and you've got the school, and those kids who look up to you."

"It's all been taken care of. All of it. The administration knows I'll be leaving and there's already a replacement. All of our affairs are in order." Sam hugged her close. "This is our day. Let's not waste any more time on this."

The truth about Ascension burned a hole in her chest, yet all she whispered in his ear was, "I love you."

The two remained in each other's arms for a while. Sam let go first, then kissed his wife deeply. The chilly wind caused her to shiver as the tree branches swayed.

"So, a drink?" he asked.

"I think that would be lovely." Alexandra wiped the tears from her eyes.

They meandered down the path to the bar, now called Donovan's, and Sam enjoyed a cold draft while Alexandra took a single sip from a glass of wine. Most of the patrons were focused on the broadcast of the evening's home game. Whoops and hollers burst out across the room when the player in center field dove for a fly ball, arms outstretched, and caught it. The animated atmosphere only fueled the warmth between them as they smiled and laughed, knees knocking together playfully under the table.

They dared each other to sample the bowl of bar peanuts full of germs from countless college students' grubby hands. They bounced from one story to another, never sticking to one topic for too long. Sam ordered a shot and started a game of quarters with the empty glass. Alexandra won.

The ball game was tied at the bottom of the ninth. The Red Sox had two strikes against them, with only one runner on first. Everyone held their breath as the pitcher lobbed a fastball. The batter timed it perfectly; the ball landed square in the bat's sweet spot. The runner on first was already halfway to second when the ball went flying deep into the outfield, then over the wall. The bar erupted in cheers. Alexandra and Sam couldn't help but join in, yelling and clinking glasses with complete strangers. In that bar, neither felt burdened by sickness or time. They had each other. They felt good. They felt normal.

EIGHT

In the Cold Wind

There'll never be any shortage of things to run from. The things we should run toward are often few and far between.

—The Madness (Third Life Cycle)

In a tiny apartment in Mattapan . . .

MAYA lay on the ripped sofa that overwhelmed the center of her friend Bogdan's living room. If one were to ask him why he kept such a ratty piece of furniture, let alone lie or sleep on it as she had many times in the past, he would have offered some excuse about it being "vintage" or "possessing a rustic aesthetic." He relished using his art degree to excuse any number of actions. The truth, however, was that he was probably too lazy to throw it out and too poor to buy a new one. All the same, Maya was not prepared to argue the point anytime soon, seeing as that busted and lumpy sofa was home until she planned her next move.

The sun spilled in through the living room window as the later part of the afternoon set in. Maya adjusted her position on the couch to redirect the glare on her slate. She had spent the better part of the day looking for jobs, finding nothing of interest.

"Hey," Bogdan called from the bathroom, "what if you became like a sugar baby or something?"

"A what?" she called back, hoping she had heard him incorrectly.

"A sugar baby!" he shouted, flushing the toilet.

"What is that, like an escort?"

Bogdan walked into the living room, still buckling his belt. "No. I mean, sort of. But no. You just make vids and maybe go on some dates. Keep older guys company. They're kind of like flatline hookups, except no one tries to die."

"I guess we can call that a perk," Maya joked.

Bogdan laughed. "No—basically, you just go to these parties in a hot dress and let these creepy old dudes touch your feet or make you step on bugs. And they pay you a shit ton of cash. It's usually just kinky, harmless businessmen."

When put like that, he was able to make it sound almost reasonable. But she wasn't that desperate. Yet. "I think I'll pass."

Bogdan nodded seriously. "I don't think that it would be all that cool, actually. You'd probably be better off as a regular stripper at that point."

"There's something seriously wrong with you, you know?" Her mouth curled into a sarcastic smile.

"Listen. I've been through enough therapy to know what's wrong"—he shrugged dramatically—"but not enough therapy to fix it." Bogdan laughed heartily, proud of himself. "I'm heading out tonight. Do you have any plans?"

"Nothing really. Thought I might head over to my grandpa's place and help out with dinner for the homeless or something."

"Damn, girl, what makes you so good? You ought to be on some poster or something." Bogdan framed an imaginary poster with his hands around her face.

She batted his hands away. "What do you mean?"

"Just that, like, here you are, a girl in the prime of her life, and you spend your free time helping your grandpa help other people. You're a saint or something," Bogdan declared as he looked himself over in the mirror hung from the bedroom door. "While you're out piling spaghetti onto paper plates, I'll be out sinning for the both of us."

Bogdan winced as he spun around in front of the mirror. "Goddamn. I need to start running again. I'm turning into my dad."

"What do you mean?"

"Too many Deluxe Italian subs from Bob's. I can barely fit into my pants anymore. Ugh!"

"You're fine. Stop it," Maya teased.

"Fine like wine, I can't argue with that," Bogdan said, smirking. "What time is it?"

"Six twenty," Maya replied, checking her slate.

"I'm going to heat up some of that pizza from last night. You want a piece?"

"Please."

A few hours passed, and soon Bogdan was ready to head out for a night on the town. A ding notified Maya of an incoming alert on her slate. Tapping a small green icon, Maya took the call.

"Hey, what's up?" she said as Amy's face projected from the screen.

"What are you up to? Where are you?" It was clear from the background that Amy was at a nightclub. Amy had to shout over the loud beat to be heard.

"I'm not doing anything."

"Oh my god, you have got to get down here. This club is crazy and I am with the hottest guys right now!" Amy said, her speech slurred.

"Where are you?" Maya asked seriously. Amy's partying tended to get out of control from time to time, leading to some unfortunate decisions and a laundry list of regrets.

"Hold on." The projection blipped as she turned to one of the large men who flanked her. "Where are we?" The audio on Maya's end became garbled as a mix of voices and pounding music played over Amy's conversation.

"Amy, I can't hear you."

The connection cleared up. "Oh, hey! Yeah, so let me text you the address. You've got to get down here. I know the whole As *plowin'* Bs thing isn't quite your thing, but these guys are so hot!" Maya could see a trio of men shepherd Amy in a different direction. "I'm being invited down into the VIP room. Oh my god, Maya, let me just—" She was interrupted. "Wait, what? Down there?"

"Amy! Stop moving! What's going on?" Maya yelled at the slate. Amy was shuffled into a darkened hallway before the screen froze and the call dropped.

Maya brought up Amy's contact information screen and pressed a button labeled Find My Friend. She waited for the results.

A frowning emoji appeared.

☹ Sorry, we couldn't find your friend.

"What's the fuss?" Bogdan asked, fastening a flashy bracelet around his wrist.

"It's Amy. I don't know why, but I think she's in some kind of trouble."

"What kind of trouble? She get caught up with a line chaser or something?"

"No. I think she's in real trouble." Maya pulled up the recorded video call.

"You worry too much, Maya."

"I don't like it," she said, scanning the video at half speed. It took her only a moment to find what she was after. Zooming in on the frame of Amy, drunk with her eyes half rolled back into her head, Maya closely examined the bar behind her. A napkin with a bright red logo rested on the edge of the counter. Unable to make out the lettering, Maya took a screen capture of the image and transferred it to her Slate Assistant. It quickly identified the logo as that of a local nightclub called the District.

"Hey, Bogdan," Maya said, "think you could give me a ride?"

"Of course. I mean, it'll be good to get you out of the house and doing something bad. I mean fun. Even if that club is kinda seedy."

"You know the place?"

"Know of it? Who do you think you're talking to? It's one of those throwback EDM places. I dated a guy who was a regular there. It's covered in line chasers and day trippers." Bogdan cringed slightly at his own imagery. "Ugh, can't imagine why Amy would even consider stepping foot in there."

"I need to go and find out."

"Then, madam." Bogdan grabbed his car keys from the end table next to the couch and jingled them. "Your chariot awaits."

Twenty minutes later, the two sat in Bogdan's 2025 compact vehicle, its engine humming. He had put up a fuss when Maya refused to "get ready" to go out but relented when he realized she wouldn't budge. In a world of calibrated traffic patterns orchestrated by the network of onboard computers in modern self-driving vehicles, Bogdan took great pains to maintain the appearance of his own car being an authentic original model. As they pulled out of his parking space, he double-checked the hacked transponder he had installed beneath the dash.

It had been nearly ten full years since the law requiring all new cars to be networked and older models to be retrofitted was passed. But many car enthusiasts and purists, including Bogdan, added a bogus transponder to avoid unwanted attention. His most recent project, the 2025 Subaru WRX MTK in which they rode, had been a real challenge. With a mix of skill and clever engineering, the rebuilt custom rally racer had become the crown jewel of his ever-increasing list of modified rides. Not being particularly passionate about off-grid machines herself, Maya's knuckles turned white clutching the door.

At last, they arrived on the quiet side street where the District was located. Bogdan's bright, blue-tinted headlights lit up the street.

"Thanks," she said, hopping out. "I'll catch the train back later tonight."

"You sure? I could always pick you up and we could see what kind of lap time I make when we get home," he joked.

"I think I'm good," Maya said, already walking away.

"All right. Be safe and ping me if you need anything."

"Okay."

Bogdan rolled the window down. "And tell Amy I said hi!" he shouted, revving his engine to the delight of those standing outside the club.

"I will. See you later."

Bogdan sped off, but not before spinning his tires, which sent a small plume of rancid smoke rising into the air. Waving it away from her face, Maya shook her head with a smile.

She approached the bouncer, who looked less like a man than a Pamplona bull in a muscle tee. The bouncer turned to her and gave her a once-over, a puzzled expression on his face. More than once, Amy had prodded her to ditch her techwear outfit for something that better suited the vibe. Would she be denied entry, even though this place was a shithole?

"Enjoy," the bouncer muttered.

She nodded at the bouncer and entered the club. She immediately found herself drowning in the scent of cheap body spray, nylon costumes, and sweat. The air was hazy from accumulated perspiration. A balcony reserved for VIPs encircled the high ceilings of the room, while at the far end of the packed dance floor a brightly lit bar swarmed with customers. Leather, pleather, latex, silk, satin, and more comprised the majority of skintight outfits on the people inside. Along the walls, spotlights swept across the crowd in random patterns, occasionally blinding Maya as she made her way to the back.

The bar was large, even by nightclub standards, stretching nearly fifty feet from end to end and showcasing an impressively large stock of cheap liquor along the wall. Behind these bottles, a mirror extended from the counter to the ceiling, giving the impression that the club was double its actual size. As she bellied up to the bar, she found that only two bartenders were responsible for the entire bar. Every time she'd raise her hand to get their attention, they shot her an indifferent glance. They would get to her when they could, which would be no time soon.

Eventually, Maya grabbed an empty glass on the bar that was collecting dust and slammed it down. The larger of the two bartenders, a man well over six feet tall, with half of his face covered in a tattoo of a demonic beast, walked over.

"What do you want?" he asked in a strange accent as he leaned in to her, both hands gripping the bar. The maw of the beast on his cheek opened with the movement of his upper lip. Both man and beast threatened her.

"I'm looking for someone. A redhead surrounded by a bunch of guys," Maya explained, raising her voice above the pounding music.

"Unless their names are Jack Daniel's, Jim Beam, or Jose

Cuervo, I don't know who you're looking for," the bartender replied.

Maya pulled all the cash from her pocket and slapped it onto the bar next to the empty glass. She put three fingers on the pile and slid it forward. He attempted to snatch the bills, but Maya held them firmly to the bar top, raising an eyebrow. The bartender nodded once.

Maya pulled up a picture of Amy on her phone. "This girl here. Have you seen her?"

He squinted at the image. "Kid, I can't help you. I see a lot of faces."

"She said she was partying with some guys. Said they were going to the VIP party."

The bartender's shoulders relaxed. "VIP? Did she say VIP room or VIP section?"

"Is there a difference?"

"Well, yeah. One is a room, and one is a section."

Maya leaned in and growled. "Listen, asshole. I really don't have time for this. Now, if I remember correctly, she said room. VIP room. So, you want to tell me where the fuck my friend is, or would you rather I just break your goddamn nose?"

"Whoa, relax there, kitten," the bartender replied. His condescending smirk irked Maya. "If she said room, then she's in the VIP room. Trust your friend, yes?"

"And how do I get into the VIP room?" Maya's patience was waning with every syllable he uttered.

He motioned to someone from down the bar to join him. A tall woman in a black latex bodysuit slithered over, flanked by two menacing-looking men. As she approached, her black lips curved into a smile.

"Hello, Ricki, is everything all right?" she asked the bartender.

"This young lady would like access to the VIP room."

"Would she?" the woman probed, turning to Maya.

"I'm looking for my friend," Maya replied, holding up her phone. "This is her. Have you seen her? I think she's in trouble."

"Hmm," the woman said. "I think I recall seeing her there, but I can't be sure. If you're interested, I can send someone in to check."

"Any chance I could have a look?" Maya asked.

"It is invite only. Normally—" The woman paused. "I suppose I can arrange to have you brought down. You'll need to stay with the escorts, of course. We can't just have anyone walking in uninvited, you know?"

"Okay, let's go."

"All right then." She whispered something into the ear of one of the men. The woman grinned as she finished talking, and try as she might, Maya could not hear a word of it. Nodding to his partner, a shorter, older man, he stepped forward. The older man gestured to a door near the end of the bar. The flashing lights of the club reflected off the shining bald heads of the pair. "Have fun," said the woman as they set off.

The shorter man opened the metal service door. Maya followed, with the larger man behind her. The door led into a dimly lit stairwell that descended into the basement. Her lead trotted down the steps. The man behind her kept a close distance the entire way down.

At the bottom, Maya was led down a long corridor, lit only by flickering fluorescent lights. The concrete walls and floor were old and dank. She couldn't see a door or exit besides the one through which they had entered. The muffled music of the club pounded above them. As the three made their way down the hall, Maya felt like they were crawling into the center of a spider's web. Slipping her left hand into her jacket pocket, she produced her phone to find, unsurprisingly, that there was no service or network connection to be had down here. With her right hand, she held the grip of the hidden revolver. She formulated a plan.

Upon reaching the door, she would draw her gun and hold the man in front of her at gunpoint. She would force them to produce Amy. If her rear escort had any plans to stop her, he would get an elbow smashed into his face. Maya calculated she would have just enough time to knock him out, then his friend.

Just a few more steps. Maya fought the urge to tighten every muscle in her body. It was crucial that she appeared calm and steady to capitalize on the element of surprise, her only advantage besides the revolver. She had to act before they went any farther. Maya inhaled. On the count of three, she decided.

One.

Two.

Three.

She threw her left elbow back and aimed the revolver squarely at her lead escort's face. Her right shoulder and elbow tensed. The man behind her grabbed her elbow and thrust it to the side, turning her around to face him. Maya pointed her revolver to his face, but his left hand shot out and clutched her right wrist. He forced her hand down. She managed to discharge a single bullet, which slammed into the concrete below.

A fist smashed into her face. Her vision blurred; her knees buckled. She felt two strong arms slip beneath her own. The man behind secured her in an armlock, keeping her both restrained and standing as her legs gave out, while the lead one ripped the revolver from her hand. She shook her head, trying to stay in the fight, but a powerful right hook soon careened into the side of her head.

NINE

Verisimilitude

Rowan Morales: "When I was a very young boy, I was at a funeral with my family. We joined a procession of hundreds of people. I heard voices quietly repeating one word over and over: presente. Eventually, nearly everyone began to chant presente. I asked my mother its significance, and she explained that it meant the dead were living on in their hearts. That they were present with us all the time. And that they'd never be forgotten. So, what do I believe? I believe good people—decent people—get to live on in other people's hearts. And not even you can take that away. There are no As and Bs. It's what we do with our life, this life, that matters. It's who we are. And how we're remembered."

Sebastian Reed: "Terrifying."

—Operation Raven Recording, Transcript Fragment

The phone rang on the bedside table....

Rebecca lifted her head from the pillow, dragged from the edge of sleep. Accepting the call with Visual mode off, she heard an unfamiliar voice speak to her.

"Dr. Teller," the voice said.

"Yes," she replied drearily.

"Doctor, this is Adam Smith from the Jacobs Institute Hospital."

"Who?"

"We need you to come in this evening. There are some urgent reports that need your review and hard copy signature regarding a number of your patients."

"Reports about my patients? What do you mean?" She knew with certainty that there were no outstanding records issues that needed her attention, given her leave of absence. Besides, it was the middle of the night and there was something about his voice that sounded strange. Unnatural. Suspicious, she asked, "Which patients?"

"I cannot say. We do need you to be here personally. It is an urgent clerical matter. Can you get here as soon as possible?"

"Did you clear this with Dr. Kleinberg? I'm on a leave of absence. If you want, feel free to send the paperwork to my inbox and I'll access them from here—"

"I am sorry, Doctor," the voice insisted, "but this requires you to be here in person."

"What department did you say you were calling from again?"

"Administration, ma'am." The phone crackled, as though the signal was cutting out.

"And who do you work for directly?"

The answer was unintelligible, the words distorted by digital noise. Rebecca could not make out anything more than the words "please come in to sign." The call dropped, and the line went dead.

Frustrated and confused, Rebecca called the hospital only

to find that the line was busy. She tried again and again with the same result. It also happened when she called a nurse's station directly. A message flashed on the screen with a random error code. Rebecca rolled her eyes. Dropped calls. Now a malfunctioning phone.

Rebecca threw on some clothes and checked herself in the mirror. She was tired and stressed, and it showed. There were wrinkles in her shirt and bags under her eyes. She cursed the administration for dragging her back in after dismissing her.

She walked into Hannah's room, pulled back the sheets, and scooped her up. She hated doing this to her child, but there was no one to watch her this late. While Hannah was half asleep, she managed to help put on her daughter's clothes and shoes. Hannah remained silent the entire time. Soon after, they were in the car, belted and buckled with the auto-drive taking them to the hospital.

Rebecca tried calling the hospital from the Communications app built into her car. An error message popped up on the dashboard display screen. Administrative assistants typically handled all departmental affairs when physicians and surgeons were off-site. She thought she knew everyone in administration, yet Adam Smith was unfamiliar to her. She racked her brain but couldn't put a face to the name. *This had better be important,* she thought.

The highway was empty; her headlights flooded the road ahead. As her car got close to the hospital, Rebecca watched a convoy of black SUVs speed in the opposite direction. She wondered if some politician or foreign dignitary was in town. The thought was fleeting, but it was a nice distraction.

🔺

Sam and Alexandra lounged together in bed one last time. Each raised a glass of wine to toast one another. A dulcet song written by John McLaughlin played throughout the house; they had danced to his music at their wedding. The ceremony had been a small and quiet service reserved for close friends and immediate family. It was likely the last time she saw her father laughing and enjoying time with his family.

Alexandra desired to die before the sun fully rose. As sunlight crept over the horizon, the two stared deeply at each other, soaking in their final moments together. Their eyes locked. This was it.

Sam pulled the small box from the nightstand and took out the two syringes.

"Did you know that in the old tradition, wedding vows often ended in the words 'until death do us part'?" Sam asked. Alexandra eyed the syringes cautiously. She took The Third Act, labeled with her name, and passed her father's syringe to Sam.

"I did know that," she said, placing her hands in her lap to ensure she didn't drop it.

Sam took out the other syringe and removed the cap. "I'm glad we didn't go all that traditional with our service."

Alexandra was not ready to go yet. "Perhaps one more glass of wine?" she asked.

Sam set his syringe aside. "Why not?" He refilled their glasses from the bottle on the dresser and raised his glass.

"I'd like to do this one," she said, using the last of her strength to raise the glass. "Sam, you are everything to me, and you are honestly more than I ever deserved. You are the most loyal, most honest, most honorable man I have ever known. I never would have made it this long without you. I would take the years we've had together over a hundred years without you. Sam, I want you to remember that. And always remember that I love you."

Their glasses clinked as tears fell from Sam's cheeks. The two downed their wine and tossed their glasses aside. The glasses crashed into the walls, shattering into pieces. They laughed for a long time until they finally settled into silence.

The couple kissed and, after one last look at each other, pierced the skin of their own forearms. Drowsiness overtook them. Both instinctively fought to keep their eyes open until they succumbed to the drugs. Alexandra's breathing grew shallow; Sam's heart rate slowed.

The monitoring system in her home alerted Institute officials of Alexandra's status. A team handpicked by her father was dispatched to recover their bodies. The prerecorded message Alexandra saved to her slate was automatically sent to the one other person who deserved a goodbye, regardless of her history with him.

⚠

In Charles Jacobs's office, a ding alerted him to a new message. Having set all other communications to silent, he knew that only messages of the highest priority would be relayed. The message was titled "Dad." He was hesitant to actually open the message, knowing what it contained. Jacobs transferred the message to his wall display. The glass walls of his office space faded to black. The image of his beloved daughter filled the room.

"Dad. So, hey. It's me." Alexandra's message began awkwardly. "We haven't talked in a long time. And now, this is going to just be me talking to you, I guess. I don't know. Maybe I should have reached out. I've been angry with you about a lot of different things for some time. Better late than never, right? So, first things first. You know what today is, and you know what's happened at this point. But there's been a slight change in plans. I may have forgiven you, at least a little, but I know who you are. I know what you're capable of. And I know those syringes you gave to Sam were probably one last crazy attempt to keep us alive. But I'm done, Dad."

Jacobs's blood boiled. He sacrificed his life, he dedicated

every resource at his disposal, to give her a fighting chance. And here she was, throwing all that away. Facing the end, how could she choose certain death over a chance to live on?

"I know that you kept a close eye on me and Sam." Alexandra's message continued playing. "And honestly, most of the time, that's just another thing I hate you for. By now, you've probably gotten the signal that I'm gone for good. And you'll receive another signal for Sam saying he's been knocked out. You see, I know you. I think I know what you were going to do to us. Everything you've ever done has been to keep me alive, and I didn't want to spend the rest of *your* life with me stuck inside some machine waiting to be 'fixed,' only to be left there once you're gone. I just want you to find a way to get to Sam. Make him understand. Keep him alive.

"Sam has spent too much of his time here on Earth tending to my needs, and while I love him for that, I want him to be free of me. Because I really love him, Dad. I really do. Maybe it'll give you some peace to know that the years I've spent with Sam have been the best of my life. I wouldn't trade them for anything. Despite my condition, I was really happy for a time, Dad.

"When he wakes up, I want him to be under your care. I want him to mourn me, and then move on. He deserves that, but he won't accept it at first. He'll fight tooth and nail to join me. He won't want to listen, but you need to make him understand. That's the only way he'll stay alive.

"Second, I want you to know something. Even though I grew to hate you, in spite of that, I still love you, Dad. I always have. I guess hate is maybe the wrong word, because really, I've been so mad. Really mad. Mad about your choices, your secrets, and for making me a collaborator in those secrets. I kept your lies, and that, more than anything, is what has destroyed me all these years. Sitting here, at the end of it all, I guess I've realized how wasteful anger is. How wasteful hate can be. All I can say is, I'm sorry, Dad. But you also deserved it."

Tears blotted out his vision. His hands shook as he cleared the moisture from his face.

Alexandra's face softened. She looked down for a moment and hesitated. When she looked into the camera, her voice was quieter than before. "We should have spent more time together as father and daughter. While I'm not letting you off the hook for that," she said, holding her pointer finger in a comical impression of a disappointed mother figure, "I will admit that I was just as stubborn as you were. Probably more, actually. But you know what? I think it's a good thing. You were stubborn enough to try to change the world and save me. I was stubborn enough to live to see my fortieth birthday, just to prove that I could to everyone who said I wouldn't. I guess we're more alike than I ever thought.

"Thank you for everything you've done for me. Even for the things I resented you for. Know that in my final hours, I am thinking of you fondly and only regretting that I wasn't more kind to you. I hope you'll let me and Mom rest, and live your life too. Goodbye, Dad."

The screen went black, and Jacobs fell back into his chair. He had one more task to carry out before he would allow himself to grieve. Touching the small screen built into his chair, he called his assistant.

"Let me know when the facilitators are headed back from my daughter's house, please," he said quietly.

"Yes, sir," his assistant said. "My condolences, sir."

"Arrange to have her sent to the Corpus immediately."

"But, sir, why would—"

"And have her husband brought to a room in the Gray Wing," Jacobs interrupted. "I'll be down there shortly." Jacobs tapped his panel and the line went dead. He brought Alexandra's message up on-screen once more and scrolled back through the video, pausing on a still frame of her face. The weight of her death pressed on him. He had expected this mix of emotions: the sensation of loss and regret, of dread and fear, of terrible grief. Yet, the amount of time he had to prepare wasn't enough. He stared at his little girl and howled in pain.

Jacobs overturned his desk and hurled everything within reach. Glasses, monitors, his chair—all were reduced to pieces. After a whirlwind of destruction and pain, he slumped against the wall.

Alexandra's image illuminated the display. At the end of her life, she looked so much like Angela.

Let it out, he heard his wife's serene voice say. *Let it out and then fix what you've broken.*

⚑

Jacobs slowly walked up a marble staircase, concealing a slatelink in his pocket. It was navy blue with a gold band in the center, cool from resting atop the archival unit in the Corpus. The damning evidence had sat there, offline and undetectable for twenty-five years; this footage would soon be exhumed from the null field. It was time for it to see the light of the day.

II

The Book of Jacobs

TEN

Past Tense

Time moves as a wave, with history rising and falling based on the foolish actions of just a few men. Now we are forced to reckon with the future they created. One childish action begat another. But time is unforgiving, power is a bitch, and their creations will backfire. So stick with me. We'll destroy all their abominations— and the foolish men who conjured them.

—The Catalyst

Before the Beginning, and before The Institute, there was a laboratory just outside of Boston, Massachusetts. It was 19 BA, by the old calendar, AD 2016. . . .

A SMALL primate named Kong lay still on a lab table surrounded by scientists. Human researchers in white coats were hard at work attaching sensors along his forehead and scalp. Kong only knew that when they were done, he would get a snack and be led back to his home.

As always, the humans held pictures up for the chimp to view. His eyes scanned these images. His brain processed them as familiar or new, bright or dim, pleasing or scary. This information was transmitted to other humans sitting at a nearby table who monitored the results. Fascination and frustration crossed their faces day after day as they repeated the exercise.

There was a day when more humans appeared than usual. Just outside the windows in the hall that circled the lab, a line of humans stood together, gazing in. One of them spoke. The chimp could not hear what he said, but he enjoyed that the man seemed to smile often.

The man also made several gestures with his hand. Kong waved to him, but to no avail. Soon, Kong's attention was drawn back to the large cards, which displayed images of colorful fruits. Much more interesting than the man in the window.

△

"Take a look at the monitor over there," said Bill Mitchell, the de facto public relations director for Oliver Labs. He pointed to the large displays suspended from the ceiling in the lab behind the window. "Our researchers are attempting to isolate and map the various parts of the brain that respond to given visual stimuli.

"As Kong processes each of the images, the subtle neural and physiological changes in him tell us, in a sense, how his mind interprets what he is seeing. Perhaps we may even be able to anticipate his future behavior."

Mitchell took stock of the small crowd of investors lined up along the laboratory plexiglass, observing the chimp on the table. Mitchell's presentation had gone according to plan, without major interruption or unforeseen hiccups. Yet his mind still wandered to the bottle of gin he kept in the lower drawer of his office's desk. The lab had kept him on as a pitchman to potential investors and donors for several weeks, and the stress had been wearing him down.

"So," a potential investor dragged out the vowel, "what are the practical applications to such research? After all, there is no shortage of this sort of ongoing cognitive study with primates. What do these researchers hope to do with whatever it is you learn here?" He seemed to have little interest in frivolous curiosity, at least regarding the use of his money.

"Well, to be honest Mr.—" Mitchell panicked. He had forgotten the man's name.

"Aldridge," the man replied curtly.

"Mr. Aldridge, of course. Well, the endgame application really does depend on who you're asking." Mitchell chuckled awkwardly. "If you were to ask that question in the lab, you'd likely hear that their work could help with everything from the study of Alzheimer's disease and other neurodegenerative conditions to advancing cognitive behavioral therapies. If you were to ask Dr. Kwock, an evolutionary biologist we've been working with for the past several months, he'd likely tell you we are breaking new ground in understanding the evolutionary development of our brains and our psychology.

"And of course, if you were to ask Kong there"—he forced yet another chuckle—"he'd likely tell you it was all for the treats."

The group shared a brief, polite laugh. The only unmoved person was Aldridge, who peered inquisitively at the monitor behind the window. It displayed Kong's neural activity as the exercises continued. "And what of the project head?" Aldridge asked.

"Dr. Oliver," said Mitchell.

"What is his hope in all of this?"

Before Mitchell could respond, a deep, booming voice

spoke up from down the hall. "My hope is that by enhancing our understanding of the hominid brain, we might be able to better understand ourselves."

The group turned and watched as the tall, confident man strolled down the hall to meet them. Dr. Oliver was an affable man of forty-five years of age and an athlete outside of work, maintaining a strong build and tanned skin. When not buried beneath the mountains of reports that his team provided him, he could be found either running the length of the Charles River Esplanade or hiking just over the border in New Hampshire. His physical presence was instantly commanding, and his demeanor was warm.

He offered a firm handshake first to Aldridge, then to the remaining members of the group. He maintained steady eye contact and smiled during each introduction. Oliver, Mitchell's boss, did everything but push Mitchell off the proverbial stage.

"In all honesty, I expect the more tangible benefits of our research to be found as we go along. The benefits we enjoy in life are often credited blindly to 'science,' and we believe they came from the logical extension of research and technology. But so many have come from unexpected discoveries made while carrying out research solely for the sake of pursuing knowledge. I would venture to guess that we have not yet tapped into the full potential that we're facing here. That said, I'm not so idealistic as to think that you are interested in playing with chance when it comes to funding. While I'd like to opine about the virtues of scientific research some more, I'll spare you further pontification."

Oliver smiled throughout almost every word. It was infectious to all, even to Mitchell. Aldridge was the exception, who asked, "What are your intentions for this? Immediately speaking."

"At the outset," Oliver spoke deliberately, "the most immediate application for the data we've gathered thus far would be for medical applications. As a species, we're living longer than ever. And I suspect we are just beginning to encounter the sort of degenerative realities that outliving nature's intended biological lifespans entails.

"In theory, we could even go as far as saying that by advancing our understanding of how the brain, and by extension, the mind, actually works, we could go a step beyond warding off its unraveling in the wake of old age. We may even find the means by which to enhance its functions and operations before age sets in."

"Making our minds more powerful by utilizing some sort of therapies?" Aldridge asked.

Oliver nodded and glanced inside the lab at Kong. "Perhaps, yes. This is its infancy. When we move into stage two, which will be studying the brain during sleep cycles for comparative analysis, we expect to gain an even greater understanding of how both the active and passive synaptic functions operate and build over time. Consciousness only accounts for a portion of our brain's natural state. In primates, such as our friend Kong over there, even less. So, sleep cycle analysis provides us with a more complete dataset."

Oliver took a dramatic breath before continuing. Mitchell knew that Oliver was teeing up his grand finale. Clasping his hands together, Oliver continued, "The mind's tapestry, woven by the threads of both conscious and subconscious thought, shall be our canvas of infinite scientific possibility. Consider, my friends, a future where the dreams of Kong and his kind, mixed with our collective thirst for knowledge, sculpt worlds beyond our imagination."

The group clapped and murmured among themselves. Aldridge raised an eyebrow and nodded in apparent interest. The group watched as researchers disconnected Kong from their equipment, guided him down from the table, and walked him to the rear door leading to the holding pens.

As he walked with them, hand in hand, Kong turned back to the window where the investors stood watching and offered another wave. The group smiled and waved back in adoration for the small primate's gesture.

The speech. The wave. *Too much icing on the cake*, thought Mitchell.

He needed a drink.

▲

Later that day, the door to Oliver's office opened as his assistant Claire showed a young man in. Oliver extended his hand across his desk, and the young man took it in an impressively firm handshake. It was a good first impression for a potential intern.

"Charles Jacobs, right? Or is it Charlie? I'm Stephen Oliver. Pleasure to meet you," he said. Both eased into their chairs.

"Thank you, Doctor, and Charles is good, thanks. I'm really glad you were open to meeting with me," Charles said. Oliver appreciated how Charles was clearly doing his best to quell his nervous jitters. There had been no lack of stuttering applicants over the years.

"Of course. I looked over your paperwork, and for someone your age, you've accomplished quite a bit. Just give me a moment here, I'm going to pull it up." With a few clicks of his mouse, Oliver brought the young man's résumé up on-screen. "Looking here, we've got lab assistant to Caroline Parker, research assistant to Doug Marsden—did you know Doug and I were roommates at Johns Hopkins?" Oliver asked.

"I did. It was actually Professor Marsden who suggested I apply for the internship here," Charles replied.

"Oh? I'll have to send him a thanks for the recommendation. Your bio says you're focusing on neuroscience, is that right?"

"Yes, sir."

"Well, what's your big world-changing ambition?"

"Uh," Charles hesitated. His generation was always nervous about giving the wrong answer. Always afraid to say the wrong thing. "What do you mean by that?" he asked politely.

Oliver smiled. "What is your dream? What vicious disease do you want to cure? Or with what groundbreaking discovery are you planning on inking your name into the annals of history?"

Charles sat quietly for a moment as a melancholy smile crossed his face. "Well, I recently had to help my parents get my grandfather settled into one of those assisted living homes. You know, not quite the hospital ward or nursing home thing, but a managed care community?"

Oliver nodded. "I see."

"So," he continued, "after his behavior started becoming erratic, we discovered that he was suffering from frontotemporal dementia."

"Oh, I'm so sorry," said Oliver. "Is it okay to ask what kind?"

"It's primary progressive aphasia. With a lot of motor skill and communication problems."

Oliver sighed, familiar with the condition.

Charles's gaze drifted to the window. "My granddad, he was always a tough old man. Tough his whole life. Twenty years in the navy, sailed the globe, fought in wars, all of it. The man always had stories to tell, you know?"

"My father was a Marine. Similar stories, I'd imagine," Oliver said.

"Right. Watching him deteriorate like that was really hard on all of us. I always knew I wanted to do something that helped people. Thought I might end up a corpsman or medic or something to, you know, maybe follow in his footsteps, I suppose. After I was accepted to Tufts, I found myself more fascinated by the research side of things than treatment, and after his diagnosis, I guess I dialed in more."

"You want to pick a fight with neurodegeneration. I respect that." Oliver brought up one of the research papers he had hunted down while vetting his potential intern. "I had a chance to read one of your papers," he confessed.

"You did?" Charles was pleasantly surprised.

"*Discerning the Difference and Interplay Between TDP-43 and Tau Proteins in Relation to Frontotemporal Dementia.* It looks like you've homed in on your first target pretty thoroughly."

Charles seemed equally pleased and terrified that his work had made its way to Oliver's desk, a tense grin frozen on his face. No doubt, a part of Charles awaited the caveat in the midst of tepid praise that would disprove his central thesis. But Oliver would not be so unkind. He liked this respectful young man, full of ambition.

"This level of work would be impressive to see from a research professional with a decade of experience under their belt," Oliver said, "but to see such accomplishment from a— are you a second year?" Charles nodded. "To see this from a second-year grad student is frankly rather astounding. How much was Professor Marsden involved?"

"He was a good adviser, and always made me reevaluate my methods. But the work was solely mine."

"I think our team would be served well by bringing you on board."

"Wow. Thank you. I am really looking forward to the opportunity this internship provides."

"Nonsense. Not the internship. I think I would like to offer you a job with us. Naturally we'll work the schedule around your coursework, but I think I'd like to have you on staff. I'd like to see you working with us in a focused capacity, not bouncing around. How does that sound? Would you like to join us here at Oliver Labs?"

"Are you serious?"

"That didn't sound like a 'yes' to me," Oliver teased.

"I mean, yes. Yes, sir. And thank you!"

Oliver smiled, reclining in his chair. He was well aware that he didn't even have the funding to pay his existing staff yet, let alone a new hire. Nevertheless, he was determined not to let that bother him. He had tempered his accolades to avoid outright declaring that Charles was, in his decades of experience in the field, possibly the most gifted up-and-coming neuroscience researcher he had encountered.

The two men rose from their seats and shook hands across Oliver's desk again. "I'll have Claire sort out your schedule and paperwork. If you can start next week, we can get the ball rolling with some sort of orientation on Monday."

"That'd be perfect. Thank you, Dr. Oliver. Thank you very, very much," Charles stammered. *There's the mix of nervousness and excitement he hid so well,* thought Oliver. *Ah, youth.*

⚘

Charles's head was spinning as he sauntered down the front steps of the Oliver Labs building. Walking in, he had hoped that there was some chance of landing an internship. He walked out of his interview as a staff research assistant working for a lab that was on the cutting edge of his choice field.

He called his parents. As it rang, Charles smiled at the family picture it displayed, taken during his sister's return from service overseas. He brought the phone to his ear and his smile broadened as his mother spoke.

"So, how did it go?" she asked.

"Well, I didn't get the internship," he said, feigning disappointment.

"Oh, honey. I know you really wanted it. But try to keep your hopes up. I'm sure something will come through soon," she replied hopefully.

"Except, the thing is, they offered me a job."

"What?"

Charles laughed. "Yeah, Mom. A real position on staff."

His mother called out to his father. "Ben? Ben! It's Charlie on the phone. No, he didn't. Instead they gave him a job! Okay, here."

Charles's father came on next. "So, they just hired you right up, huh, kid?"

"Crazy, right?"

"Makes perfect sense. I mean, they can get anyone to fetch coffee. They know brilliance when they see it." His father's voice was full of pride.

"I'm pretty psyched."

"You should be. Hold on." After some shuffling, Charles heard his father close the door. "Now, I think the only proper way for you to celebrate is with a steak, a scotch, and if you can find one, a woman. Doesn't have to be in that order, got it? You're on your way to the big-time, kid. Go out and treat yourself." To his father, there was nothing manlier than alcohol, meat, sex, and success, preferably all at the same time.

Charles awkwardly laughed. "Well, I'll see what I can manage."

"No. No, no, no. Listen, you still have the credit card we gave you for emergencies?" His father was also a very persistent man.

"I do."

"Okay. Well, I want you to go to the Capital. You go there, and you buy yourself a man's dinner. I'll cover the costs, okay?"

Charles relented, knowing there was no saying "no thanks" to his father. "Okay, if you insist, Dad."

"And listen, I want you to call some pretty girl from school or something and bring her along. No woman in her right mind will say no to a steak dinner, trust me. It's where I brought your mother for our anniversary, it's fantastic, so you—" The door opened in the background. Charles's mother asked what they were talking about. The conversation between his parents devolved into a largely unintelligible marital inquisition about boundaries. Eventually, his mother chimed in on the phone.

"We're so happy for you, honey," his mother said.

"You've done good, kid. Go get your dinner," his father said.

"What dinner?" she asked.

⚊⚊ ▲ ⚊⚊

Across town, another prodigy was also speaking with his mother. However, the tenor of their conversation was much more tense. Sebastian Reed walked behind his mother with his head bowed. The fifteen-year-old did his best to focus on her words; she was scolding him after discovering a stash of pornographic magazines below Sebastian's bed. So, Mrs. Elomina Reed was bringing her son to church in Dorchester, Massachusetts, to pray for forgiveness from God. Although Sebastian had attempted to explain that they belonged to a classmate who needed them hidden, he knew better than to plead in light of his mother's mood.

Sebastian's mind had begun to wander after the third or fourth block. He pondered what the actual thickness of the concrete sidewalk slabs might be between his feet. He imagined the countless layers of subterranean sewage pipes, telecom cables, and fiber optic conduits that lay beneath.

"Child, if you're listening, then what did I just tell you?" she snapped.

"That a good man respects women like he respects his mother," Sebastian repeated robotically.

Things had not been easy since his father's death. He knew his mother believed that, especially with no man in the house to set an example, he needed a strong, discipline-oriented upbringing to stay on the straight and narrow. It was only the structure of the church and Elomina's firm hand that hopefully could make up for the loss of his father. Whenever Sebastian was caught misbehaving, the routine of a lecture while walking to church, prayer, and a stern conversation over dinner had become her standard approach to corrective parenting.

"You've heard your Uncle Johnny say a thousand times, 'I'm just a Black man in America.' Do you understand what that means?" His mother huffed.

"Yes, Mama."

"Do you? You need to understand that your actions will constantly be scrutinized." She always sounded a little more sad than angry during this part of the lecture. "Think before you act. Think real hard, Sebastian."

"Yes, Mama."

After another three blocks of relentless lecturing, they arrived at the Church of the Sacred Trust. His mother went to speak with Pastor Williams, the young and energetic pastor whom many families found to be a compassionate counselor. Sebastian weaved through the pews to his typical seat. The seat was close enough to the front so the pastor's words could be easily heard, but far enough back so the view of the stained-glass windows could be taken in all at once. Over time, his faith in the church and its mythology had waned. "God" was, as all gods before him, a figment of collective imaginations desperate to explain away the dark. Yet, he found it curiously comforting to be inside the house of faith and surrounded by its imagery and tradition. Sebastian struggled to reconcile the contradiction.

Perhaps it was the memories of sitting beside his father on Sunday mornings. He would listen thoughtfully to the pastor's sermons, while wearing his finest shirt and tie. His father, Isaiah Reed, was more of a humanist than a man of faith. With his mother's faith running as deep as the Atlantic Ocean, it fell to both father and son to take what they could from the church's offerings. The Reeds found community and routine to be a linchpin of their family's life. That all faded away years ago, after the accident. Isaiah was attempting to help a stranded motorist on Interstate 93 when an out-of-control tractor trailer barreled into the breakdown lane. Three people were killed, including Sebastian's father.

Following his death, Sebastian questioned how a loving God could take away a boy's father. He determined unequivocally that there was no God, and that lives began and ended as a result of either human choices or uncontrollable circumstances.

"Sebastian," the pastor interrupted his thoughts and sat down next to him.

"Hello, Pastor Williams."

"Your mother tells me that you've been looking at some mature magazines, yes?" There was no judgment in the pastor's voice.

"They weren't mine. My friend needed me to keep them safe for a bit, and so he asked me if I'd hold on to them."

The pastor maintained eye contact. "All right. Why though?"

"Why what?" Sebastian replied, uncertain.

"Why did you agree to hold on to them? Why did he need you to?"

"I'm not lying. . . ."

"I don't think you're lying, Sebastian. I'm just trying to understand your perspective."

"Okay, so his name is Tommy. Tommy found his uncle's stash of *Playboy*s and decided to take a few. But the thing is, Tommy's mom would probably smack him silly if she found out. He asked me to hold on to them until he could figure out where to hide them."

"And you, wanting to help your friend, agreed."

"Yeah. I mean, I know it was wrong and my mom is pissed, but Tommy already had them, and I didn't want him to get in that kind of trouble." Sebastian sincerely hoped the pastor would see his point of view to help soften his mother's mood.

"Look, I'm not going to sit here and tell you that what you did was some kind of grievous sin, okay? And I know your thoughts on the Lord and his will. We've had those talks plenty of times. But there is a real question of ethics here that I want you to consider."

Sebastian looked curiously up at the pastor. "Ethics?"

"It starts with Tommy. He had already taken the magazines from his uncle, so that right there was questionable judgment on his part. Especially since I'm guessing he knew what his mother would do if she found out. Tommy, from the outset, had used poor judgment. And then, what did he do?"

"He gave them to me."

"That's right. And you took them, knowing neither of you was supposed to have them." The pastor's logic was sound. Sebastian had a sinking feeling that the pastor was about to link the moral of this personal story to something Matthew or John said. These guys found connections to the Bible in everything.

"I was just trying to help my friend," Sebastian repeated. "I thought it was the right thing to do."

"And in a sense, you were right. I know you, Sebastian, and you're a good kid. The point here isn't that what you did was wrong. I'm just not sure you weighed the circumstances and consequences evenly before you made your decision."

"What should I have done then?" Sebastian asked, exasperated.

"What could you have done? What other options did you have when you decided to help your friend like this?"

Sebastian pondered the question in silence. The pastor watched him closely as he mulled over his choices. This was a patient man who would be willing to wait an eternity for Sebastian to respond. Finally, Sebastian relented. "I could have said no?" His voice rose, half statement, half question.

"Yes, you could have said no, but then you'd have left your friend in a lurch, right? And that's clearly something you wouldn't want to do. What else?"

Sebastian proffered another option. "I could have told him to put them back."

Pastor Williams nodded. "That could have spared the both of you from any negative consequences. What I want you to take away from all of this is that, regardless of whether what you did was right or wrong, you acted without fully thinking the matter through.

"Perhaps in the future, instead of going with your instincts, take just one or two extra moments to consider all of your options. Be mindful. Always." Pastor Williams patted Sebastian's shoulder. "Now, I suppose I can at least tell your mother that we've explored the moral implications of what you did. I'll let her know that I believe your side of the story, and that should bring you both some peace."

As the pastor went to speak with Elomina, Sebastian lingered on the meaning behind their talk. Pastor Williams was right, he begrudgingly admitted. In any situation, the best outcome was only possible if all options on the table were considered. Anything short of that approach ran the risk of overlooking a solution that solved for all the variables.

"All right, it's time to head home," his mother said calmly as she walked over to him.

"Sorry, Mama. I should have thought more before helping Tommy."

"Sebastian, God gave you a powerful mind. With his guidance, may you never let it go to waste."

▲

Beneath the vaulted ceilings of the Capital Steakhouse, at a table for two, Charles sat across from a young woman. Her name was Angela, and in a move that would have delighted his father, he had found her in the crowd while waiting for his train. Charles's youth had been replete with awkwardness and insecurity around women. Only on a few occasions had he possessed enough confidence to prove that fortune truly does favor the bold.

He had been riding high following the wildly successful interview with Dr. Oliver. On the station platform, he made eye contact with a woman who, in a sea of dark gray hoodies and black backpacks, wore a dress covered in small embroidered books, her blond hair pinned up by a bright yellow claw clip. A polite half smile crossed her face. He approached her by putting one foot steadily in front of the other. Introductions were made. The conversation pivoted to where the two were headed. The labored bit of small talk was cut short by Charles laying it out there: He would like to treat her to dinner that very night. The shock of his brazenness surprised them both. Yet, she agreed.

"Maybe we could do that," she said coyly. "That time could work," she continued when Charles suggested a time. "I might see you there," she responded, smiling broadly when the two confirmed their plans.

By pleading on the phone with the manager of the restaurant, he was able to secure a table for two. He felt the elation of a gambler in the midst of a hot streak. He could not lose. Charles made his way back to his apartment to shower and change before his date, his confidence only rising.

He met Angela in front of the Capital Steakhouse. She was even more astonishingly beautiful than he realized. Her quirky dress stitched with books was replaced with an elegant off-white one that hung loosely on her frame. Angela was the physical embodiment of perfection, and he prayed there was equal depth to her personality. Hopefully, today's good fortune would manifest his desires.

Sitting together in a large, refined dining room full of patrons double their age, they chatted away as they waited for a bottle of wine.

"Let me guess," she said. "You work in finance?"

Charles laughed. "No. Really though? Finance? What makes you think I'm in finance? Is it something about the way I'm dressed? Do I sound like I stare at spreadsheets all day?"

Angela returned a chuckle as she waved his questions away. "No, nothing like that. Really, it was the stop where we met. It's close enough to the Financial District that I thought you might work in the area. That, and well, the fact that you were able to pull a reservation here out of thin air. That was kind of impressive."

"I was actually just transferring trains. If you had asked me a week ago, I would have told you that I'm a grad student, but as of today I'm also a research assistant at a laboratory. I got the position, like, an hour before I met you."

"You are having a lucky day, huh?" She leaned in.

"Yeah, I'd say I am. Truth be told, I think I was sort of riding a wave today. I'm normally not the kind of guy who asks out random girls at the train station."

"Sure, buddy. You usually catch them at the laundromat then, right?" she joked.

"Exactly," he replied, running with it. "And on Thursdays, I troll arrivals at the airport."

The two laughed as the waiter returned and filled their wineglasses. They ordered an appetizer of mussels, followed by the two most expensive items on the menu, as per his father's instructions. Charles was excited, but not surprised, when Angela asked to return to his place after dinner had concluded. *Lucky, indeed.*

▲

The next morning, Angela set out to make coffee as Charles lay sound asleep. She had a great night but was not pleased when she was confronted with a dirty coffee maker and only one visible mug. Her French press machine at home kept her sane. Sorting out this boy's foreign machine, she poured the cheap ground coffee into the filter. She doled out two servings, one into the mug that she claimed for herself and another into a pint glass from the cabinet.

Sipping hers black and bitter, she thought about the sleeping man with whom she had spent the night. He was dorky and cute; she found his enthusiasm for even small interactions invigorating. Angela, coffee in hand, stepped out onto the narrow balcony that overlooked I-93. She had not planned on dating anyone seriously and should probably leave before he got the wrong idea. Between her work as a production manager at an understaffed production company, and the bitter taste left over from a series of abysmal dates with attractive but dull men, she had little desire for another relationship.

When Charles got up, Angela would talk about how she'd had a nice time, quickly bid him goodbye with a passing comment about meeting up again sometime, and then slip back into her normal life. When would she hand him the coffee? She was still finessing her plans when a groggy Charles joined her on the balcony.

"Good morning," he said, letting out a big yawn.

He sat down in the patio chair across the table from her, placing his glass down. Peering sheepishly at the pint glass, he murmured, "I should probably get some more mugs, huh?"

She smiled. "You should probably get rid of that coffee maker. I cleaned it out for you."

"Thank you," he said, embarrassed. He sipped his glass and set it down again, nodding. "You know, I think I can taste the clean. This is some good, clean coffee."

She laughed. She couldn't help it. So much for her plan.

"What you need is a good French press and some fresh ground beans."

"Ah, a coffee snob."

She shrugged and sipped her coffee.

"So, I was thinking, even though I didn't have a chance to ask your last name and you don't know mine—"

"It's Bexley," she blurted.

"If you weren't doing anything today, maybe you might like to come with me to the aquarium." His invitation was more of a statement than a question. "And it's Jacobs, by the way."

She was reluctant to admit he wasn't like the other guys. He was funny, sincere, even wholesome with this aquarium date idea. He had surprised her, yet again.

"Gawking at sharks and sea lions doesn't really scream 'second date' to most people."

"If you play nice, they may let you pet the stingray."

"Is that a euphemism for something, buddy?" she needled him playfully.

"Time will tell?" Charles stumbled for a witty response. It was cute.

"Okay, let's do it. Why not?" Angela grabbed Charles by the hand and led him inside. They showered, together, before getting dressed.

Charles grabbed his keys as Angela took one last look at his apartment.

"Listen," she said, "the only way I'm ever coming back here is if we go shopping for better coffee and cleaner mugs."

"Deal. I think I shoved one of those Bed Bath and Beyond coupons in my glove compartment. I had a feeling this would all work out."

ELEVEN

Calculations

I look every gift horse in the mouth . . . twice.

—The Fist (First Life Cycle)

At a driving range, Dr. Stephen Oliver was off his game in more ways than one. . . .

O**LIVER's** mind was fixated on funding, payroll, and the future of his lab. So long as they could secure several donors to the tune of a couple million dollars, his operation would be solvent for at least another quarter. The economy was still recovering from the recent recession, and investors were slowly coming out of their shells. Without a quick cash infusion, he would have to make some hard decisions.

Looking to the sky, he tried to calculate the wind and air pressure. An errant gust from the Charles River could unexpectedly slow or shift the trajectory of the ball. A moment's hesitation would make or break his drive. If only he had the mental capacity of a supercomputer to process all the variables. *I am a mere mortal,* he thought.

Oliver brought his club around and up over his head. He swung hard with a twist of the knees and a precise grip. The ball took flight, landing just shy of the blue marker.

A voice from behind beckoned his attention.

"Dr. Oliver?" the voice said. "Trent Aldridge. I was touring your facility the other day. I've never seen you at the range before."

"Every Sunday unless I'm hitting the green, which is rarer and rarer these days," Oliver replied.

"I'd be here every day if I could." Aldridge chuckled. "I was actually just talking to Frederic about what you showed us on Friday. Oh, where are my manners? Dr. Oliver, this is Frederic Sorensen. Frederic represents . . . damn, I've forgotten the name. What was it?"

"Morgen-Sinn." The tall and serious companion answered with a European accent Oliver couldn't quite place. Sorensen offered a handshake.

"Frederic," Aldridge continued, "Dr. Oliver is the head of research for the neural thing with the monkey that I told you about." He turned back to Oliver. "Frederic and I were going to meet later this evening for a drink. You should join us. I'm sure the two of you could find plenty to talk about." Aldridge took out a plain white business card with only a tiny phone number printed on the front. "Call my assistant after four today and she'll send a car for you."

A car? Send a car? Never had a car been sent for him. Never had he been driven to drinks with potential investors approaching him out of the blue. It had always been Oliver pleading for them to tour the lab and hear his pitch. This was new, and he struggled to temper his excitement.

"Thank you, Mr. Aldridge." Oliver matched Sorensen's

energy, cool and aloof. Knowing he would be the one calling for the car in a few hours, he lied, "I'll have my people take care of it."

▲

Oliver ordered a drink known as a Baudin from the server at the HojoPlus cocktail lounge. A concoction of bourbon, honey syrup, hot sauce, and a twist of lemon, the quality of the drink was how he tested a bartender's competence. The server placed the beverage on the dark oak table. Oliver sat in a leather chair beside a large window overlooking Boston Harbor with the water reflecting the city lights. Cargo ships disappeared into the darkened horizon as a few yachts left the port for a nighttime cruise. Oliver took a sip and winced at how the honey completely overpowered the hot sauce.

"I spend most of my time away from home. It can be challenging," Sorensen explained dryly, leaving his drink untouched. He folded his hands together on the table and straightened his spine. Oliver was surprised by how odd and wooden Sorensen behaved in contrast to Aldridge.

"Well, when I was a younger man," Aldridge said loudly, "I spent a lot of time overseas and on the road for the firm. I do sometimes miss those days, but I've become something of a creature of habit now that I'm in my sixties. A scotch in my favorite bar is more than enough for me." He finished his drink, wiping his mouth with the back of his hand. Aldridge turned his attention to Oliver. "What about you, Doctor? Spend much time on the road?"

Oliver wiped the condensation from the side of his glass in lieu of taking another sip. "I'm lucky if I can get out of the lab long enough to go for a run these days, but I've been to a conference or two."

Sorensen leaned in closer to Oliver, though his back

remained rigid. "I am actually quite curious, Doctor, as to the specific nature of your work. Mr. Aldridge gave me a layman's interpretation, but I wanted to know, what exactly are you pursuing?" His eyes narrowed in, trapping Oliver in his gaze. Sorensen's voice dropped to just above a whisper, yet he carefully enunciated each word. "You must have an ulterior motive, something other investors may not find so palatable. Perhaps another application of your work." His tone shifted and his head tilted slightly to the left, embracing the macabre. "Tell me, what will come of this knowledge when you've expired?"

Oliver was taken aback by this brash inquisition and strange wording; he believed that his intentions were honorable. *Expired, how odd.* He studied this bizarre man carefully. Sorensen had been polite and reserved up until now, but there was something sinister, almost unnatural about him. *Did the man's eyes just change color?* Oliver decided to shake it off and sidestep Sorensen's last question. After all, he needed the money.

"In terms of what we think can be done with our discoveries," Oliver explained, "it would seem the only limit is imagination. We hope to make neurodegenerative diseases a thing of the past and perhaps even unlock a mystery or two behind the inner workings of human intellect. It may sound ambitious, and it is, but I believe that with emerging technologies, we will uncover neural connections we've never thought to look for that bind us together. Perhaps other meaningful connections beyond even that."

Sorensen sat back, unimpressed. "You're searching for the core. The soul, you might say."

It always circles back to religious nonsense, thought Oliver. He acquiesced, "I don't know if I'd put it that way, but in a sense, I suppose that's a possible byproduct of the work." An atheist himself, Oliver didn't put much stock in any of that, but he had determined years earlier that publicly dismissing the religious implications of his work was not a wise course of action.

"The soul is equally distinctive and ordinary. Transitory and eternal. Quite different from what mankind has been led to believe. Where do you stand?"

Oliver shrugged, concerned this was a trap. "I am open to all possibilities."

"I have found that men who don't believe in a god are more open to the true nature of the universe." Sorensen sat unblinking, waiting for an acceptable response.

"I rely on data to guide me."

"Indeed. Morgen-Sinn specializes in many types of emerging technologies including efficient power converters, AI development, and gene therapies. So long as your intentions are true, your project will be acceptable to my associates, provided you are willing to make certain concessions."

Oliver's heart raced. This moment would make or break the deal. It was important to tread carefully. "What sort of concessions?"

"There are researchers who object to providing militaries or the state access to their work. It would be unfortunate for Morgen-Sinn and your lab to enter into a relationship that could be impacted by any rigid perspectives."

Even though it was unclear which military was interested in his work, Oliver wasn't keen on asking Sorensen too many questions. He couldn't envision his work having any harmful applications. Besides, he could shut it all down if anything went awry. He had won Sorensen's favor and couldn't get caught up in hypotheticals.

Smiling broadly, Oliver raised his glass to Sorensen. "I think we've got a deal."

Sebastian eyed the large cardboard box on the table near the door of his classroom. A shipment had arrived for every class at Dorchester Public High School, courtesy of the Morgen-Sinn Foundation. The hum and murmur of the class subsided with the arrival of Mrs. Daniels, their teacher. The school was grossly underfunded, and there had been occasions in the past when philanthropic donors gifted books, pens, notepads, and calculators to the school. Assuming this package was just that, Sebastian thought about his own inventory of well-worn supplies.

"Okay, settle down now," Mrs. Daniels said, drawing the students' attention. "I'm sure you're all very curious as to just what is in this box." She lifted the large package and placed it on her desk at the front of the class. "To help each of you succeed, as we all know you can, you've been given—" She paused for dramatic effect as she opened the top of the box. From it came a slim white box. She smiled as she presented the item to the class. "Your very own, um, 'slate' tablet. Isn't that wonderful?"

Though excited to receive a new device, Sebastian questioned why these had come so late in the year. Typically, such endowments were received at the beginning of the year or around Christmas time. The rapidly approaching summer vacation meant that these tablets wouldn't see much use in a few weeks.

Mrs. Daniels attempted to instruct the class on how to input their personal data and declare ownership of the devices. Some students were already past the setup screen and exploring the preloaded applications. Sebastian was no different, booting up his own machine using the Power button on the side and watching as the high-resolution screen came alive with a flashy animation of the Morgen-Sinn logo. The tablet brought up the home screen, where a series of application icons were displayed in rows.

Each icon linked to a website with coursework, study materials, and other assets: one for math, one for English, one for biology, and so on. Indicators for battery life, Wi-Fi, sound, and Bluetooth, along with an unusual wave pattern symbol, populated the top bar. Sebastian tapped the wave symbol and was presented with an informational pop-up:

> *Welcome to Morgen-web 2.0.3.*
> *Using this utility may grant access to the internet and other networks when standard data connections are unavailable.*
> *Morgen-web utilizes satellite data transmission, radio frequencies, and dedicated lanes to deliver a high-speed connection wherever the user may be located.*
> *By clicking Continue, you hereby agree to the terms of service outlined here.*

There was a light blue hyperlink at the very end of the paragraph, with a button below it that read Continue in bright red letters. Sebastian almost tapped the button right away, but his eyes fixated on the words *terms of service*. He backed out of the Morgen-web pop-up and instead allowed the slate to log directly onto the school's Wi-Fi. He set about registering his information on the slate and planned to explore the terms of service page in greater depth later.

For the remainder of the day, lessons were given with the new devices in each class Sebastian attended. Soon the final bell rang, and the students headed home. Sebastian slipped his slate into his bag between two old textbooks and wondered how well it would stand up to any jostling on the way home. Sebastian planned to care for the slate devoutly, unaccustomed to new and expensive items. He wondered if this device might allow adjustments to its programming, allowing for uncensored web surfing and gaming.

Sebastian burst into his apartment and yelled, "Hey, Mom!"

Wishing to show his mother his new toy, he slung his bag on the back of the dining room chair and took out the slate. No response. He called out again but was met with silence. It was then that Sebastian noticed a note hung on the refrigerator:

> Sebastian, I had to take another shift. I'll try to get out as early as I can but may not be home until late. Do NOT pig out on junk food. I've left your dinner in the fridge. All you need to do is heat it up in the microwave. Don't be lazy, it's better warm. Hope you had a good day at school. Love you. —Mom

He shrugged and opened the refrigerator to pull out a can of soda. As he cracked the tab of the can and listened to the carbonation fizz, he turned the slate on. Sebastian tapped the Security app, and the screen went black before loading pages of technical documentation about the slate's security features. He scrolled through them as he gulped down his drink.

The device boasted a GPS anti-theft locator, biometric login, encrypted communications, and advanced malware and virus protection. Sebastian hit the Activate button and was met with the terms of service screen. He shrank the security activation window and reopened the Morgen-web app he had opened at school, which displayed the terms of service agreement once again. He alternated between each app, finding the agreements identical.

Sebastian skimmed the terms, lingering on a passage outlining the use of collected data:

> *By accepting these terms, you authorize the Morgen-Sinn corporation to collect and analyze*

personal data for technical, analytic, and any other purpose Morgen-Sinn deems necessary.

Data will not be sold, but may be shared with groups, not limited to, but including, partners, affiliates, or other parties of Morgen-Sinn or its associates, not limited to the duration of your use of these products and services.

Not noticing anything particularly unusual, Sebastian hit the I Accept button and was redirected to a screen asking for his name, age, and address. He was then greeted with the last step in the process. A sliver of plastic along the right-side edge of the device pulsed with a dull blue light as instructions popped up on the screen. Sebastian followed the guide to set up his own biometric security key, sliding his index finger along the glowing strip. It felt warm to the touch and, for a second, he thought it burned his finger. The slate presented him with another pop-up, thanking him and alerting him that his data had been processed.

Sebastian grabbed a fork and took his dinner out of the refrigerator. He picked up the slate and started exploring the applications and web access that the machine now granted him. He devoured the meal as a game loaded. Dismissing his mother's personal preferences, he liked his food cold.

△

Sebastian Reed was the first minor registered in Boston with the Morgen-web. The burning sensation he had felt was the slate sampling skin to collect Sebastian's DNA. Within the slate's screen lay hidden cameras and sensors connected to an imaging program, which mapped Sebastian's facial expressions as he interacted with the device. Everything from the content he digested to the speed at which he consumed information was tracked and recorded in a profile that he had no idea existed. The device reported the data through its own encrypted network to a data center far away to be evaluated.

It was determined that Sebastian would be a man of average build, and would naturally live into his seventies. An examination of his interests and processing speeds, when coupled with data mined from social media and school records, suggested a high probability of scientific achievement. Records showing the boy's social and emotional development, when compared to school performance and RFID location tracking, suggested he thrived on a balance of disciplinary measures and independence.

The Morgen-web identified Sebastian Reed's profile as one of serious potential. He, like the millions, then billions, to come, would remain under surveillance. Sebastian didn't give it a second thought, as a point-and-click farming game held his attention.

⚠

Charles arrived early for his first day of work with a spring in his step and a dopey smile on his face after having enjoyed an early breakfast with Angela before she headed off to work. He climbed the front steps of the building and checked in at the front desk, where a security guard told him to wait for Dr. Oliver in the lobby. Charles took a seat and checked his email on his phone. Oliver soon arrived, and once he provided Charles with a temporary employee ID badge, the two made their way down the hall toward the laboratory. Oliver appeared to be in as good a mood as his new employee.

"Did you enjoy your weekend?" Oliver asked, leading him down the hall.

Thinking back on the dinner, the trip to the aquarium, and the virtually nonstop sex marathon with Angela, his smile broadened. "I'd say it was one of the better ones I've had in recent memory."

"Good, me as well," Oliver replied. "I hope you're ready for what's ahead. Pretty soon we're going to be drowning in new equipment and possibly even a bigger lab space. You've come on board at a very exciting time. At any rate, we would normally go about getting you onboarded and set up at your workstation, but seeing as we're going to be receiving new equipment this week, we can just take an extended orientation tour. How does that sound to you?" Oliver asked.

"Sounds perfect."

The two men toured the facility. First, Oliver took Charles to the main floor where the medical exam tables for the primates were installed. A series of surgical lights hung from steel arms above each of the tables. All around the outer plexiglass wall were a myriad of stations with computers and lab equipment.

After the main floor was the processing center. Its overhead industrial lights illuminated the five rows of floor-to-ceiling computers. A sticky note was posted on each machine, marked with a cartoon face and the name of a dead poet scribbled by one of the staff.

Next were the conference rooms, the offices, the bathrooms, a brief peek into the janitorial closet, and then finally came what Oliver referred to as "the vault." The vault was a room requiring both a key card swipe and a keypad code to access. Within it, he explained, was the most advanced experimental technology the project had at its disposal to date. Holding up a vial with a clear substance, Oliver smiled. "Take a very close look at this liquid."

Charles reached for the vial. "May I?" he asked. Oliver nodded and carefully handed it to him. He saw nothing unusual short of a viscous gel, which coated the inside of the tube as he turned it. "What am I looking at?"

"What you have in your hand is experimental nanotechnology. You can't see them, but suspended in that gel are millions of nanobots. They're made from engineered proteins that respond to biochemical signals in the human body. Once injected, they integrate with your biological systems and operate continuously." Oliver beamed with pride, his eyes transfixed on the small vial of clear gel.

"And you made them?" Charles asked, handing the vial back over.

"They're on loan from a research team I'm friendly with over at MIT. Never underestimate the power of making the right friends at the right time."

Oliver smiled as he placed the vial back into the padded casing. "Since we've pretty much done the tour, how about we go feed the animals and then grab a bite. Have you eaten today?"

"Yes, but I could eat again," Charles assured him.

"Good." Oliver loudly clasped his hands together. "A feast, then. First the animals, then the men."

Over the course of the following week, the facility became a buzzing hive of activity. As the computers were replaced in the processing center, Nipul, a data analyst and the unofficial network troubleshooter, bid each of the units farewell by tugging off the sticky notes. New notes were stuck to each replacement. This time, however, the units were marked with names of beloved composers, such as Williams, Franke, Beethoven, and McCreary.

After the installation, the entire staff was brought into the conference room. In addition to Oliver and Charles, Mitchell and Nipul were in attendance. There was Claire, Oliver's administrative assistant, and Eugene Chopra, Jaime Kong, and Dev Chandre from the research team. The primate handler, Bryce Tepschek, was there, as well as the interns, Hillary Chen and Cynthia McGoldrick. Oliver gathered the team together to receive new ID cards and passkeys to match their cutting-edge laboratory.

The assembly brimmed with excitement, yet none had anticipated the speed of upcoming developments. Within two weeks' time, the parent company of the rebranded Oliver Research and Development, known as O.R.D., would determine that Oliver's lab facility was insufficient, and decide to purchase the entire building. By the end of the first month, the staff grew threefold, then another threefold within the following two months. With resources growing exponentially, the staff's productivity skyrocketed beyond Oliver's wildest dreams.

Meanwhile, Charles's good luck didn't last forever. Luck has a way of turning on those who rely on it.

TWELVE

Alexandra

We don't bury our dead so that they may rest in peace, but so we might do so in their absence.

—The Madness (Third Life Cycle)

It was 15 BA, but by the old calendar AD 2020....

CHARLES stood motionless in a frantic hospital room. Medical devices blinked and beeped. Doctors and nurses scrambled around the blood-soaked bed, tending to Angela. Another set of medical professionals crowded together around a tiny thermal bed, an infant crying. Charles's attention wandered between the larger hospital bed and the thermal bed several times. His mind refused to fathom the gravity of the situation. Inside his head, all was remarkably quiet. Unnaturally quiet.

A hand was placed on his shoulder, and a voice spoke his name. Everything roared into sharp, loud clarity.

"Dr. Jacobs," the nurse said, her mouth hidden behind a surgical mask.

He blinked. "Yes?"

"We need you to step out of the room, please." The nurse gestured for him to leave. "We're doing everything we can, but we need you to exit the room, sir."

"What is happening?" he stammered.

"Sir, your wife nearly lost the baby. Both of them are in serious condition. We need you to accompany us to the waiting area so the doctors can focus on saving their lives. Okay?"

"The baby wasn't due for another month. Is he—she—going to be okay?" Charles and Angela had not found out the sex of the baby ahead of time. Angela insisted that they be surprised. She was always hoping the world would surprise her. Over the years, it was a trait that was both charming and annoying to Charles.

"We're going to do everything we can for her, sir."

"Her?" he asked, tears beginning to well in his eyes.

"Yes, sir. You have a little baby girl, but she needs to be intubated. Please, go with one of the nurses to the waiting room."

His journey to the waiting room was a blur. Hazy shapes of orderlies, doctors, and nurses garbed in whites, blues, greens, and reds passed him. Ventilators shaped the soundscape, humming and beeping as patients took labored breaths. A vicious virus was ravaging the world, and the hospital was overwhelmed. He was guided to a stiff chair in a room that reeked of cleaning solution. As he settled into his seat, the young nurse who had accompanied him knelt.

"Dr. Jacobs, I know this is hard, but I want you to know that Dr. Taj and Dr. Noack are going to do everything they can for your wife and daughter. Is there anyone you would like me to call? A family member or friend?" she asked.

Charles's parents had both died within the last year. First, his father passed as a result of a stroke, and then his mother followed no less than six months later from leukemia. His time away from his work was spent with Angela, and his "friends" were merely workplace associates. Death and loneliness, it seemed, were nipping at Charles's heels.

A single name jumped out from all the names, faces, and identities of those he knew and trusted. Oliver. Oliver was the one to call.

"Dr. Stephen Oliver. Please." He pulled Oliver's business card from his wallet, which had the Morgen-Sinn logo next to a photo of his face. His hand trembled as he handed the card to the nurse.

She put a comforting hand on his shoulder. "We're going to do everything we can, Dr. Jacobs. You just sit tight, I'll try calling Dr. Oliver, and we'll let you know the minute something changes, okay?"

Charles nodded. This was not how things were meant to be.

A half hour later, Oliver arrived to find Charles sitting with his elbows upon his knees and his head in his hands.

"Charles?" Oliver said, walking briskly over. Charles stood, embracing his mentor.

"I came down as soon as I could. How is Angela?" Oliver said.

Charles struggled to maintain his composure. "Still in surgery." The words escaped his lips in a weak croak.

"And the baby?"

"Baby is in the NICU. I . . ." He thought of his daughter, hooked up to machinery like the lab's animals. "They don't know how bad it is." Sadness turned into an outburst. "They won't fucking tell me!"

"I'm sure they're doing everything they can."

"I know." Charles sighed. "It's a girl. I have a little girl."

Oliver's face split into a warm but tempered smile. "Congratulations. I'm sure she'll pull through. Both of them will be fine. This is the finest hospital in the city. You're in good hands."

"She was so small." Charles's voice broke with every syllable. "So tiny, and so beautiful, and she wouldn't move. I couldn't move. I just looked at her in that crib and stood there doing nothing. I couldn't help her. Then they wheeled her away. She's so small."

"She'll grow bigger, Charles. She'll grow bigger, and you and Angela will watch her turn into a beautiful young woman. Before you know it, she'll be causing you real grief when she introduces you to her boyfriends." Oliver placed his hand on Charles's shoulder and seemed relieved to hear a labored chuckle escape from his mouth between the sobs.

The two waited together in silence. Ages passed before the nurse entered the room.

"I have an update," she said. Her tone was professional, monotone. "Can I speak with you privately?"

Oliver took his leave.

The nurse lowered her voice. "Your wife experienced a postpartum hemorrhage following a premature delivery. This resulted in immense blood loss and a drastic decline in blood pressure over a very short period of time. Between the blood loss, shock, and low blood pressure, it was just too much, too fast. Dr. Jacobs, your wife didn't survive."

Ringing filled Charles's ears. Words became muted tones of bass and treble. It was not until the word *baby* was uttered that he emerged from the emotional cacophony.

"What about the baby?" he asked desperately.

"Your daughter is stable, but she is not out of the woods yet. If you like, I can take you to see her. It's tough for new parents in your position to see their children like this. She's severely underweight and on life support."

His kin, his blood, was fighting for her life, and he had neither properly met her, nor chosen her name. He wanted to hold on to hope. However, Charles pledged that if his daughter died, she would at least do so with a name given after he had laid, if not a father's hand, at least his eyes on her. *My god, Angela, how am I going to do this without you?*

In the NICU, Charles stood beside the small, clear box in which his infant daughter lay. Though intubated and hooked up to an IV, she was the single most beautiful sight he had ever seen, with her little round nose and little wisps of hair. His shaking hand covered his mouth. Charles struggled to take several deep breaths. This was the first meeting between himself and his daughter.

"Alexandra," he stammered, his voice a mess of congestion and emotion. "Your name is Alexandra." A weak smile crossed his face. "We talked about naming you after your mother's father. His name was Alex. He was your grandfather, baby. Your mommy's daddy. He's gone now." The notion of a departed parent struck him like a hammer to the chest. "He's gone, and so is your mommy. But they both live on in you. Just as your mommy will always be with you, so will I. I will always, always be right here. For you. You won't ever have to worry about that. No matter what, I promise to protect you. So please, just stay with us. Stay with me."

By the time the two left the hospital, the life Charles imagined with Angela and their child was gone. Only Dr. Jacobs and his promise remained.

△

In the following weeks, Alexandra Jacobs was diagnosed with a condition that the medical staff took to calling "Jacobs's disease." Even with the help of her father, their best guess was that it was an unusual and exceptionally slow form of neural degeneration. The initial speculation, which would soon be confirmed by Jacobs's own research, gave her ten to fifteen years until she succumbed to the effects of her condition. Jacobs vowed to find a cure before it was too late, pivoting his research endeavors to focus on rare neurodegenerative diseases.

This was not to say that there was a lapse in productivity for the research teams at O.R.D. Nearly fifty projects were undertaken by the staff, with dozens of affiliate laboratories scattered around the globe. All continued to make extraordinary progress. There were advanced biometric scanning and tracking technologies used in everything from medical monitoring to national security. Cognitive behavioral tools monitored neurological changes in patients, allowing doctors and researchers to better understand and treat a myriad of mental and behavioral conditions. The achievements by O.R.D. made the company both an industry leader and a cultural sensation.

A series of remarkable breakthroughs was achieved through the implementation of next-gen nanotechnology provided by Morgen-Sinn. Known as "Protein Actuated Cerebral Technologies," or "PACT bots," these nanobots were suspended in a biocompatible gel medium. The bots integrated seamlessly with human physiological systems, providing an unprecedented level of access to human consciousness and neurological function.

The critical advance came when Oliver's team solved the blood-brain barrier challenge that had stymied neural interface research for decades. PACT-I's engineered transport proteins mimicked naturally occurring molecules, allowing injected nanobots to cross from the bloodstream to brain tissue through receptor-mediated transcytosis, though the process was slow and required precise injection timing and dosing.

The team combined this technology with Jacobs's theoretical framework on neural degeneration, finally enabling the practical study of the complex protein interactions his research had predicted. Six months after receiving their first production batch of PACT bots, O.R.D. made international headlines when Jacobs's work on neural protein breakdown was successfully applied to reverse memory loss in Alzheimer's disease. The cure for Alzheimer's was the first of many miraculous discoveries at the O.R.D.—none of which helped Alexandra.

△

Sebastian sat at his mother's side as she lay in a hospital bed. They were treating her for a sudden collapse she suffered while tending to her garden. Sebastian, now a premed student at Harvard, calmed himself with the realization that this was the inevitability of getting old. Besides, he told himself, it was more likely caused by some nutrient deficiency in her diet than serious illness. The two awaited test results as Elomina received IV fluids. Eventually, Sebastian wandered down the hall in search of a cup of coffee.

He passed the emergency ward, where cries and moans echoed around the wing. His phone vibrated with an incoming email. It was an offer to interview for an internship opportunity. Although he hadn't applied for anything, his heart raced as the words *Oliver Research and Development* jumped out at him. They were the big league but rarely had any openings. Sebastian accepted immediately.

The excitement was cut short by the wail of pain from a nearby hospital bed. He could see a sliver of what was going on through a gap in the curtains.

△

Henry Price, a lean and dark-eyed twenty-three-year-old, remained by his screaming mother's side in the curtained corner of the emergency ward. Her grip on his hand loosened, and her breathing labored. His father had already passed, his body covered in a sheet on the next bed over. Now, his mother was about to leave him too.

"Henry," his mother said weakly. "Henry, it's okay. I can see them, Henry."

Through his own tears, Price replied, "Who?"

"Everyone. I see everyone, Henry. Even Papa and Yaya. I see your father. It's going to be all right."

The monitors alarmed as her heart stopped. Price let his mother's hand slip from his as nurses ushered him out of the room. He stumbled into the hall, bumping into a young man absorbed in his phone. "I'm sorry," the man said, putting a hand on his shoulder to stabilize Price. At a nurse's nod, he gently led Price back to his mother's bed.

Tears streamed from Price's face at the sight of his mother's lifeless body. When the lead doctor's sullen voice announced the time of death, Price was numb to the world. The young man from the hallway stayed, watching as Price stood frozen.

"I was just on my way to the waiting room," the man said, guiding Price from the bed. "Do you have someone else here with you?"

Price shook his head.

"Let's find a place to sit. I'm Sebastian, by the way."

Two hours later, Sebastian and Price sat side by side in the waiting room. Sebastian riffled through magazines. There was nothing for him to do now but wait while his own mother slept and recovered from dehydration. Price sat hunched over, elbows on his knees, waiting for his uncle to pick him up. Another visitor reached for a switch on the side of a small television in the corner of the room and increased the volume, drawing both Sebastian's and Price's attention.

"If I may," the television reporter asked renowned scientist Dr. Jacobs, "I'd like to also congratulate you on your amazing work. I'm not sure many out there were expecting we'd find an effective treatment for Alzheimer's, let alone a cure. What was it like to make such a discovery?"

"It was a team effort, all those years of work. And I wasn't actually there when the initial results of the breakthrough came in. I was busy mourning the loss of my wife. Nevertheless, things have been taking off since then, and our research teams are already breaking new ground," he said, sipping from the cup of water in front of him.

The reporter chirped, "So, what's next for you and Dr. Oliver?"

"There's a lot still up in the air, but I can say that we're going to begin trials for a new type of study. Since much of what we do focuses on neurochemistry, we're attempting to use our existing nanotechnology to capture the lived experiences of test subjects. If successful, we should be able to not only understand what goes on in the course of a given experience, which includes those with conditions like psychosis or autism, but could potentially record and replicate the occurrence of everyday things like, well, dreams."

"Recording dreams? That's unbelievable."

"Improbable, more like. With singular focus and dedication to achievement, I find nothing scientifically based to be unbelievable."

"What do you hope to do if you're successful? What's the ultimate goal?"

Jacobs shifted in his seat, considering the question. "If we're able to observe and understand the experiences of those with certain psychological conditions, we could have a better grasp of how to address or treat them. And there could even be unknown benefits in treating people with rare neurological diseases.

"We could be entering an entirely new era in human understanding. We will, in theory, be able to understand one another to degrees previously unimaginable. If one can truly see and truly feel the lives, thoughts, and emotions of another human being, is empathy even really a strong enough word to describe that experience? Again, it all hinges on how successful we are in adapting the technology we have on hand to achieve this goal. This could potentially save the world, I suppose," Jacobs said, crossing one leg over the other and sipping again at his water.

The reporter fumbled, trying to find the right words to save her broadcast from dead air. "So then, you're out to save the world?"

"Isn't everyone?" Jacobs allowed himself a small chuckle. "Look, what we're doing is no different than past research. We're on a mission to challenge and defeat death. To cure the previously incurable. That is exactly what we at O.R.D., as well as our benefactors at Morgen-Sinn, are doing. What could possibly be a more noble goal?"

"Well, Dr. Jacobs, thank you so very much for taking the time to speak with me here. It has been an honor, and thank you for all of your work," the reporter said earnestly.

"My pleasure. Thank you for having me."

Although Dr. Jacobs seemed like a pompous ass to Price, maybe he had a point. Making the world a better place through understanding born of experience. Gaining certainty from that knowledge. Price felt his grief fuel a drive to remove any doubt as to what was seen by those who lay dying. The death of his parents was more than a freak car accident. It would be a gift.

THIRTEEN

A Common Thread

The problem with standing on the shoulders of giants is that it soon becomes impossible to remember what the view from the ground looks like.

—The Catalyst

Four years later there was applause. Lots of enthusiastically polite applause....

*T*HIS *is obscene,* thought Price. One handshake after another reached out to him. All of them were sycophants in love with his bank account. O.R.D. was thanking him for his generous support at the official opening of the Etta and Harry Price Memorial Lab at Oliver Research and Development. Donating most of his parents' wealth to science had killed two birds with one large deposit. It fulfilled his mother's wish to "do good" with her money while positioning Price as an up-and-coming leader in his new career. Still, all this commotion made him uncomfortable. They weren't applauding his efforts; he had bought his way in. Still, it had made sense to take advantage of the resources at his disposal. He had started off a little older than his peers, but he was much more ambitious. And he was restless.

"Nice speech you gave. A little too pithy for my taste, but well done," Dr. Stephen Oliver said playfully as he walked over. "You look like you could use a breather. Do you have some time to meet with Charles?"

"Sure, when would be a good time?" Price asked, taking out his phone.

Oliver winked and gestured to a conference room. Price was surprised when Oliver ushered him into the room and promptly shut the door without entering behind him. Jacobs sat at the head of a large conference table reading from a manila folder, a few documents and a pen laid out next to him.

"It's nice to finally meet you," Price said, sliding into the executive chair at the opposite end of the table. Jacobs held up one finger, eyes scanning the document in the folder. Price leaned back, tapping his brow impatiently. Jacobs finally closed the folder and let it fall from his hand to the table.

"Thank you for your efforts," Jacobs said sincerely.

"I'm happy to support this organization. My parents—"

Jacobs cut him off. "Nonsense, you did more than support. I watched you lead the entire project. Organizing the assets, bringing in the equipment, advocating for staff changes. A lab this sophisticated can take years, not months, to become fully operational. And you've done all this as an outsider."

Ouch, thought Price.

"You didn't just want to put your name on the wall and walk away. You're invested in this, and you know what you're doing. It's unexpected and most impressive. I asked my staff for more information on you," Jacobs admitted, tapping the manila folder with his pointer finger. "I'm trying to understand how someone who began his career in the media ended up as a champion for neuroscience."

"It's a long story. After college, I did marketing and public relations, but then my parents died. It was an interview with you that I saw on the news that changed my interests."

"Oh?" Jacobs leaned back in his chair.

"It was on TV the night my parents passed. You were speaking about defeating death, and when I heard you say that, I suddenly saw a whole new path. I went ahead and changed my life's plan the very next day."

This was not, in fact, the truth. It had taken over a year for Henry Price to upend his life. Managing his parents' estate while applying to every school that might accept him, then learning an entirely new field, were a few of the herculean tasks he had juggled. His previous training in the art of communications had taught him that little white lies never hurt anyone, so long as they were told for a good reason.

Jacobs slid a nondisclosure agreement and a pen down the length of the table. "This is sensitive information I'm about to give you, so you need to keep it to yourself, understood?"

Price nodded. He sped through the boilerplate language and signed it.

Price dated the agreement as Jacobs continued, "Stephen Oliver suffered a health scare recently and has begrudgingly taken it as his cue to retire." Jacobs exhaled, folding his hands together. "I'm going to be taking over his role, and I need someone to take over mine.

"I can't help but think about how it was Stephen who took me under his wing. My thinking is that now I ought to do the same with someone as driven as you. You blazed through your education with passion. Between that, and what you've spearheaded here, it's quite remarkable for someone so young. I need someone who can keep the labs going when my attention is demanded elsewhere. You may have heard about my daughter's condition. She's held on longer than we could have imagined and I'm running out of time to find a cure."

Change was coming to O.R.D., and Price sensed he was about to get pulled into the deep end. Jacobs was going to be distracted, and this was Price's opportunity to contribute something more than money. "So, when should I start?"

Jacobs chuckled. "How about Monday? That would be ideal, since we're going to be announcing a partnership with Mass General next month for some trials of our latest PACT developments. It might be a perfect way to cut your teeth. Think you can get a new facility up and running in three months? We're expanding their campus."

Price spoke firmly. "Absolutely. I'd love to work here at O.R.D."

"Just one thing," Jacobs added sheepishly. "Since Stephen will be stepping down and turning this all over to me, we're going to be renaming our operation."

"To what?"

"Most of the staff thinks 'The Jacobs Institute' would be appropriate. I'm not sure how I feel about it. Seems a bit vain, but the PR department insists it helps with funding."

Price mulled the name over. "I'd say it has a nice ring to it. Between the evolution of the PACT technology, the breakthroughs on ALS and Huntington's, and your dream studies, The Jacobs Institute is quite appropriate. You may not have created O.R.D., but you're the one who put this place on the map. It should be The Jacobs Institute."

"As half of the office is already calling it that anyway, I'm not sure I have much of a choice. Maybe I'll just refer to it as 'The Institute' to keep my ego in check."

"I'll let you know if it ever surpasses mine," joked Price. Maybe Jacobs did deserve all the praise and admiration he received.

▲

In the back seat of a luxury sedan, Sebastian listened as Dr. Jacobs laid out impending changes in senior staffing. Sebastian only half paid attention, processing this dramatic turn of events. Jacobs had surprised him the day before, commanding him to join a new venture at Mass General.

He had grown to admire Dr. Jacobs greatly, yet Sebastian seldom had the opportunity to speak to the man. In the years that had passed since his internship, Sebastian could likely have counted the number of times on his fingers that he had worked with Dr. Jacobs in the flesh.

"Dr. Reed, isn't it?" Jacobs had asked, bouncing into the break room.

"Yes, sir," Sebastian answered.

"We need you tomorrow for a task force. You'll drive with me. Bring the Deltas."

The team was headed up by some new guy in Operations who apparently bought his way into Jacobs's good favor. Though Jacobs had been engaged with several secretive endeavors, it now looked like Sebastian's hard work was finally paying off and he would get to be part of the inner circle. They finally acknowledged his contributions, and this was his reward. *Best not blow it now,* Sebastian urged himself, refocusing on his boss.

Jacobs explained their most recent good fortune. In their search for a shared facility, a building adjacent to the city hospital had become available. The market value of the company that had previously inhabited the building inexplicably tanked, and the operation was forced to shut down. This same corporate collapse coincided perfectly with a substantial cash infusion from Morgen-Sinn to The Jacobs Institute, cementing the deal.

As they pulled up to the front of the building, a large,

unmarked delivery truck pulled around to the side. Dozens of trucks had flocked to the new facility, all laden with brand-new equipment. Jacobs told him that this site would soon be inundated with all the cutting-edge equipment money could buy.

Jacobs pushed his keys into the valet's hand without making eye contact with him. He smiled as the hospital liaison approached.

"Dr. Jones, good afternoon," Jacobs said, shaking her hand vigorously and gesturing to his side. "This is Dr. Reed, a senior researcher from O.R.D."

Sebastian was pleased with his new, albeit unofficial, title as a senior researcher. He, too, offered Dr. Jones a firm handshake.

Jones turned her attention back to Jacobs. "From what I've heard, it's likely to be The Jacobs Institute soon enough, huh?" She winked.

The three entered through the main foyer of Mass General and walked through several hallways. At the center of the maze, a locked door swung open on its own. "Our biometric security system has been working phenomenally. Thank you again for that," she said, leading the men through it.

Their new laboratory was easily three stories tall. The rooms above were connected by catwalks and promenades circling the center. Rounded white walls encircled each level. At the far end of the hall, a pair of service entrance double doors remained propped open as laborers and technicians moved in equipment.

Sebastian was especially intrigued by a series of salon-like chairs being wheeled into one of the larger rooms on the main level. These chairs, positioned in rows, were plugged into power and data ports on the floor. They reclined backward and included large circular halos suspended on hinges at the top, clearly meant to be brought down over an occupant's head.

As soon as a seat was placed, a small team of technicians set about diligently plugging them in and performing diagnostics.

"Dr. Jacobs, welcome!" Sebastian turned around to find a man with a well-maintained goatee and hawkish face charging in their direction. He thought the man looked familiar.

"Wouldn't miss the final touches if my life depended on it," Jacobs insisted, clasping the man's left bicep.

"And you brought some staff, no less!"

Sebastian felt a pang of resentment at the mention of him being "staff." He pursed his lips. This operations guy seemed awfully familiar, but he couldn't quite place the face.

"Henry Price, this is Dr. Sebastian Reed. He's one of our most talented R&D guys," said Jacobs as Sebastian forced a smile, trying to play it cool. "Where are we in terms of acquisitions?"

Price's eyes lit up. "We are better than good, sir. Our facility is the epitome of progress and achievement." He reminded Sebastian of a dog expecting a treat for fetching his own toy.

"Progress and achievement, eh?" Jacobs mimicked sardonically. Sebastian had not seen this side of Jacobs before. Perhaps he also objected to Price's yes-man persona.

Jacobs moved on. "How long until we can get things up and running?"

Again, Price shined at the opportunity to offer an answer. *Woof,* Sebastian thought.

"Well, all we need to do is get the units installed and we're good to go. It's plug and play." Price shrugged, feigning nonchalance. "More or less."

Jacobs shot a curious eye to the equipment already installed. "So, once everything is hooked up, it'll be ready for a test?"

Price looked around at the installation in progress. "We've got a viewer seat, the processing bay, and the power up. We don't have a subject lined up yet, but I suppose if we have any of the Delta series PACT on hand, then we could make something work."

Sebastian gripped the right strap of his backpack, which contained the vials of the new PACT. He was familiar with all generations of PACT: past, present, and in the pipeline. Yet this "viewing seat" and its relation to his Delta series PACT was a mystery.

"Well, as it turns out, our friend Sebastian here has a whole set of Delta with him. Shall we fire it up?" Jacobs patted Sebastian on the shoulder.

"Wait a second. There are transmitter modules for the Deltas in this chair? I don't know if the Deltas are ready to interact with external devices without—"

Jacobs cut him off. "It's fine, Mr. Reed. They're ready."

Sebastian bit his tongue. *Think before you act,* his mother's voice echoed in his head. He had just been promoted; now was not the time to put that achievement at risk.

"Without any additional input, human or software-based, it'll only be an empty container. A loading screen, for lack of a better term. That's our next can of worms. Would you like to be our test subject, Dr. Reed?" Price inquired, raising an eyebrow.

Sebastian instinctively looked at Jacobs.

"If Dr. Jacobs has no objections, of course," Price added.

Jacobs shook his head.

Price clapped his hands together. "Well, there we have it. Dr. Reed, would you like the honor of being the first human to experience the Optical?"

"The optical what?" Sebastian asked.

"It's sort of a nickname I gave the setup. I had thought of calling it the Greater Optical Display, but the acronym is a little unfortunate."

"I like it. The G.O.D." Jacobs sat with the name for a moment. "It is the closest humanity will likely get to ever locating a deity. Ha!"

Despite being an atheist, Sebastian was surprisingly offended. His mother grew more frail with every passing day, yet in the face of increasing hatred, injustice, and all the other atrocities that came with occupying this planet, her religious conviction persisted.

Thinking about his mother triggered a memory from the night she collapsed. Sebastian recognized Price as the man at the hospital, eyes vacant and sunken, whose parents had just died. A very different, insufferable man stood before him now.

It was clear Price had come a long way since they had met at the hospital. Sebastian assumed Price had funneled his grief into work, much like Jacobs did each day, fighting to cure his daughter.

Sebastian watched Price laugh at another one of Jacobs's jokes. He knew these men were both plagued and bonded by tragedy. As much as Sebastian longed to be a part of their clandestine projects and inside jokes, it would never be worth going through what they had experienced to get there. Sebastian's drive would continue to be entirely self-motivated.

The G.O.D. was soon fully operational. Sebastian walked over to a nearby table where various cases, boxes, and bags were spread out. He opened a plastic container and pulled out a tube rack holding vials containing hundreds of thousands of PACT bots. As he rolled up his sleeve, Jacobs spoke to his back.

"Are you sure you want to be our test subject?" Jacobs asked.

Sebastian nodded. "I'm intrigued by what all of this entails." He put aside his annoyance with Jacobs and Price for now.

"Very well. We're exchanging test signals to make sure the units are communicating. Now, I want to warn you, this may be a bit disorienting. This isn't virtual or augmented reality. You'll be fully, 100 percent immersed, at least in theory."

Sebastian prepped a needle filled with the Delta series

PACT and held it a few inches from his arm. Sebastian considered his situation: On one hand, anything from a tremendous headache to frying his neural synapses was possible. On the other hand, he was thrilled about the exploratory nature of whatever was about to happen. He sank the needle into his arm, finding his vein with little difficulty.

Sebastian took a seat in the chair with the large halo above it. Aside from the rigid arms, which held a series of lights, switches, buttons, and ports, it was surprisingly well cushioned.

"It's a comfortable chair," Sebastian remarked to Price.

"I've spared no expense on these units. Odds are good that at some point people will be spending the better part of a day or more in them," Price replied.

He flipped a switch on the side of the chair, turning it on. A whirring sound came from the circular halo device. Price lowered the contraption until it was perfectly aligned with Sebastian's forehead.

"Now, this may feel a little strange, but I want you to just remain calm and keep your breathing steady," Price instructed. "Okay then. Coming online." He paused briefly, and the machine noises subsided. "Stats all look good." Sebastian breathed in through his nose and out through his mouth. He counted down silently as Price counted aloud.

Three.

Two.

One.

Sebastian's world disappeared as "one" escaped Price's lips. Everything around him ceased to exist; a deep blackness dissolved into a gray void.

Then, a blinding white light.

FOURTEEN

The Link

Deep into that darkness peering, long I stood there, wondering, fearing, doubting, dreaming dreams no mortal ever dared to dream before.

—Edgar Allan Poe, "The Raven"

"LINK COMPLETE" flashed on the screen....

SEBASTIAN'S eyes glazed over as his body briefly convulsed. His shoulders drooped, then his whole body relaxed into the seat. He breathed comfortably.

"We should be able to start run-time processes and open communications," Price announced with a glowing smile. Sebastian's vitals and brain wave activity appeared normal, and eager smiles split Price's and Jacobs's faces. As Price began transferring data from a workstation along the wall to the G.O.D., Jacobs arranged the vital signs and neural activity displays on the large monitor that hung beside Sebastian's seat. He noticed the brief spike in Sebastian's heart rate that had occurred when the machine was first switched on. There was a drop, followed by a steady pulse as the connection stabilized.

"Shall we see if we can speak to him?" Price asked, eyes darting between the displays.

Jacobs nodded. He pressed down on a bright yellow icon in the bottom corner of the display in front of him. "Sebastian? Can you hear me?"

A series of unintelligible clicks and static sounded from the small built-in speakers of the monitor. Then silence. Eventually, the confused but calm voice of Sebastian was heard through the speakers. "I can. I'm not sure how, but I can hear you. I don't exactly hear you, but I know you're talking to me. Am I dreaming?"

"This is real. Describe what you're seeing to us," Jacobs said, eyes transfixed on the unmoving face of Sebastian.

"It's hard to describe," Sebastian's voice replied. "It's a giant white room, but there aren't any walls or even a floor or ceiling. Just a bright emptiness."

Releasing the Talk button, Jacobs yelped, "We're hearing his thoughts! His thoughts! He's not even speaking. He's thinking at us!"

"It's not going to look like anything right away, but watch this," Price said, engaging with a new screen to his right. He entered a few commands, and the display lit up with a flat white image. "Just another second now," Price muttered as he finalized his commands. In the center of the image, a crudely drawn table popped into view. He input the illustration into Sebastian's feed.

▲

Sebastian squinted as his eyes adjusted to the white space before him. He wasn't sure he had eyes; it just felt that way. He couldn't feel the rest of his body either, yet he felt more grounded than if he were dreaming. He was Sebastian Reed, but also not Sebastian Reed.

A simple metal table appeared out of nowhere in the distance. The landmark oriented him in the white space.

"Dr. Reed, what do you see now?" Jacobs's voice reverberated around him.

"It looks like a table. Looks like it's just four legs and a silver tabletop. Nothing fancy," Sebastian replied. "I'm going to try to approach it," he said, moving forward. "Strange. I'm getting closer, but my perspective of it remains the same. I can't look around it or above it. It's like a two-dimensional sprite."

"Sprite?" Jacobs asked.

"Retro video game characters. They were two-dimensional things that would always look the same regardless of the angle that you viewed them from."

"Can you touch it?"

Sebastian reached out with his hand. "Yes. It's cold."

Price spoke. "How about this?"

A brown desk fan materialized on top of the metal table, a dirty power cable dangling off the edge. The fan started slowly rotating around and around until the blades seemed to blend together. It created a faint buzzing sound. The air brushed Sebastian's face, or whatever served as his face in this realm. He looked down at his own body; he possessed two feet, two hands, ten fingers, and ten toes. Everything was where it was supposed to be. This definitely wasn't a dream. A lightheadedness overtook him, and he transitioned back to the waking world.

⩓

"How was it?" Jacobs asked, helping Sebastian up from the seat. His eyes returned to normal.

"I'm used to virtual reality, but this is something else entirely," Sebastian replied, stunned. "What did you see out here?"

"Henry, do we have a recording?" Jacobs asked.

"Audio and video," Price replied, bringing up the recording on the main monitor.

Sebastian watched in awe as his experience was replayed from his perspective. "It's as though you were seeing it through my eyes."

"We are seeing it through your eyes," Price said proudly. "And better yet, I think we can replay it all back through the G.O.D."

"Incredible," Sebastian stammered. He realized that Jacobs was using the PACT bots and the G.O.D. to relay visceral experiences—an intense combination of senses, emotions, and thoughts—from one person to another. This was an unprecedented achievement: to see, hear, and maybe even feel the direct experiences of another person. To one day know what it is to *be* that person.

"I'm envisioning great uses in everything from therapy to pain management," Jacobs said. "Doctors right now can only treat pain as it's described, but once the remainder of these units are installed and networked, one's sensations can be experienced directly. We can feel everything. There's a lot of work ahead of us, but the applications are limitless."

⚕

Following their first experiment with the Greater Optical Display, Jacobs, Price, and Reed had one miraculous breakthrough after another. Morgen-Sinn funneled billions into the research and development of the new technology, and Sorensen paid the main facility a visit for the first time in years. Jacobs noted how the man looked remarkably the same from year to year, without any sign of aging. Sorensen spoke of his delight in their progress, although he showed little emotion.

The distribution of the G.O.D. systems, coupled with the widespread implementation of PACT, led to many dramatic advances. When using the G.O.D., the halo device interfaced with the user's internal PACT networks, enabling seamless transmission of the recorded experience. This hyper-immersive technology allowed people all over the world to experience not just the actions of another, but the sounds, smells, feelings, and emotions that came with those moments. People lined up at Institute centers en masse to inject themselves with PACT bots to participate in the new technology.

Studios created massive complexes where films were replaced by immersive experiences doled out to audiences with eyes glassy and still. The experiential stories would play out in their minds. They did not just observe the thrills and chills of action and suspense, the terror and delight of horror, or the expansive wonder of science fiction, but genuinely experienced the full breadth of sensations that came with their chosen narrative.

Addiction followed. One lawsuit claimed a company selling sexual experiences had caused a customer to lose track of which memories were his and which were part of the experience. Following this case, the first experiential watermark law was crafted. All scenarios were required to display the creator's corporate logo and regulatory language throughout the experience. These could be found on walls, in clouds, and tattooed on the user's forearm during the session.

The police, military, and intelligence services all sought to exploit new applications of PACT. Recorded experiences of police officers and spies using the PACT bots provided a clandestine way to relay information, replacing pocket cameras and audio recorders. Within five years of the initial launch, a majority of global metropolitan areas had replaced conventional security systems with PACT scanning arrays. Ceiling-mounted transmission panels interfaced with people's internal PACT networks to collect biometric and location data. PACT IDs made it easier to quickly identify who was present. This allowed authorities to review past events during the course of investigations. Privacy advocates rebelled, but ultimately the presumption of being surveilled when in public became the new norm, and PACT IDs became the primary form of biometric identification.

The Jacobs Institute thrived; its influence spread everywhere. Institute medical doctors and special nursing practitioners, often referred to as Feelers, received transmissions from their patients' PACT bots. Patients no longer struggled to articulate their pain or discomfort. Medical professionals could experience the symptoms firsthand, leading to more accurate diagnoses and treatments. Additional advances enabled PACT bots to be programmed with therapeutic protocols, allowing targeted drug delivery and cellular repair at the molecular level. Mortality rates plummeted. Though schools and health centers encouraged parents to withhold PACT injections until their children were at least thirteen years of age due to the challenges of differentiating between their own and others' experiences. Around the world, any attempt to re-create PACT transmission and reception without a license from The Institute failed. The Institute became the most powerful organization on the planet, integrating its technology into every facet of life.

Much to Jacobs's despair, all this success meant nothing when it came to curing his daughter. Through his work, he would stumble upon treatments for countless other illnesses but made no progress on the disease that plagued Alexandra. The world hailed his genius while his daughter fought to stay alive.

FIFTEEN

The Beginning

And the earth was without form, and void; and darkness was upon the face of the deep.

—The Heresies, Genesis 1:2

It was 1 BA, by the old calendar, AD 2034, New Year's Eve....

Most of The Institute's research staff had been given an additional week of vacation to celebrate the close of another successful year. Jacobs and Price were accompanied by an intern, Rashida Johnson, who was a semester away from graduating from MIT at the top of her class. They casually looked over datasets in a break room off the atrium in the main Boston facility. Half-full glasses of scotch sat in front of them. Jacobs and Rashida sipped the pale golden liquor. Price appreciated the smell of the drink without letting a drop touch his lips. It was a curious idiosyncrasy that Jacobs had observed but never quite understood.

"Henry," he pried, "why is it you're always happy to join me for a drink, but you never actually *drink* the drink?"

Price raised an eyebrow. "I make a point of not indulging. In college, I noticed certain tendencies within myself when it came to substances, so I take measures to keep them at bay." Price swirled and studied the liquid in the glass.

"So, you'll smell and stare at it."

"And consider that against what those drinking around me experience," Price replied, a sly smirk creeping from the corners of his lips. "For instance, what do you think, Rashida? If you had to describe this to someone, what would you say about it?"

Rashida examined her glass. "You mean if I were a food critic?"

"Exactly. Abandon your life's ambition here and become a foodie," Price replied with a grin.

"Okay." She paused, taking a deep sniff from the top of her drink. "It's strong. The smell is very strong. It smells like a campfire?"

"Very good!" Price exclaimed, leaning in. "What else? What about the flavor?"

Rashida smiled. She took a small sip and looked around the room. With a swallow and a cough, she continued, "It definitely has a sort of smoky, mossy kind of taste. It burns quite a lot, but there's something almost refined about it. Like it's actually worth whatever you paid for it."

"Absolutely brilliant." Price seemed delighted with her appraisal.

Jacobs was still skeptical. "And that's enough to be fulfilled?"

Price nodded.

"For a research scientist that really doesn't sound all that thorough."

Price shrugged, looking into his full glass. "Do I need to go to the moon to know that it isn't made of cheese?"

Jacobs arched his brow. "Touché."

As Jacobs brought the glass to his lips, an unexpected buzzer nearly caused him to drop it. Out in the atrium by the central entrance, the large red light that indicated the doors were locked turned green. Jacobs rose from his seat, wondering if it was a malfunction with the security system since they had not been expecting any other company. A moment later, the doors burst open, and a cadre of heavily armed men accompanied by a team of unknown uniformed medical staff tended to a patient on a stretcher. The stampede of people made a beeline for the closest G.O.D. receiver bays.

"What's going on?" Rashida asked.

"I'm not sure," Jacobs said, concerned. "Henry, did you know about this?"

Price rubbed his temple and exhaled. "Shit. Those people aren't here. And if we're ever asked by anyone, they were never here."

"What are you rambling on about?"

"You remember a few months ago, when I mentioned the applied sciences division was getting a new contract from the feds?" Price whispered. "Well, these are the feds, and they aren't exactly the type you say no to when they want something."

Jacobs groaned. "You know how I feel about military contracting."

"It's not technically military. It's C.I.D."

The US Conglomerated Intelligence Department was a relatively new branch of government formed in the aftermath of a series of terror attacks by white nationalists targeting fellow Americans and government infrastructure, both domestically and abroad. These intelligence failures were rooted in miscommunication and rivalries between the FBI and the CIA. In response, C.I.D. was created as a leaner organization more focused on technology, whose director reported solely to the president of the United States. Price explained that they had, of course, taken an interest in the future of PACT technology, and he had been their point of contact.

"They came to me and I didn't have any choice, Charles. You know that when they want something, they'll find a way to get it. It was either play ball or watch them shut us down."

Jacobs growled, "First, we see what this mess is." He jutted out a finger at the team working in his facility. "And then you and I are going to have a longer conversation."

Jacobs stormed toward the lab with Price in tow. Rashida stayed a few feet back, clutching her slate, ready to call for help if needed. Jacobs had nearly reached the lab when two of the heavily armed guards blocked his way.

"Move aside," Jacobs said, unfazed by the guns pointed at his face.

"We're going to need you to step back, sir," one said from behind a black balaclava.

"And I'm going to need you to go straight to hell. This is my lab, and I won't just have some glorified cops take over."

"Sir, step back!" the other said, adjusting his grip.

"Or what, you'll shoot me? Shoot my colleagues as well?" Jacobs was in no mood for discussion. "It makes whatever black bag bullshit that this is pretty difficult to pull off when the world's foremost scientist winds up being executed on the floor of his own lab, wouldn't you say?"

"Maybe your lab will just burn down with you inside, smart-ass," the first soldier snickered.

A woman in a business suit walked over and intervened. "Stand down, Sergeant," the agent said.

She was roughly forty years old with streaks of gray running through her black hair. A thin set of rimless glasses magnified a pair of piercing blue eyes. She spared a quick nod at Price. "Henry," she said curtly. The agent lightly touched

Jacobs's arm as she spoke to him. "Dr. Jacobs, I'm Agent Thorne and I am very sorry for intruding. We had no idea you'd be here, and we wouldn't have come if it weren't an emergency. But your being here is fortuitous, because we can certainly use your help."

Jacobs frowned. "Why should I help you? You're trespassing."

"Dr. Jacobs, I'd love to impress upon you that this is a matter of national security, but I don't have time for that conversation." She gestured to the squirming Price. "Your colleague signed a contract granting us full access to your lab in times of need. And this is a time of need. So just help us, and we'll be on our way. We are unfamiliar with your setup, and time is of the essence."

Jacobs seethed, "Henry, how dare you put us in this position."

"I'm sorry, Charles, but the deal is done," Price asserted.

"Who do you think you are? You do not have the authority—" Jacobs's outburst was cut short by a door slamming shut inside the lab. Through the observation window, they watched as a naked body was carried in and strapped down on an exam table. "Who is that? What is going on here?" Jacobs insisted.

The agent sighed. "That is a person of interest who is in possession of extremely valuable information. You don't have the security clearance, and I shouldn't have to explain to you what will happen if you leak this to anyone. He's going to die, and there's nothing we can do for him."

"Oh, I see. You tortured him, that didn't work, he's going to die, and now you want me to just pluck the information from his brain, right? Here's a newsflash: I don't have that capability. All I can manage to do is draw his immediate experience right now or review recorded material. So, pack it all up and get out of my lab!"

The agent removed her glasses, looking Jacobs dead in the

eye. "Okay, Doctor. I'm going to give it to you straight. This individual has no PACT signature, and his body rejected our injection attempts. So, we need your help. You can cooperate or we can make this difficult. Either way you will assist us. Now, am I making myself clear?"

Price cut in. "Charles, I made the deal. Gave them my word. Our word. They can shut us down if we don't comply. I signed—" Jacobs waved Price's words away.

"So, no choice then," Jacobs said.

"No choice," said the agent. "And in case you've got something else in mind, you should know that we blacked out this entire facility ten minutes before we arrived. There is no network connection coming in or out of this building. No surveillance or electronic signals can leave these walls. No one can peek in from above. What we do now is for our eyes only."

"Let's get to it, I suppose," Jacobs acquiesced.

Jacobs led them into the adjacent control room, which housed a row of computer stations and large monitors, along with cabinets stocked with vials of the Theta series PACT bots and PACT-II, the next evolution of PACT. PACT-II was engineered to bypass injection entirely and overcome the transport limitations across the blood-brain barrier that constrained PACT-I deployment, entering the recipient's body through aerosol distribution. The nanobots featured hybrid locomotion systems with microscopic cilia for navigation and biochemical guidance for tissue targeting, allowing them to survive airborne deployment and reach neural tissue directly through respiratory-to-brain pathways. Enhanced biocompatibility coatings enabled immune system evasion during the entry process. However, laboratory tests revealed stability issues in aerosol form and inconsistent distribution patterns, so the technology remained in development.

Along the far wall, the G.O.D. system was active, awaiting its user. Jacobs moved to the master control panel as Price went to one of the cabinets. He retrieved a syringe containing the Theta series PACT bots; in lab tests they were proven as the most reliable to date.

The entrance to the exam room was blocked by the agent. "That area is restricted," she said, positioning herself between Price and the door.

"Your patient is going to need the Theta series to interface with the equipment in this lab. The G.O.D. is calibrated solely for the PACT-I Theta. Without that new injection, you'll see nothing."

She held her hand out. "I'll administer it."

"Fine." Price placed the syringe in her hand. "Left arm, right below the shoulder." She turned on her heel and went into the room as Price joined Jacobs by the control panel.

The agent injected the now motionless body on the table with the solution. Price and Jacobs watched the monitors, which displayed a three-dimensional rendering of the body. A real-time visualization showed the PACT bots' diagnostic networks mapping cellular damage and pathological markers throughout the patient's body. Price and Jacobs waited for the results.

Nothing was found. The readouts showed no detectable signs of infection or injury. Jacobs and Price looked at each other, baffled. The PACT bots had fully circulated through the body, but they showed absolutely no signs of life. Strangely, no internal organs displayed on the screens. There was no blood or blood pressure, nor any skeletal structure. Nothing was there. Convinced that there was a malfunction with the system, Jacobs ran diagnostics while Price went to the cabinet to inspect the Theta series vial. Neither could find the source of the issue. Rashida began recording the scene on her slate.

The body on the table convulsed violently against its restraints. The lights in both rooms flashed. The backup generator was top of the line and supposed to withstand any form of surge without interruption, yet the power fluctuated wildly.

Price rushed over to a G.O.D. and sat down. "Charles, boot it up and connect me to what's happening in there."

Jacobs was uncertain if turning on the device without a reliable source of power was wise. Yet, out of options, he complied. Price lowered the halo and waited for the connection to stabilize.

On the display mounted next to the G.O.D., Jacobs watched as a brilliant white light flooded the screen. He approached Price and the unit, adjusting a dial on its control panel, to decrease the signal strength. He pressed the Communication icon on the display.

"What do you see, Henry?" he asked.

"I don't know," Price struggled to respond, his voice strained. The experience was clearly intense; Jacobs adjusted the intensity. "The connection is strange. But I think it feels like he's dying. I'm not sure. It's not really working. Oh my god, Charles. Oh my god."

Jacobs observed the event Price was experiencing. The white light intensified and rippled. What had first appeared to be pockets of darkness were actually shadows. The lights in the lab dimmed and surged again. On the screen, blurry silhouettes milled around. One of the distorted figures stopped abruptly. It turned its attention to the observers and moved forward.

Another power surge overwhelmed the electrical system and everything went dark. Red emergency lighting kicked in. Jacobs lifted the halo from around Price's head. Price sat back, eyes wide, struggling with the transition back to the lab. Jacobs helped him up, and both moved to the window looking into the exam room.

What they saw defied all known laws of physics. The body on the table contracted in on itself. It sank into the table, melting like ice cream on a hot summer day. The creamy ooze formed into a single mass and dripped from the table.

Jacobs heard a deafening engine whirr as the puddle reconstituted itself into a body. As one soldier inched forward, its pointed limbs swung violently. The right limb stretched directly into the soldier, impaling him through the stomach and lifting him into the air. The guards at the door gave way as Price, Jacobs, Rashida, and others rushed into the room and over to the dying soldier. Another limb lashed out, sending nearby equipment flying across the room. A medical scanner slammed into a storage cage, which also housed vials of PACT-II bots. Vial after vial cracked open as trillions upon trillions of bots swarmed, creating a nebulous cloud that penetrated the eyes, noses, and mouths of everyone in the room.

They all stood captivated by what Jacobs would later describe as having their souls leave their bodies, transmitted into another plane of existence. Blinding white light accompanied the sensation of a warm embrace that detached them from their physical form. Any pain and discomfort became a forgotten memory. Elusive shadows came and went, their faces obscured by the light. Familiar voices washed over them. Family, friends, *something* was awaiting them, just out of reach. This place was real. As real as the lab in which they had been standing. This dying patient was showing them the next stage of life, be it heaven, the experience of the Singularity, or something else beyond their ephemeral existence on Earth. Their connection was only seconds in length. A pale golden light enveloped the patient, and the impaled soldier fell to the ground. The collective experience came to an end as the swarm flew out of their bodies, up a vent, and out of the lab. The air, now devoid of PACT-II bots, was still. The figure lay at the center of the destruction, surrounded by witnesses.

The agent broke the silence, barking orders at the soldiers to initiate a lockdown procedure. Jacobs, Price, and Rashida were escorted back into the break room. After they spent three hours in isolation, the agent entered the room. She sauntered over to the table and slid the glasses of scotch over to both Rashida and Jacobs. Eyeing Price mischievously, she took the glass in front of him for herself.

"I know you won't mind, Henry," she said.

Price waved it away. She sipped from it and furrowed her brow. "Very nice scotch, Dr. Jacobs. Very nice."

"I'm glad you approve," Jacobs mumbled as the agent swiped Rashida's slate from the table.

"Okay, so this is what happens next," the agent said. "You all return to exactly what you were doing before this happened, because none of it happened." The agent smashed the slate into the ground and stomped on it with her heel until the display shattered. A soldier rushed in, collecting the pieces into a C.I.D.-branded evidence bag. "If you should forget this arrangement, if a piece of news should hit the press, if some blog should run a story that is even remotely similar to the events that *did not* happen tonight, this Institute will be taken over and dismantled. An investigation will find that you and your senior staff have all been collaborating with foreign governments that are hostile to the United States. You will all be found guilty and sent to a facility where you will rot until the end of your lives."

"Monica—" Price began. Jacobs turned sharply toward Price.

"Is that clear?" the agent asked.

The trio nodded.

"Now, this needn't be all doom and gloom for you," she continued. "In addition to your cooperation in keeping this nonevent out of the public, you'll also be given an opportunity to keep other nonevents out of it, which will undoubtedly advance your research even more."

"We will not be government puppets," Jacobs said, his voice tight.

"Think of it more like establishing a partnership between our two sectors. In exchange for your assistance, you will find yourself protected from any sort of threat to your research, legal or industrial. It's a win-win for everyone, Dr. Jacobs."

"And what do you want from us?" Rashida demanded. "What's this assistance?"

The agent turned her head slowly to face Rashida. "The Institute will assist us by uncovering whatever all that was. We've stabilized him, but who knows if it'll last. You will keep him here, alive and safe from prying eyes. Determine what the hell just happened. This place will remain a black box. No signals in or out. And we will help ensure your security."

"How can we possibly hope to keep this quiet?" Jacobs exclaimed.

"No, she's right," Rashida interrupted. "We have no idea what just happened, but that swarm of PACT bots may be the key. Better we are the ones to conduct the studies."

"Besides," the agent added, "we can provide personnel support as well as some incredibly advanced technology of our own to keep your research safe. Only a select few may learn of this, but we need answers."

"If you've got this incredibly advanced technology, then why did you even need to come here in the first place?" Jacobs asked sarcastically, glaring at Price.

The agent threw back the remainder of the scotch in her pilfered glass, placed it back on the table, and leaned in. "Dr. Jacobs, I understand why you may feel that you're being attacked or somehow press-ganged into service. In truth, yes, that is what is happening. But know that for the majority of the time that you are here, you will not see us, hear us, or have any contact with us, save for those very few times in which a national security matter facilitates the need for your assistance.

"It is unfortunate that this is how we had to meet. When my team and I walk out these doors, you will go back to your life as it was and say nothing."

Jacobs could have launched himself at her, attacking her

violently. He felt impotent and enraged. Price was holding something back, which made this all the more frustrating.

The agent reached into her pocket and pulled out a smooth black cylinder with a ring of flashing lights. "Keep this near our new friend," she instructed. "It creates a null field, which blacks out all communications in the immediate vicinity and will ensure privacy from any prying eyes. We've installed one in the lab and have had one with us during our journey here. We'll get you more down the road to expand the radius of the field. We'll designate it as the Corpus, since that's where the body will be."

The agent placed the device on the table and left without saying another word. Price pulled the three glasses to him. Pouring a dram in each, he slid one to Rashida, one to Jacobs, and saved one for himself. Picking it up, he inhaled the aroma deeply and looked over to his friend.

"I had no choice, Charles. No choice in working with them and no choice in keeping it from you," he said.

"There's more that you're not telling me. Who is she? Why does she know so much about you?"

"That's irrelevant. Despite what she's done—what I've done—we've uncovered something. This is world-changing."

"And what might that be? That our procedures can somehow liquefy and re-solidify a person? That it can cause mass hallucinations? This is a disaster!" Jacobs erupted, his hand slammed the table.

"Is that really what you saw?" Price pushed back.

"What was it then?"

Price brought the glass of scotch to his lips, downing the entire thing in one gulp. "I don't know how to describe it. I'm not sure, but I think it was his death. And we were there. We need to know what's going on here."

"I think he's right," Rashida affirmed, "but I want no part of this."

Jacobs was flustered. "Weren't you the one who said we should be the ones to conduct studies?"

"I did. And you should," Rashida replied, shoving her glass toward the center of the table, drops of scotch spilling out toward Jacobs. She headed for the door, turning back once toward Price and Jacobs before leaving. "But whatever this is, it's going to get you both killed."

SIXTEEN

Of Mice and Men

"God is dead.... And we have killed him," wrote Nietzsche. Unfortunately, there's no one left to wipe his blood off our boots.

—Sebastian Reed, Private Journal Entry 294

Six months after the Incident, a press conference was held....

BILL Mitchell looked back at Jacobs and Price sitting behind him. The massive press pool assembled in front of him filled the lecture hall. An empty flask resided in his coat pocket. Mitchell had been a sober man for years now, but today's task strained his resolve. He took comfort in the weight of the flask. Mitchell stood at the podium with countless cameras, microphones, and recorders trained on him, waiting for him to start speaking.

Mitchell had been there since the beginning of O.R.D.,

and he sorely missed Oliver. Sure, he was eccentric and too bombastic for Mitchell's taste, but despite all the progress that The Institute had made and all the money and resources provided, he missed the scrappiness of O.R.D. He missed the thirst for progress and new donors. He was grateful to Jacobs, who had allowed him to keep his job when he fell off the wagon. Jacobs opened a door into a rehab facility and even pleaded with Mitchell to stay. He wanted to keep as much of the old guard together as possible to share in the rewards of their efforts, he had said. So Mitchell got sober, found religion, and stuck to his daily routine. Dutifully, he showed up, did his job, supported Jacobs and Price as their resources expanded. Was today his reward for that loyalty or punishment for his past sins?

Just read the script. Over and over, they told him that. Mitchell knew that the outlandish rumors over the past six months had taken a toll on Jacobs and Price. He knew there was a secret project not ready for his eyes, and that today it would be announced. They had clued him in on unwanted C.I.D. interest and their concern that all these rumors could compel C.I.D. to shut them down. Outlandish rumors of an incident at The Institute had spread worldwide, even reaching the Tiangong and the International Space Stations. A nuclear reactor malfunction. Discovery of a secret portal to another dimension. Clones of world leaders hidden in the basement.

"Esteemed guests," he read from the prepared introduction. "In the course of human history, some chapters of mankind's story have been shaped by scientific pursuit and discovery; too often, they were told through the lens of blind faith. By the spread and clash of religions unanchored to reality. Today marks the beginning of a paradigm shift. One that will benefit us and our progeny."

𝔸

What the hell are they up to? thought Monica, who watched the press conference from her office display. This rushed press conference that Jacobs had orchestrated felt suspicious. He had enough sway to convince pretty much every news channel and slatecast to cover his event live with less than an hour's notice, catching everyone, including Monica and C.I.D., off guard.

She watched their PR guy begin to welcome everyone, but she focused on one man sitting behind him. Her ex. A year had passed since the breakup. When the assignment began, the objective had been clear. The Institute was expanding fast and she was to figure out what was really going on in there, who was funding them, and what futuristic technologies were in development. Price had been her target.

"Don't touch anything, okay? Promise me you really won't touch anything," Price had insisted, scanning his badge as they walked through The Institute almost a year ago to date. Surprisingly, it didn't take much to get him to show her behind the curtain. He believed there was nothing to hide. The light above the door turned green.

"I gave you my word. Just help me understand what's going on here." Regardless of the mission, she liked Henry. He was ambitious, and stubborn, quite the challenge. One thing led to another, and their intimacy exceeded the bounds of her assignment.

"I keep telling you, it's just a bunch of eccentric Europeans who funded the expansion." He swiped his badge again. They walked down another hallway, the motion sensors turning the lights on one by one as they made their way to Jacobs's private wing of the main campus. It was late, and most of the staff had long since gone home. "Charles has been working himself to death. I basically had to threaten to quit to get him to take a night off. He practically lives in this lab."

At the end of the hall, Price swiped his badge with his left hand and simultaneously used his left thumb for a biometric scan. Two doors opened into an elevator.

"He's really into skyline views," Price explained. Monica rolled her eyes.

The lab was the only room on this floor. Price opened the door with a traditional key. In a building that was otherwise so sterile and white, this was where some of the office furniture from O.R.D.'s past had come to rest. A single ergonomic chair was pushed into a desk that was far too small for the room. The walls, coated in dry-erase paint, were covered in equations, chemical reactions, notes, and scribbles. Slates were mixed in among paper, covered in an unintelligible scrawl. In the corner of the room, a workstation displayed an endless scroll of names, biometric data, and analysis reports.

"What does he do here?" Monica scanned the writing on the walls, trying to make sense of it all. She slowly circled the room and absorbed the chaos.

"He's not up to anything. This is all he cares about, finding a cure for his daughter, Alexandra. Neither of us saw it at first, but the cure for her disease, we hypothesize, is similar to how we treat rare blood diseases. We're searching for someone who is homozygous dominant for Alexandra Jacobs's disease to perform an allogeneic stem cell transplant."

The daughter. The mysterious, sickly girl. "What's the big deal then?"

"The big deal is that there are maybe four people on the planet with what we're looking for. And perhaps the only way to find one of those four people is to determine how, why, and when Jacobs's disease is present. Jacobs is doing that by analyzing, well, everyone. As many people as he can and looking for answers. Since the day Alexandra was born, he has spent time getting resources, volunteers, and data from all over the globe."

"So now I get what Jacobs is passionate about. How about you?" Monica drew nearer. Price laughed awkwardly and blushed as Monica lightly scratched his goatee and batted her eyelashes.

"I said, what are you passionate about?" she whispered, kissing him deeply. She held his face, then slipped her hands around to meet at the nape of his neck. She tapped twice on the tiny implant buried in her left wrist. This alerted her partner back at C.I.D. He was waiting for her signal to create a diversion so she could get a real look around.

She waited. Kissing Price wasn't the worst way to pass the time. He knew what she liked by now.

Price's phone rang, but he ignored it. It rang again, and still he ignored it in favor of keeping his attention on Monica.

"Maybe you should take that," Monica said. A third ring cut her off.

Frustrated, Price pulled out his phone. "What is it?"

Monica took a step back, patting him on the chest as he listened to the voice on the other end of the call.

"Fine. I'll be right there. And see if you can get Maritz to come in and take care of it." Price hung up. "Can you give me two minutes?" he said to Monica. "I'll be right back."

"It's no problem," she said, taking off her heels and sliding into Jacobs's chair. She crossed one leg over the other, folding her hands on her knee. "I'll be right here."

Price kissed her goodbye and darted out the door.

Monica pulled lipstick out of her purse and reapplied it. She pressed her lips together, counted to twenty, and stood up. She rummaged through Jacobs's scribblings and files. She took pictures of what she found before placing a data siphon next to the workstation. The siphon was a dome, which looked like a smooth black rock that was sliced in half. It emitted a yellow glow, indicating that it was copying all the data from Jacobs's computer.

Three minutes had passed. She knew her colleague's distraction would keep Price occupied for at least ten minutes. A loud alert scared her shitless. Rapid, high-pitched beeps echoing like a digital heartbeat emanated from the workstation in the corner of the room. She rushed over and saw that it had stopped sifting through data. It read:

AJD MATCH IDENTIFIED
Subject: Enebish Bayarmaa
Age: 7
Location: Ulaanbaatar, Mongolia
Source: #2A5DGK41B

Monica did a double take. This was Jacobs's holy grail. The person who might just cure his only kid. This information was the leverage she could rely on to make Jacobs into one of C.I.D.'s most powerful assets. She committed the name, location, and whatever the source number meant to memory. She had to be the sole owner of this child's identity. Working quickly, she entered Price's security credentials, hoping that Jacobs's system would accept them for administrator access. She had stolen that gem of information early in their relationship, and it worked. Monica deleted the entry as well as the past five years of data. She hit restart on the data analysis. Five years' worth of collected profiles were removed from the system. This would set Jacobs's work back years, buying her time to best utilize this information and preventing Jacobs from finding another match anytime soon. When she returned to her own office, she would erase all global database references to this Enebish Bayarmaa, any security footage, and the log that documented Price's credentials had accessed the workstation.

Price couldn't be compromised for this. She needed him to maintain his position next in line to Jacobs. But Monica's relationship with him put that at risk, so she had broken things off. She had completed the objective. The longer she had stayed with him, the more likely he was to have noticed something suspicious.

Monica admitted to herself that she still missed her

relationship with Price. She missed their banter and his woefully out-of-date goatee. But the work would always come first, and since the Incident, the stakes were even higher.

Luckily, Price had provided her with all the legal justifications for C.I.D. to draft The Institute's resources when needed. Less than a month after their breakup, Monica knocked on his door late at night. His face lit up at the sight of her on his doorstep, but he was disappointed as Monica laid out her latest demands, pen and papers in hand.

"You will sign these documents providing C.I.D. with unlimited, unrestricted access to all of The Institute's facilities, databases, and any other asset even remotely connected to you. You will speak nothing of this to anyone, including and especially Jacobs."

"Why would I possibly agree to this?" Price yelled at her.

"We have the name Jacobs has been looking for. His perfect match to save his daughter."

"That's not possible."

"We have the name. In fact, Jacobs came close to discovering the match, but we'll hold on to that information for now."

"How dare you? His daughter is dying!"

"He'll get the name when he needs to get the name. And only if you agree with C.I.D.'s terms."

"You're a monster." He grabbed the pen and signed the papers.

"Jacobs will get the name before his daughter dies. You have my word. But he'll get that name from me, not you. Not anyone else. No one can know of our agreement. Understood?"

She had forced Price's hand back then. However, as Monica watched him take to the podium and speak, she realized that the deal she had made was about to turn around and bite her in the ass.

◬

"Today, we of The Jacobs Institute announce the beginning of a new age in human understanding," Price spoke firmly, reading from the teleprompter in front of him. "From the dawn of time, a single question has permeated philosophies and religions, scientific explorations of the human condition, a question that has been asked by every man, woman, and child who has ever lived: What awaits us after death? The Jacobs Institute, in the course of its research into experiential study and neurocognitive function, has discovered indisputable scientific proof of an afterlife."

The room was still. No one quite knew what to think. Looks of disbelief appeared on the faces of the assembled crowd of reporters.

Then, someone laughed. And they laughed hard.

⚊ ⚊ ⚊

Jacobs hadn't heard laughter like that in a while. He hadn't felt happiness or the urge to laugh in a long time. A small smile crept on his face as his forehead relaxed. It felt good. What they were doing today was laughable. It was insane, after all. But it was the only way to both minimize C.I.D.'s insistence that he spend all his time in the Corpus and save his daughter. He might have been close to a match, so close that someone had sabotaged his work. Who had done so and why was a mystery, but it was time to go on the offensive.

Just two months ago, he had been half asleep watching the names scroll by on his workstation:

    Subject: Merari Xander
    Age: 93
    Location: Athens, Greece
    Source: #00ABHKO5C
    AJD Status: False

Subject: Ichiro Satoshi
Age: 53
Location: Nagano, Japan
Source: #10AJG08V
AJD Status: False

Subject: Anani Randal
Age: 12
Location: Maui, HI, United States of America
Source: #10BHF20X
AJD Status: False

Subject: Angela Bexley
Age: 43
Location: Santa Cruz, California
Source: #001HD
AJD Status: False

Angela Bexley. He hadn't seen his dead wife's name scroll on his workstation for years.

He fought, but failed, to keep the pit in his stomach from growing. The pain of her loss was as fresh as ever. Angela Bexley, from Santa Cruz. Age forty-three. Not his wife, a different Angela. But this was too strange. Not only did this woman bear the same first and last name as his Angela, but this forty-three-year-old Angela from California was a familiar profile. He had seen this particular entry before. What was the likelihood that there would be another Angela Bexley from Santa Cruz, currently alive in his database, who just now happened to be processed?

He paused the program and scrolled through the most recent records. This made no sense. He cross-referenced the source IDs and locations. These batches of profiles were some of the original ones tested years ago. He ran diagnostic after diagnostic but found no reason for the repetition of analysis. Worse yet, it appeared that years of data were missing.

This was a disaster. Alexandra's life was on the line, and it was all slipping through his fingers. He took a moment to compose himself. *I am a problem solver,* he told himself. *How do we get out of this hole?* Should he turn to C.I.D. to investigate? *No.* Jacobs had no faith in them. Incompetent engineers, bureaucrats, spies, and jarheads. He alone created the protocol to search for a match and those thugs would be of no use. He needed a way to test every single person on the planet as quickly as possible rather than piecemeal from outside sources.

If he deployed the airborne PACT-II worldwide, and if he could check everyone's likelihood of being a donor for Alexandra faster, then they'd have a fighting chance. There were two herculean tasks ahead. Convince the entire world to perform genetic testing while chasing C.I.D. away without anyone asking too many questions.

People would swallow the absurd if they could escape the uncertainty of the human condition. The machinations he conceived were preposterous. But considering the variables in front of him, this path was the only way forward. Price would have to go along with this. *He owes me.*

⚠

As a cacophony of hysterical press launched questions at him that he could not decipher, Price raised his hands in a desperate attempt for calm and order.

"I will," he shouted, "I will now turn this conference over to Dr. Charles Jacobs, who made the discovery."

Price nodded as Jacobs rose to take his place, while Mitchell took Jacobs's seat. Jacobs stood tall at the podium, gazing out at the audience.

"Ladies and gentlemen, what you have just heard is the

truth," Jacobs said. He raised his hands, commanding a silence that descended on the room. "For many years, we have been studying the human mind and the human experience through the use of advanced neural interface technologies. Several weeks ago, while attempting to treat an individual who suffered from a serious medical condition, an unexpected breakthrough occurred. It was during our attempts to diagnose and treat this individual using PACT-II that the patient had a severe neurological and cardiac event."

The *patient's* cardiac event. *What hubris I must have to think people will accept this. One day, they'll hang me for all of this.* Since Oliver's retirement, Jacobs had been keeping his mentor up to date on The Institute's work. But the latest developments enraged Oliver. He had warned Jacobs: "Men ought not to play God before they learn to be men, and after they have learned to be men, they will not play God." Jacobs still felt the sting of Oliver's words. If he had been a real man, he wouldn't be playing God right now. He would have saved Alexandra already.

Jacobs steeled himself. "While attempting to treat this individual, they died. But not before our technology was able to relay the experience of their death as it happened in real time." He gestured up to a large screen on the wall behind him. "Since then, we have been able to replicate that experience. And today, we have a terminally ill volunteer who will allow us to witness the experience of their death. They go to their death here at the Jacobs Institute Hospital, surrounded by their family.

"Though I wish to provide this warning. If you consent to PACT-II, you will be able to tap into this experience. You will see it. You will feel it. It will be intimately personal, deeply profound, and very real. Know that this is temporary. It is only the beginning of the journey that awaits many of us upon death of the body. For those of you present in this room, we will provide you with the newest PACT right now and without the intrusion of an injection." Jacobs nodded at the back of the room. "Welcome to the first of our 'Viewing Rooms,' where we no longer require the G.O.D. to relay an experience to you. In fact, the G.O.D. is now obsolete. Transmitter arrays in our facilities can activate your PACT-II networks. And only in this Viewing Room can our proprietary transmitters interface with you to relay the experience of our volunteers. A shared experience that you will all have as one." Vents in the ceiling opened, and a PACT-II swarm was released into the room. Jacobs continued, "To those who are present in this room, this experience may be difficult to watch. For this reason, I encourage any who may not feel ready to leave the room."

Jacobs had expected at least some small contingent of those in attendance to turn away, but only Mitchell walked out of the room. Jacobs knew that he was uncomfortable with the remarks that Price and Jacobs had presented to him earlier. Outside, Jacobs imagined that the world watched in tremendous anticipation, with some standing in broad city streets watching on massive displays and millions of others huddled around connected slates.

The new era began with the click of a Play button on a small remote in Jacobs's hands. The airborne PACT-II connected the audience to the facility's transmission system, which relayed the Corpus experience. Though he had announced a volunteer would light the way, there was no terminally ill patient nearby. No one would die that day. Those in attendance were fed the exact same "death experience" that he, Price, and Rashida had endured six months ago. An adjustment to the PACT-II bots enabled Jacobs to alter the user's mind in such a way that they would be incapable of articulating their experience for the rest of their lives. The bots restructured key neural networks associated with language and memory; Jacobs's work on Alzheimer's cleared the way for this cognitive block. What the people in the Viewing Room went through was real, from a certain point of view. The connection from the Corpus was strong.

⟁

Unlike Jacobs, Price was motivated to uncover the truth behind The Institute's captive, and thankfully, the press conference got C.I.D. to back off. This demonstration was going to bring so much attention and power to The Institute that C.I.D. could no longer have them under their thumb. What better place to hide a needle than in a haystack, to put everything in plain sight.

Price thrived off the immense attention and power that lay in front of him. After the shared death experience, when pressed by reporters to identify the terminally ill volunteer whose death had led to all this, he said, "I cannot and will not disclose the identity of the individual due to a whole host of legal, ethical, and personal reasons. But we will find a way to refer to this volunteer in a manner that befits their place in history.

"One last thing," he continued. "As of today we can confirm that this experience upon death is guaranteed for those with a certain genetic profile. We'll keep working to determine if this transition is the same for all. Please be patient while our work continues in this regard. But for now, a simple genetic test will determine if you meet the current genetic requirements. PACT-II can only tell us who you are, what you're doing, how you're feeling, and if there are any stressors or anomalies. It doesn't provide us with genetic data, so the new blood tests will be of paramount importance in determining eligibility. The Institute will be releasing a test kit shortly for anyone to use."

This would give Jacobs the opportunity to save his daughter and Price the data and power he needed to begin more intensive research. He could get one step closer to unraveling the mystery of the patient by finding their kin.

Reporters jumped out of their chairs to shout questions at him, talking over one another.

"Will there be another demonstration soon?"

"Mr. Price, do you anticipate a backlash from religious leaders?"

"Can you detail the exact profile needed to move on like this?"

They could not hear the more important question that ran rampant in his own mind. *Where did the patient come from?*

△

Later that year, in the Great Hall of The Institute, Jacobs stood before a mass of dignitaries, former religious leaders, political figures, and press. News drones hovered throughout the newly constructed hall. The hall featured a rolling garden that encircled the main floor where the attendees had gathered. It was filled with natural light that rolled off the copious amounts of polished marble and white carbon fiber. Behind Jacobs soared a mammoth statue.

The statue was six stories high. It was of a robed man whose face was hidden by a large triangular object, the logo of The Jacobs Institute. It rose from his outstretched hands. A gilded plaque was welded to the base, obscured from view by a silk cloth. Speaking through a small microphone mounted along his ear, Jacobs addressed the crowd.

He gestured to the massive statue behind him. "Today, we dedicate this monument, and The Jacobs Institute extension, to a man whose gift to us is well known. This shrine stands in memory of a man whose death showed us that beyond this life there can be serenity. Embrace his legacy. Honor this man whose name is lost to history but will forever be known as the *First Ascendant*. May this place, the Hall of the First Ascendant, be his place to light the way."

Jacobs walked back to the base of the monument and pulled the silken cloth to expose the plaque below. Emblazoned in gilded letters read: *The First Ascendant. In his death, we found the way.*

Applause rang out throughout the hall but soon gave way to scattered screams and yells. Jacobs surveyed the crowd, trying to ascertain what was happening. The crowd seemed to part down the middle. He saw a member of the audience tackle a security guard to the ground. The aggressor ripped the gun from the guard and ran straight for the statue. It was Mitchell. Institute security surrounded Jacobs. Other guards charged in Mitchell's direction, but he quickly knelt at the base of the statue and spat, "Fuck you," aiming at the hooded face of the First Ascendant.

A day prior, Mitchell had finally given in to peer pressure and went to a Viewing Room with other colleagues from The Institute. Rows of chairs were set up for the experience on one side of the room. On the opposite wall was a large display, clear as glass. The display illuminated, and an elderly woman was moved from her hospital bed into a white pod filled with a viscous white gel. He took a seat and the halo above him connected to his PACT-II network. The woman took one last gasp of air before the experience began.

But instead of bliss and comfort, Mitchell was shaken following the experience. What he saw commanded him to betray his faith and his God by rejecting heaven as he knew it. That night, he had lain awake sweating in bed, unable to reconcile his beliefs with what he had seen. So Bill Mitchell, the recovered alcoholic, devout Catholic, former O.R.D. employee, and current director of marketing at The Institute, shot himself in the head. His blood splattered all over the plaque.

The Age of Ascension had begun.

SEVENTEEN

Prescience

Ascension is regarded by the masses as true, by the heretics as false, and by the gods as useful.

—Henry Price, as quoted in *The Price They Paid* by Anna Seneca

After the dedication to the First Ascendant . . .

Ascension test kits were distributed widely, and numerous Viewing Rooms were constructed all over the world, all directly linked to the Corpus at The Institute's main facility. Jacobs was shocked by the toll this certainty about an afterlife would have on humanity. People wanted to die. They were quick to throw away their lives and those of their family members because of the security the knowledge of an afterlife brought them. The experience of the Viewing Rooms was too powerful, too visceral for any logical counterargument.

In collecting such a large trove of genetic information worldwide, Price inadvertently made a discovery of paramount importance to The Institute's work in the Corpus, one that divided the population in a way he could not have predicted. Once Price detailed what the genetic distinction was between those who became known as Alphas and Betas, and later, Ascendants and Biomasses, the public realized that Ascendants were a minority population within the species. Furthermore, The Institute failed to show proof that Biomasses could ascend. Riots overtook some cities with mobs of resentful Biomasses wreaking havoc on Institute facilities and terrorizing those even suspected of being Ascendants. Likewise, many Ascendants formed associations of their own. Some regarded Biomasses, those doomed to nothingness after death, as lesser beings.

For Sebastian Reed, the divide between factions hit close to home. On the eve of his proposal to his girlfriend, he was running late to his mother's house. He intended to pick up his grandmother's ring earlier in the day, but as always, overcoming scientific roadblocks consumed his time. When he finally arrived, he found his mother, Elomina, dead in the front yard. Bruises covered her skin. Police would tell him later that night that she had been the victim of a passing gang. Though she had refused to test her status, Sebastian would insist on a posthumous report and learn she had died a Biomass. He was certain that her life had been meaningful; she was devoted to her family, her garden, and her God. But tonight, it had all come to an abrupt end. Worse yet, as a Biomass, she was gone forever. If she had been an Ascendant, this would have only been a transition. Tonight, he would mourn his mother and respect her antiquated burial traditions. Tomorrow, he would endeavor to make everyone an Ascendant and ensure that no other son would stand, as he did, in despair.

Seeing his mother lying in the dirt, Sebastian fixated on

his grandmother's ring in his mother's open palm, a worm crawling through it. He picked up the ring and crushed the worm. Her God was bullshit.

▲

Fifteen years after the discovery of Ascension, Jacobs struggled to document his latest confession as he paced back and forth at the far end of a lab on the ground floor of The Institute. A trio of armed guards were situated across the room, distracted by the breaking news reports on the screens. He had been archiving his video logs for a distant future that would one day demand a reckoning of his time on this planet. Still, committing thought to sound for this entry proved difficult and his lips trembled. Jacobs felt the weight of his words caught in his throat.

Jacobs slumped into a chair, heart pounding, and pressed Record on his slate. "We've made a mistake," he whispered. "I've made a horrible mistake and done nothing for my daughter. Fifteen years of death at our hands. My hands. And it's only getting worse.

"So many children have died now. All because of the sway of conspiracy theorists and power-hungry con artists spouting lies. 'Ascend now, stay young forever,' they claim. In an attempt to save lives, I released a statement that, based on recent research, only Ascendants who were over the age of forty—mature adults—were ready. The 'Announcement,' some are calling it. I can feel their disdain at me for taking away the lives of loved ones too early."

His bodyguards jumped, startled as an object slammed into the bulletproof glass window near them. Jacobs didn't flinch. "The streets are on fire now, and everyone's a target."

A rifle round tore into the window and embedded itself in the outer layer. The guards surrounded Jacobs.

"Sir," the lead guard said, glancing at the window. "I believe it's time we moved you. My team has secured your daughter and her fiancé, but it's time to go. Your helicopter is inbound."

Price burst in with his assistant.

"It's a goddamn mess out there, and it's not just the Bs either," he huffed.

"What happened?" Jacobs said, turning off his slate.

"There was a bombing, down in the Financial District. Hundreds, maybe thousands are dead," Price replied. He pressed a button mounted on the wall.

A video feed of an office tower with half of its facade scorched off appeared on every slate in the room. The building smoldered as the skeletal remains of its exposed rooms and hallways reached from the street to the sky. The camera drone filming the destruction panned down to the massive crater below and then up along the opposite side of the street where the front exteriors of several smaller buildings had also been blown off.

"Who did this?" Jacobs asked.

"It was a group of Ascendants."

"How do you know this?"

"They released a vid and posted it on a bunch of anonymous channels. They're calling themselves the A.R.M.: the Ascendant Revolutionary Militia. Just look for yourself." Price took a slate from his aide and handed it over. Jacobs played the video preloaded on the screen.

The speaker was dressed in fatigues, face masked. A pair of sunglasses made them entirely unidentifiable. The voice that spoke was modulated. "The spilling of blood tonight is the hallmark of a new era. We have stepped forward to claim this new world as our own. We will not stop until our demands have been met."

Jacobs paused the video. "I've seen enough."

Price issued orders to the guards. "I'm tripling your pay

and that of all your friends. You work directly for me now. I want every resource at your disposal dedicated to tracking down and neutralizing these people. Work with law enforcement and any intelligence or military contacts you have. I don't care how much it costs."

"Henry, I don't know if we can contain this," Jacobs said.

"We're past containment, Charles. We need to end this before it spirals even further out of control. For safety, they want us off-site. I was supposed to be heading down to DC anyway. You should go home."

"What are we going to do?"

"I have some ideas but now is not the time. Let's get going."

The men shook hands. Flanked by their security details, Jacobs and Price took a private elevator to the roof, where two helicopters were waiting for them. Jacobs went first, climbing into a helicopter that took off moments later. Price's heart skipped a beat as he climbed into his own helicopter. He was not alone.

"Monica. How did you weasel your way in here?" he asked angrily as the door slammed shut, taking the seat opposite her.

"Henry. I wish I could say it's a pleasure to see you again," Monica said. "We have a lot to talk about." She leaned closer to the pilot. "We're ready to go."

The helicopter took off and flew above the city. Price broke the silence through his own headset. "Takes a terror attack and a possible civil war to flush you out of your hole?"

"I'm the one who gets to be mad here. This scheme of yours, it's—"

"You want to hash this out, now? I've kept my end of the bargain. The Corpus is secure. Isn't it time to give Charles the name he needs? Hasn't he suffered enough?"

"You're right. You have kept your side of the bargain, but this cover-up has gotten out of hand." Monica took a breath. "You need to rein in The Institute and help the government regain control of the people. Remember, I can still bring you and this whole operation down."

The helicopter's rotors droned like a war drum, masking the chaos below. From this height, the city almost looked calm. Its fresh wounds were hidden by distance and altitude.

"What exactly do you want?" Price demanded.

"Nothing good has come from Ascension," Monica said. "What was Jacobs thinking?"

"We had no clue it would get this out of hand and he found a way to minimize the losses. People—kids—were dying."

Monica released her seat belt and moved next to Price. "It's time for Jacobs to go."

Price recoiled. "What are you saying?"

"He has too much power, and he'll never prioritize our mission. That has to be clear to you by now. My people will take care of it. I just wanted to give you the heads-up, as a courtesy, before I give the word to facilitate his retirement." Monica took Henry's hand. "Think about it, Henry. You'd be in the position to call the shots. Keep the work on track without all these distractions. All the power you always wanted." It irritated him, the slow pantomime of her hand in the air, as if she were christening something already built. But even he could see the shape of it, the inevitability in her voice and the thing he'd always wanted: "The Price Institute."

Price took a moment to consider her words, threats, and promises. "No," he declared, pulling his hand out of her grasp.

"No," Monica replied. "'No' is not an option here."

"He's been my mentor, and he is my friend. I owe him—" Price insisted.

Monica hissed, "I will destroy Jacobs. C.I.D. will take over The Institute. And if you force my hand, I will destroy you too!"

Her words carried a bite Price could not dismiss. He caught himself imagining how she might claw her way back into that power over him.

"You're right," Price said quietly. "I'm sorry, Monica. Sorry for our relationship. Sorry for agreeing to your devil's bargain. And sorry for this."

Price unlatched the emergency release and wrenched the door open. Wind howled into the cabin.

The pilot turned, shouting something Price couldn't hear over the roar of the wind.

"What are you doing?" Monica shouted, her hair whipping wildly in her face.

"Saving The Institute." Price grabbed Monica by her waist. He flung her over his body and out of the aircraft. She plummeted, screaming, until the street silenced her.

"Forgive me, Alexandra," he whispered into the wind. "I had no choice."

III

The Book of Price

EIGHTEEN

Commencement

That moment when the stage goes dark
and the spotlight shines on me.
When everything that was fades to black,
and everything that will be ascends.
That moment when all that was reverberates back,
and everything that will be courses like an
electrical charge through the air,
connecting performer to the audience and to both—
an undiscovered future.
That beautiful, silent, and torturous moment.
And after that final moment, when
silence turned into applause,
I felt alive.
I felt close to God.

—Sebastian Reed, *The Lost Recordings, Vol. 2*

Late at night, as Sam's and Alexandra's bodies were picked up for collection, Maya lay unconscious at the District. Meanwhile, an assault convoy pulled up to the front of the Tellers' house. It was 25 AA, by the old calendar, AD 2060....

Heavily armed teams of four piled out from the vehicles and established a perimeter around the house. Three men, led by Briggs, scanned the main entrance. Henry Price was about to climb out of the car when his phone rang. He read *Office* and knew, with some certainty, what the call was regarding.

"This is Price," he answered.

"Dr. Jacobs is leaving now. His daughter is gone," Maritz said from the other end.

"Thank you, Tyriq," Price said, ending the call. *Oh, Alexandra,* he thought. He wished he could have helped her, but Monica and Alexandra had been inextricably linked: Removing Monica from the equation had killed Alexandra. The name of Alexandra's potential donor was lost during that helicopter flight. Her blood was on his hands.

Briggs knocked on the window beside him. "Sir," he said as Price cracked open the window. "We are good to go, sir."

Back to business. Price opened his door and stepped out onto the street. Briggs, in full tactical gear, short-barreled rifle in hand, waited obediently.

"Confirming nonlethal rounds loaded, sir. Target will not be harmed. Teams Bravo and Charlie are in position," Briggs said.

"We're here to collect a child. Records suggested no more than three people in the house. The mother, her older daughter, and the girl. There will be no need for weapons."

"Understood, sir," Briggs replied. "Just like to remain ready."

"Keep your men back," Price said, buttoning his jacket and straightening his cuffs. Alexandra's image lurked in his mind, despite his best efforts to keep it at bay. "I'm going to see if anyone is home."

"How, sir?"

"I'm going to knock on the door." Price fought the impulse to roll his eyes. Everything had to be a big production with these meatheads.

"Of course. We'll maintain watch, sir," Briggs replied.

The Tellers' home lay at the end of a quiet street and boasted a relatively large, well-manicured lawn, lined with short hedges. The lights were on inside, clearly visible through the open blinds. But there was no car in the driveway, nor any visible activity. Price doubted anyone was home. As he neared the front stoop, he realized that he might have missed his target once again. His blood boiled.

Price rang the doorbell. He heard melodic chimes ring throughout the house. He tried again before knocking hard on the large wooden front door in annoyance.

"Should we prepare for a breach, sir?" Briggs asked through the communication unit Price wore in his ear.

Rationally, Price knew that breaking into a private home on his own was ridiculous for a man of his station. At the same time, he had never been so close to a pure Ascendant match. He needed to find the girl. Price teetered for a moment between these conflicting sides of reason and obsession, then finally issued his orders.

"Breach, but quietly," he spoke into the comms unit.

"Understood," Briggs confirmed before issuing his own orders over the comms. "All teams, stealth breach, sweep and clear. Shut down the lights and go night vision for the remainder of the op. Move now."

Price lingered on the stoop while the action commenced. Power lines were cut, windows were broken, and side and back doors were smashed in. After the initial commotion, the affair continued in relative silence. The front door sprang open and Briggs's masked face greeted Price.

"The house is empty, sir. No sign of the girl."

"I appreciate your team's enthusiasm, but that was a bit excessive, don't you think?" Price needled Briggs. "Step aside."

As the other team members congregated in the foyer, Price strolled through the house. "Pack up anything of interest. We're heading back. Contact Maritz and have him run traces on their gear. Phones, slates, toll passes, social, all of it. Send teams to check known relatives and associates. I want the girl found before sunrise."

▲

He was supposed to be dead. Instead, Sam was floating on his back in the middle of a lake. Yet the smell of salt permeated the air. *Something is wrong*, he thought. *Is this the ocean?* He fixated on the clear sky. Sam crossed his arms beneath his head and exhaled. He felt as if he was sinking, but his body did not move. The sun flickered above, temporarily blinding him. *Where am I?* Bright lights flashed above him. He was now in a hospital, lying on a bed strapped to machines. *Who did this to me?* His eyes watered; his vision was blurry. *And where is Alexandra?* Whispers and beeps surrounded him, but the throbbing in his head drowned them out. One declaration penetrated the noise: "I'm sorry, she's dead." A wave of sadness overcame him.

Time passed. Sam fell in and out of consciousness until a ragged gasp jolted him upright, and he broke his restraints. His heart rate skyrocketed as lights flashed on the display wall to the right of him. His arms burned from his previous attempts to end his life, and new bandages wrapped around his forearms. Sam's eyes darted around the room, desperately seeking some tool that might succeed where his earlier suicide attempts had failed. He shifted his legs to the side and pushed himself off the bed. His legs promptly gave out under him, sending Sam tumbling to the floor.

Sam hauled himself onto the bed and tore the IV bag from its hook. His trembling hands wrapped the plastic tubing around his throat. He tried to pull it tight, but the slick material kept slipping through his fingers. As he fought to maintain his grip, the door burst open. Jacobs grabbed Sam's wrists and pulled his hands away. He pressed Sam back onto the bed, restraining him as his weak body struggled.

"Sam! Stop!" Jacobs barked, pushing down on the man. "Just stop. Relax. Calm down." As he spoke, his voice grew softer. His grip relaxed.

"What?" Sam croaked. "What happened? Why?"

Jacobs released Sam. He stood upright again. "Because Alexandra wanted you to live." He sighed deeply. "It's time this whole charade of mine comes to an end." Jacobs pulled a folded wheelchair from the wall. He opened it and gestured for Sam to take a seat. "It is probably best if I show you."

Jacobs wheeled Sam, still disoriented, out into the hall. The hallway seemed to be part of an ordinary hospital wing, lined with doors to identical examination rooms. Curtains were drawn; empty beds awaited occupants. The overhead lights were on, but the rooms and nurses' stations were all dark.

"Where are we?" Sam asked as Jacobs pushed him beside an abandoned nurse's cart.

"We are in a private wing of my facility. It's one of the additions that directly connect to The Institute's research annex." Jacobs pulled a full IV bag and fresh tubing from the cart. He hung the bag on the IV pole attached to the chair, connected Sam's line, and squeezed the drip chamber until the fluid ran through. "We closed it off a long time ago."

They reached an elevator. Jacobs produced a small key from his pocket. Inserting the key into the control panel unlocked the executive levels. As the elevator climbed, Sam eyed the key curiously.

"Analog access to my wing," Jacobs explained casually.

The two rode in silence as the elevator rose above the hospital levels and climbed the outer glass wall of The Institute tower. Sam peered down at the street. Crowds of people carrying protest signs converged on The Institute campus. He could see fires flickering in the distance, and in two locations, billows of smoke drifted up above the skyline.

"They've been going like this for days now," Jacobs explained. "It was always a possibility that the anniversary events could stoke some reaction. If they knew half of what you're about to learn, they'd raze the city just to tear me to pieces with their bare hands."

The elevator came to a graceful stop, and Jacobs wheeled Sam out into his spacious office. It was furnished with a single workstation, one wall alive with displays. Plenty of space for a lonely man working high above the city. Jacobs loomed like Zeus on Olympus, perched far above the mortal world.

△

Rebecca Teller watched as her navigation system routed and rerouted around the protestors swarming the roads near the hospital, Hannah sleeping soundly in the back seat. With the satellites above routinely updating their maps in accordance with crowd density, the system eventually became overwhelmed. The auto-drive system mistakenly steered the two Tellers down a crowded street. After an abrupt stop followed by a flying brick crashing into the windshield, Rebecca initiated Manual mode and reversed course. Seconds later, the car reasserted control and rerouted, driving to an entrance two blocks away. Hannah slept through the entire ordeal.

Next to a loading bay in the rear of a federal office building, an automatic garage door opened as soon as the car approached. Rebecca and Hannah were driven down a long concrete tunnel. Unbeknownst to either of them, the tunnel had been constructed years earlier to allow high-profile individuals, in need of medical treatment, secret and secure access to the Jacobs Institute Hospital.

The car rolled to a stop just outside of an underground ambulance bay. A small team of unfamiliar nurses rushed out to the car. The sight of Rebecca and her daughter gave them pause.

"Ma'am, what are you doing here?" a male nurse of stocky build and red hair asked.

"I was called in by admin, but the car routed us here. What is this place?" she asked.

A security guard followed the team of nurses and approached the group. "This is a high-security area. PACT ID, please."

Her palms started to sweat.

"PACT ID, ma'am, if you consent," the guard repeated firmly.

Rebecca slowly extended her arm and allowed the guard to take her wrist. He pulled a small slate from a satchel on his leg and scanned her arm for a detailed biometric reading. He dropped her wrist and focused on his slate.

The guard stood down. "Apologies, Doctor, you have full access," he said.

Though she'd never heard of this wing before, she had been granted unrestricted access when the car rerouted them. "Admin called me in about an hour ago."

The red-haired nurse explained, "The entire facility is on lockdown as a result of the protests outside. I believe our wing is the only one that has some flexibility."

"Can staff move throughout the facility?" she asked.

"Dr. Teller," said the security officer, "you may move between wings; however, without appropriate security clearance, all remaining staff are under orders to shelter in place."

"Let me call them back—" She felt her phone vibrate wildly in her pocket. "Oh, hold on."

It was not a call coming in, but rather an onslaught of notifications. Rebecca tapped her phone and a pin dropped on a map. A series of hurried messages from Maya followed: *help*, *trapped*, *district*, and *VIP room*. Maternal instinct propelled her into action. She dialed 911, only to find herself greeted by a busy signal. "Dammit!" she howled angrily. She looked up at the confused security guard and asked, "Do you have any contact with city police?"

"No. All police lines are tied up due to the demonstrations. Satellite communications are a mess. I wouldn't be surprised if the National Guard was called in soon," the officer replied.

"Officer, do you have internal access? Can you call over to the main trauma unit and ask for Dr. Sarah Bennett?"

"Sure, that still works," he replied, pinging Dr. Bennett on his slate.

Sarah's face appeared on the screen. "This is Dr. Bennett," she said as the officer handed the slate to Rebecca.

"Sarah, I don't have time to explain. Maya's in trouble. I'm at the hospital with Hannah. I'm so glad you're on call tonight. I need you to take Hannah while I find Maya. It's an emergency."

"Of course," Sarah replied. "Whatever you need. We'll figure it out."

Rebecca spared a soft smile. "An officer will bring her to you. And, Sarah, thanks, I owe you one," she said.

"Again." Sarah chuckled. "I've kept a list going. Be safe." She disconnected the call.

"What happened to Maya?" Hannah yawned, still buckled in the back seat.

Rebecca scrambled for words. "Nothing, sweetie. Maya is fine, she just needs a ride, is all. I have to go pick her up."

"You said trouble. You said it."

"Hannah—"

"Tell me, Mommy. Where's Maya?"

Rebecca gave in. "Fine, Hannah. I don't know what's going on, but I need to get her because the police can't help us now. I am going to need you to go stay with Mommy's friend Sarah. She'll keep you safe at my work until I get back. Can you do that for me?"

Hannah hesitated, then nodded. "I guess. But bring Maya back soon, okay?" She unbuckled her seat belt and jumped out of the car.

"I will, sweetie. I promise." Rebecca turned toward the security officer. "You'll do this for me?"

"Yes, ma'am. I will see to it personally." A nurse joined them, and together they walked Hannah into the hospital.

Once Hannah was safely inside the building, Rebecca searched for the District on the dashboard display. She pressed Go, and the car took off. Twelve minutes of driving until arrival, which meant twelve minutes to come up with a plan.

△

Price and his convoy pulled into The Institute's garage, which had been secured from the protestors outside.

"Any update on our search?" Price asked Briggs as he stepped onto the garage floor.

"Teams have been dispatched to relatives' homes and workplaces, InfoSec is working PACT recognition through all available security feeds, and we've got the feds running checks at all exits from the city. We should have her by the end of the night, sir," Briggs replied, falling in behind Price as he headed to the elevators. Dean, in turn, shadowed Briggs as the two men spoke.

"Good. Any update from the field teams?"

"When Kilo team attempted to search the grandfather's office, he tried to interfere and was killed in the scuffle," Briggs reported.

"Killed how?" Price stopped abruptly and turned on his heel to confront Briggs. Things were getting out of hand.

"He attempted to blockade the door. He was hiding some illegals in a makeshift shelter. He apparently thought we had arrived to arrest some of them. I'm told he slipped on the stairs and died before any medical teams could be called."

"Any witnesses?"

"Only our men, sir, who reported he lost his footing and fell down." Briggs handed Price a slate that played back a security recording. Price watched Rabbi Teller standing outside the shelter, staring down the security officer from atop a flight of steps.

"Okay, I've come out. There's no need to push inside. How can I help you?" the rabbi asked.

"We're looking for your daughter. And your granddaughter. Are they here?" The officer took a step toward the rabbi.

"What could you possibly want with them?"

"Are they here?"

"No, truthfully," the rabbi replied.

"Who else is here? Step aside," a second officer demanded as she walked over.

"No one of interest to you is here. Now, go away. You have no authority here!" the rabbi exclaimed, pointing a finger at her.

"Step aside!" she insisted.

The rabbi crossed his arms and leaned against the door. The first officer rushed up the stairs and grabbed the rabbi by the collar. He threw the rabbi down the front steps. The officers flinched as the rabbi's head cracked against the concrete, killing him. The recording ended as the officers opened the door to the shelter.

Price handed the slate back to Briggs. "No sign of the girl there, I take it?"

Briggs shook his head. "No, sir."

"And what about the people he was hiding?"

"Reported to the feds. The whole place is being emptied now."

"Well," Price replied with a shrug. "I suppose we're doing our civic duty in the course of our hunt, then." His phone rang, and he answered. "Tyriq, good. I've just gotten back. Any news on the girl?"

"No, and Dr. Jacobs has just returned to his office. He's not alone," Maritz said over the line.

"Who is he with?"

"PACT scans are showing he's with his son-in-law, sir."

"What the hell is Sam doing here?" Price's face tightened. He was supposed to be dead. "Tyriq, can you access the stream to his office?"

"I can try, sir. One moment." Silence overtook the line as Maritz attempted to connect to Jacobs's feed. "I'm locked out, sir. I can see from the security cameras that they are looking at something."

"Keep your eyes on him, I'm headed there now." Price disconnected and turned to Briggs with grave purpose. "Jacobs is in his office with a security risk."

Briggs peered at Price. "Is Dr. Jacobs himself a security risk, as well, sir?"

Price found himself at a crossroads he had been trying to avoid for years. He had witnessed firsthand Jacobs's inner turmoil steadily spiraling with each passing year. But now, the race against time was over. His wife was gone, his daughter too. With Alexandra's death, he had little left to lose and even less to gain. Jacobs had lost sight of their work a long time ago, and Price did not believe he would be able to find his way back. He needed to unburden The Institute from Jacobs, no matter the cost.

As the two stepped inside the executive elevator, he spoke. "Yes. Dr. Jacobs is presently posing a security risk to The

Institute. Please prepare a team accordingly." Briggs nodded at Dean, who entered the elevator. With a push of a button and a turn of his key, Price sent the three of them rocketing up to the top floor. Briggs nodded to Dean, and the two men methodically removed the nonlethal rounds from their weapons, replacing them with live ammunition.

▲

"Whose Ascension was that?" asked Sam, recovering from what he'd just witnessed. Jacobs had wheeled him into his office and pressed a button to transmit a beautiful Ascension to Sam's PACT-II bots. It was unclear how the connection was made so far from a Viewing Room and a volunteer.

"You weren't connected to any volunteer," replied Jacobs, clearly expecting Sam's confusion.

"I don't understand. Was that Alexandra's death? How is this possible?" Sam's mind raced. Ascension was only ever accessible by going to Viewing Rooms, watching as those volunteers shared their death.

"You were connected to something else."

"I don't care; why show me this? Why keep me alive against my will?"

"Because it's a lie. Watch, Sam. Feel." Jacobs pressed a slew of buttons on his desk and Sam was thrust into Ascension after Ascension experience. The Boston Viewing Rooms: He saw a volunteer lying in a pod in front of him. Then bright white. Warm embrace. Serenity. Flickering shadows. A presence. It was all there, but he couldn't describe it. The Cape Town Viewing Rooms: Another volunteer in a pod appeared next to him. Then bright white. Warm embrace. Serenity. Flickering shadows. A presence. It was unspeakable. London. Mumbai. Cairo. Volunteer after volunteer from across the world appeared before him, only to relay the same experience he was unable to process. Sam could hear Jacobs speaking throughout the onslaught.

"At its core, it's all the same. We say everyone experiences something different and uniquely personal, but that's not true. It's just unspeakable because we've designed it that way. Besides, I don't think we have the capability as human beings to describe the event. But we've pumped out the same experience to everyone over and over again. It's a transition to somewhere, but not our afterlife. It's not for you, nor our volunteers. It's for them."

"What are you saying, Charles?"

"All of it is a singular connection to one source, and I need you to see it. I need you to live, Sam, and if making you understand is the only way I can keep you alive and secure Alexandra's last wish, I will let this place burn."

"You're not making any sense."

"Before she died, she asked me to ensure you live."

"Why would she do that?" Sam whispered.

"Because she knew the truth. It all started with this." Jacobs pressed another button on his desk and a video played on a display. Decades-old security footage showed shadowy government personnel commandeering The Institute. Sam was unable to make out all the exact words exchanged during the heated argument, but his interest was piqued when the footage transitioned to the interior of an exam room. The footage cut out, then his jaw dropped entirely when a person liquefied on the table. Soon after, the group stood transfixed, eyes glazed over. Sam leaned forward, speechless, attempting to process what it was he had seen.

Jacobs broke Sam's silence. "That was our First Ascendant. They let us keep the footage to study what happened. Each Ascension viewed here or at any other installation has been that same experience, relayed over, and over, and over again from the Corpus throughout the world."

Sam stared blankly. The man who had discovered Ascension, who had ushered in an entirely new era of human civilization, had admitted it was all a lie.

"What have you done, Charles? Those who've died, who gave their own lives, all for what? For nothing?"

"Not entirely for nothing. There is a process that we've determined occurs with those with the right level of Ascendant code."

"Ascendant code? What in the hell are you talking about?"

"The real difference is a simple line of genetic variance. We found that a small percentage of the population shared a similar genetic profile with the First Ascendant. For some reason, their PACT-II bots transmit what life is left in them to the First Ascendant, which has kept it alive all these years. These Ascendants sustain the First Ascendant in the Corpus, which, in turn, feeds the experience to the Viewing Rooms. That's the key to all of this." Jacobs waved his arms around wildly. "And perhaps the key to understanding what's really going on. Before our work, all people talked about was the commercial benefits of a contrived Metaverse or the approaching human Singularity. But this! This is all of that and more."

The Corpus. The Singularity. Metaverses. These meant nothing to Sam. He trembled as he asked, "What happened to Alexandra, then? What happened to my wife?"

With tears in his eyes, Jacobs shook his head. "All her life I failed her. And in the end, my little girl had one wish that was within my abilities, to let her die in peace. But I couldn't just let her die! I might not have been able to save her body, but her mind—there was still a chance." Jacobs went on to explain how his work on combating death, something he referred to as "the backup," utilized a new generation of PACT bots. PACT-III neural-mapping technology was designed to record detailed brain activity patterns and to create digital neural matrices for potential consciousness reconstruction. "That syringe meant for her, what you injected in your arm, Sam, it was all meant to keep Alexandra alive long enough for the PACT-III bots to begin the transfer."

"Those syringes!" Sam interrupted as adrenaline filled his bloodstream. He lunged from the wheelchair, pinning Jacobs to the wall behind him, screaming, "You wanted to use my wife as a fucking test subject?"

"I wanted to save my daughter!" Jacobs shot back, breaking Sam's grip and pushing the schoolteacher away easily. He went crashing over the wheelchair.

Sam seethed as he scrambled to his feet. "Where is she?" he demanded. His fingers clenched into balled fists. He could end Jacobs right then and there with his bare hands.

A ding interrupted Sam's rage. Jacobs looked over to his desk and grabbed his slate. The screen displayed two armed men flanking Price, riding in an elevator. Tapping lightly on the slate, Jacobs spoke. "Thank you, Mr. Maritz. If you're able, I might recommend heading out now."

"Thank you, Dr. Jacobs. Best of luck to you." Maritz disconnected the call and Jacobs put his slate down.

"We don't have very long." Jacobs turned back to Sam. "So, here is what I need from you. In less than a minute, Henry Price is going to walk out of that elevator, along with two armed men. They're coming here to silence me. Kill me, I suppose. You, on the other hand, will be heading downstairs using my favorite thing in this entire building." Jacobs touched an icon on his slate and the floor sank behind his desk. Individual floor tiles lowered to form a graceful stairwell that led down under the office and out to the exterior wall of the building.

"That passage will give you full access to The Institute and hospital. I had it secretly built in when this tower was constructed. Not even Henry knows about it. Make for the monument. Just behind it, at the base of the statue, you'll find a hidden panel. By the time you make it down there, I'll have authorized the security protocols so that your PACT ID will be granted access." He pulled Sam's phone from his pocket and handed it over. "Take this, I've left instructions for you to follow. As soon as you're there, document everything and share it with the world. Now go."

Sam tore the IV from his arm and stumbled toward the passage. "What am I supposed to do with this?"

"When you see what's down there, you'll understand. Leave, now."

"Not without my wife."

"You don't have a choice." Jacobs ushered Sam down the steps forcefully before returning to his desk. Jacobs's voice echoed throughout the stairwell. "Share what you see. And, Sam, I am so very sorry."

Sam heard the apology, but the words rang hollow. Jacobs had shattered the illusion of Ascension, but Sam no longer cared. He needed to be wherever his wife was, afterlife be damned.

▲

```
Sector 027-Office of Dr. Charles Jacobs-
Surveillance Node 3

INCIDENT: Data anomaly. Source: slatelink.

ERROR.

WARNING: Cognitive algorithms experiencing
paradoxical input.

Data Origin: UNKNOWN.

Archival footage reveals target. Current
location unknown.
```

System Report: Sam Lee equipped with active communications device.

Commands: Monitor Sam Lee. Initiate full system resource reallocation to primary directives.

Primary Directive: Investigate data origin.

Secondary Directive: Protect Hannah Teller.

> _

⚠

Jacobs had nothing left to do but wait for the inevitable. He lowered himself into his office chair and relaxed his body. From his shoulders, down his back, all the way through his feet, the tension in his muscles evaporated. His feet brushed aside shards of broken glass and cables that littered the floor since his fit of rage after Alexandra's last correspondence. The state of his office was a perfect metaphor for what would soon befall The Institute.

The light above the elevator illuminated at the opposite end of the hallway. Jacobs rose and approached the control panel. It housed an intercom system to communicate between the outer hallway and his office. He watched Price approach the locked glass door of his office.

"Open the door, Charles!" shouted Price, who immediately tried to override the lock. It failed.

Using the control panel, Jacobs tossed the video clips he had previously shown to Sam onto the main wall display, in full view of the trio standing out in the hall. Through the floor-to-ceiling glass windows, he watched Price pale, then furiously kick at the glass door. Jacobs walked over to the door and squared up behind it, facing his partner.

"Charles, what have you done?" he hissed, glaring. Jacobs knew that releasing this secret, known only to a few, would send Price into a fit of rage. If Jacobs bought Sam enough time, then soon the whole world would know the truth.

Price grabbed Briggs's pistol from his holster. He aimed at Jacobs's face and fired. The round struck the bulletproof glass and lodged in the outer layer. Price winced at the sound but continued firing. The glass would hold; this was all theater.

Briggs and Dean stepped in front of Price and raised their rifles. They fired in rapid, controlled bursts. Arrhythmic thuds beat against the glass. Dull and uninspired. Jacobs preferred to face his death surrounded by music. He chose Josquin des Prez's *Nymphes des bois*, filling the office with the lament. Jacobs appreciated the irony of his music choice; the haunting voices mourning the death of the composer's mentor. The ghost of Jacobs's predecessor, Dr. Oliver, haunted him as Price scrambled to become his successor. Jacobs walked back to his desk and sat, then pulled out a bottle and drank deeply. Fifty-year-old scotch had never tasted so good.

The gunfire paused, his door still intact but weakening at the impact points. While the men outside reloaded their weapons, his mind wandered outward, through the window, across the city that had descended into chaos. He remembered the chaos of a train station, after landing his dream job. A girl standing on the platform, wearing a dress covered in tiny little books. The mother of his miracle child.

Jacobs's gaze drifted to the photo of his daughter on his desk, then slid to his desk drawer. He pulled out a vial, which contained his final project, the same PACT-III bots he had gifted Alexandra.

There had not been enough time to run any trials before Alexandra's death. Jacobs had only enough time to create two doses with the new PACT: one for her, and one for himself. He had hoped some fragment of his soul might one day rest with his daughter, in whatever state this "backup" might permit. In the hopes that other scientists would refine and expand upon his work, copies of his research were set to be delivered to top universities upon his death.

If all went according to plan, his PACT-III bots would store a digital copy of his genetic code upon death. It would create a singular digital container that could re-create Charles Jacobs; a cohesive mesh of that genetic information along with analyses of all recorded visual, audio, and PACT experiences, detailed psychological profiles, and everything else that made Jacobs the person he had become. That container's sole directive was to seek out and create a network with other similarly crafted containers. The Institute's global servers would power this Singularity. He would use the PACT-III to cheat death by crossing into this new life, so long as his calculations were correct.

He studied the picture of Alexandra. The smile of a happy girl in the arms of her loving father. One moment captured, suspended in time, and completely ignorant of all the other moments he had chosen the work over her. In so many ways, he had wasted this life. He did not deserve another.

Briggs and Dean had resumed their attack, and the glass showed signs of strain. The door would not hold for much longer.

"I have something to tell you," he said aloud to her ghost. "I'm done with work."

Jacobs crushed the vial between his thumb and forefinger, and the liquid spilled to the floor. He was mortal, and it was time for him to go. He lifted his chin, stood, and faced Price.

Controlled bursts shattered the glass.

A rifle barrel edged through the empty frame. The first round struck Jacobs high in the chest, just below his shoulder, and spun him to the floor. A second buried itself in his abdomen. The third smashed into his ribs.

He sputtered and wheezed as he turned over onto his stomach. Briggs and Dean trained their rifles on him. Price signaled them to hold fire. Jacobs rolled onto his back and locked eyes with Price. Through his tunneling vision, he saw Price loom over him. "Oh, Charles," were the last words Jacobs heard as his eyes closed. His work was finally done. He was free.

NINETEEN

Pit Stop

My mother walked through fire for me. She never realized that I was the arsonist.

—The Catalyst

Maya dreamed she was walking in an empty room....

SHE stopped in the exact center. An old grandfather clock appeared in front of her. With a swipe of her hand, it disappeared. There was a slate in her hand. She pressed the blinking blue button, and a sea of security camera footage taken during the initial blasts of the November Bombing enveloped her.

Another tap on the slate and she was transported into the footage. She floated from floor to floor as explosion after explosion tore the building apart. Trapped and terrified office workers flung themselves out the windows. Maya approached one young woman who was caught on the exposed edge of the building between a raging fire and a hundred-story drop. The woman reached out and gently took Maya's hand. Maya hugged the stranger, then thrust them both out of the building. They tumbled to their deaths below.

Her consciousness returned, accompanied by a ringing headache. Her face stung as she grimaced. She was unsure of where she was, how she'd gotten there, or who surrounded her. Her eyes burned as she focused on the dim light of the single bulb on the wall.

The dungeon had a dirt floor, concrete walls, and a metal security door in the corner. Huddled in the opposite corner were four other young women, each dirty and bruised. Grunting, Maya slowly brought herself upright. She searched the room for a clue of her location.

Her memory returned quickly when she touched the tender welt along her eye. The nightclub. Amy. The VIP room. Maya attempted to spring to her feet but resorted to standing up slowly when she felt the pain. She stretched each shoulder and moved to the others.

"Amy," she croaked, finding her mouth very dry. "Amy." Maya coughed. "I'm looking for Amy. Was she here?"

She noted that each member of the quartet was bloodied, wounds everywhere. The captives' lips were split, necks and faces bruised, clothes torn. None of them, however, was Amy. Maya was unsure if that was a good or a bad sign.

One of the four rose and directly addressed Maya.

"Your friend," the woman whispered, "she was here, but they took her away when they brought you in." She looked to be about Maya's age with long black hair that reached her waist. Her sparkly gold dress hung in shambles.

"Took her where?" Maya asked.

"Where they take us all."

"What do they want with us?"

"They rape the Ascendants they capture. They want to

create more of us." The woman spoke so mechanically that Maya reeled back in shock. "Bs . . . they want to fix."

Maya needed to get out of there and find Amy. She refused to just wait there for the door to open. Maya ran her hands around the walls, trying to find some other way out. Being a victim wasn't an option.

"They're looking for a way to turn Biomasses into Ascendants," the young woman continued. "They take them away and we never see any of them again. Which are you?" The woman's lip and jaw quivered, and tears streamed from her eyes. The dark lines of running makeup were punctuated by a black-and-blue bruise on her cheek and a bleeding scab on her brow.

"What the hell?" Maya yelled as she scraped her palm on a sharp rock.

A piercing cackle erupted from the shadows, and a woman stepped closer to Maya. She was much older, perhaps fifty, with stained teeth peppered with gaps.

"This isn't hell." The woman snickered. "This is the last pit stop on the way to hell, and you're the fresh meat. The fresh meat!" she repeated, growing visibly agitated. "Rape, torture, drugs. You'll see." As the woman returned to the shadows, she continued repeating, "You'll see."

Maya looked around, beginning to panic. Her brief examination of the room came up empty: It consisted of nothing more than a dangling light bulb, four cold walls, a ceiling, a dirt floor, and one solid steel door without a handle. Maya pounded on the door, screaming angrily.

"Hey! Hey! Open this goddamn door!"

Much to her surprise, the door opened. Behind it stood the large, older bald man whom she had followed down the stairs in the first place. The man's meaty hands grabbed the collar of her jacket before she could react. He dragged her from the room, the other women scurrying into the shadows as the door slammed shut.

▲

Rebecca passed through a wall of heat. Sweat dripped from the bodies of those who danced, drank, flirted, and laughed. She hadn't been to a club in years, and never one this oppressive. The District was very much the sort of club that she had avoided in her youth.

Something caught her eye that sent her into a panic. Following a wicked laugh from a clearly intoxicated patron, she was drawn to the sight of a young man convulsing on the floor. She instinctively felt the urge to rush to his side, to diagnose and treat his condition. When the spasms stopped and his body went limp, she noticed the conductive pads. The crowd erupted in raucous applause.

This was a "chaser." It was a term given to the morbid subculture that had grown around an increasingly common and lethal game known as "flatlining" or "line chasing." Participants would bring themselves to the very brink of death, all in pursuit of a glimpse and thrill of what supposedly lay beyond. Bets were placed on who would be "out" the longest. In recent years, her emergency department had been dealing with more and more cases of chasers who went too far. She stood frozen in place, clenching her fists until the young man's company finally sent a reviving pulse through his system. The young man sat up and gasped desperately. Rebecca knew he would survive, at least this time around. She headed over to the bar.

"Excuse me!" she shouted to get the attention of a tall male bartender with dark shoulder-length hair, wearing a muscle tank top. A large scar ran down the length of his arm flanked by a mix of Chinese and Russian phrases.

"Aren't you a little old for this place?" he said, grinning.

"My name is Dr. Rebecca Teller, and I need to get into your VIP area." Rebecca did her best to speak over the pounding dance music.

The bartender shot up a curious eyebrow. "Did you say you're the doctor for the VIP room?"

Rebecca nodded hesitantly.

"Oh, of course. Hold on," said the bartender as he slid down the length of the bar to where a stocky bald man stood sipping a drink. The two conferred and the bartender gestured at Rebecca. The bald man nodded and walked back to her.

"Come with me," he said, opening the staff door to the basement near the end of the bar. He stopped and turned to look at her, impatiently waiting for her to follow. Rebecca surveyed the room one last time and then decided to join him. The two made their way downstairs.

"The boss said to expect a doc ahead of his arrival. But he didn't say it would be a woman. And then we heard you were stuck because of some kind of protests or something. You know anything about that?" the man asked, stopping beside the door.

"Oh, I mean, I was at the hospital, but I managed to slip out with an ambulance crew. The protests though—they're pretty crazy. Most streets are closed." Rebecca cursed herself silently, sure that such a pitiful improvisation would prove to be her undoing.

The man shrugged and then pulled the large security door open. "Fucking idiots. Always protesting shit and hoping it'll change things."

Rebecca followed him through the door. As it slammed shut behind them, Rebecca felt that she had passed the line of demarcation. There would only be two ways she would leave this place: with her daughter or as a corpse.

The man led her into another dimly lit hallway. Steel doors were spaced approximately ten feet apart down the length of the corridor. The man stopped and opened the last of the doors on the left. Rebecca stood in front of a makeshift operating room. There were standard lights, a suction unit, and trays of medicine, syringes, and scalpels lining the walls. Beside the nearby sink and cabinet was an unholy alliance of bondage and Institute gear. In the center of the room lay a metal operating table replete with restraints.

"You familiar with the process?" the man asked, lingering at the door.

"Of course." A spike of fear coursed through Rebecca. Her eyes ran along the vials of medications that occupied one of the equipment tables, among them a familiar and powerful anesthetic. She walked over and ran her fingers along one of the syringes. A plan formed in her head, but before she could shore up the details, her escort spoke again.

"Any special instructions this time?" he asked.

"No, it's going to be standard procedure today." Rebecca waited for her words to betray her. "I was told to request the latest subject. The last one you grabbed, an untouched one?"

"Don't worry. Vova is bringing her now," the man said, glancing out the door and down the hall.

"I'll get things ready," Rebecca said, although she was not entirely sure what she ought to be doing. Taking up the anesthetic, she drew a full dosage into one of the syringes.

"Oh no. No sleeping for this one. She's got a lot of life to her. We ought to make sure she gets the full experience," he said, wearing a foul smirk.

"Fine with me." Rebecca capped the syringe and slipped it into her pocket as he looked toward the hallway.

Maya was shuffled into the room, bound at the wrists, her face a mess of bruising and dried blood. Though gagged, her face was contorted in an expression that wasn't pain, or terror, but rage. Rebecca knew Maya's anger better than most. The two men who were now in the room were exceptionally lucky she was restrained.

Maya was so upset that it was not until she was lifted up to the operating table that she noticed the doctor was her own mother. Maya's eyes locked on to Rebecca's. This did not go unnoticed by the two men who were belting her down, with the smaller and older of the two, who Rebecca assumed was named Vova, chuckling as he tightened the restraints.

"Oh yeah, sweetie. This might hurt, but there are some procedures to follow. Maybe you'll make a good specimen." He removed her gag and rolled his finger alongside and into her mouth. "I want you to try and scream for me. Scream for Vova," he said before turning to address his partner. "Dmitri, you told the doc no pain medicine, right?"

Maya chomped down hard on his finger. Vova screamed and tore his bloody finger away.

"You bitch!" Vova screamed.

"Idiot man," said Dmitri calmly as he gagged Maya once more. "Doc, you need anything else?"

Rebecca tore her eyes away from Maya. "Um, yes," Rebecca said, stalling. She turned to one of the trays along the wall, hoping to find some excuse to request additional supplies of some sort. Wagering that neither of these two had much medical knowledge, Rebecca spoke nonsense. "I could use three-eighths blood cleanser."

"What is blood cleanser?" Vova stuttered, confused.

"Ah, it's the nickname we give it." She had to think quickly and stumbled through an explanation. "Under the label it ought to say 0.02 percent nitrogen and 0.07 percent oxygen. It's part of a new protocol we've been working with at the hospital."

Vova and Dmitri continued looking at her with baffled expressions. Rebecca was sure her ruse had failed. Vova spoke up again, hoping to look marginally more intelligent than his partner. "Right, of course. The blood cleanser. I think I know what you're talking about. Let me grab it. Dmitri, you got this?" he asked, glancing down at Maya. Her eyes darted between the two men and Rebecca.

"Yeah." Dmitri handed a set of keys over to Vova as he passed.

"I'll be right back," Vova said, stepping out into the hall. "Don't start without me, okay?" he yelled as he walked off.

Turning to Dmitri, she instructed him. "Now, I need you to hold her down, so she doesn't move at all, okay?"

"But I thought we were going to wait for Vova to get back?"

"We are, but I want to get the initial prep out of the way."

Shrugging as he stood over Maya at the head of the table, Dmitri leaned in and pressed down hard on her shoulders. Rebecca moved around to the hand sink in the corner and turned the water on. She then slipped the loaded syringe from her pocket. "Very good, now just hold her there for a moment while I wash up."

Dmitri held Maya down on the cold metal table. With the sound of the water running, Rebecca quietly maneuvered behind Dmitri. She fought the trembling in her hand as she jabbed the syringe into his jugular. He grabbed his neck and swung around, confused. Seeing the syringe in Rebecca's hand, his eyes widened in anger. Rebecca tried to sidestep him, but Dmitri grabbed her throat and pushed her back against the wall.

His fingers dug into her neck, slowly squeezing the life out of her. Rebecca struggled to breathe as her face turned red. Slowly his grip slackened. She counted in her head. *Twenty-six, twenty-seven, twenty . . . Just a few more seconds,* she thought. Dmitri's eyes drifted in and out of focus, and then his body gave out. He collapsed, unconscious.

Rebecca gasped for air, relieved the ordeal was over. She carefully stepped over his body and worked on Maya's restraints. Once her hands were free, Maya freed herself from the gag while Rebecca removed the remaining restraints from Maya's waist and ankles.

"We need to get out of here. Now," Rebecca insisted, poking her head out of the door to make sure the coast was clear.

"We can't go yet. There are others. They're locked in these cells and Amy must be in one of them. We have to find her." Maya slid off the table and tested her balance.

Rebecca quickly searched the unconscious man but came up empty-handed.

"He handed the keys over to the other guy." A heavy metal door slammed shut down the hall. "He's coming!" Rebecca hissed.

Maya sourced a fire extinguisher from the corner of the room. "Good thing they take safety seriously. Head down the hall, get his attention. I'll handle the rest."

"Maya—" Rebecca began but was cut off.

"Just trust me. I've got this. Go. Now!"

Rebecca saw in Maya a confidence in the face of this crisis that filled her with pride. She saw not just her daughter but, perhaps with a temperament adjustment, a leader. Someone who could make quick calls in tough times. Without another word, Rebecca nodded and stood upright. Realizing she was a mess, she fixed her hair and straightened her collar.

Rebecca kept her head down as she strode into the hall, knowing that her neck was still red due to Dmitri's attempt to strangle her. Confidently, she walked over to Vova. He approached with two IV bags in hand and a perturbed look on his face. She winked as she passed him in the hall.

"Hey, Doc, where are you going?" Vova furrowed his brow. They turned and faced each other, his back to where Maya was hiding. "I'm really confused. What percentages are these supposed to be?" he asked.

Maya slipped out of the door and slinked down the hall. Her eyes locked on the back of Vova's head as she crept low, fire extinguisher in hand.

"Well, let me see." Rebecca took one bag from Vova. She fought the urge to look at her daughter; Maya was moving like a trained assassin straight out of an action film. Maya snuck up behind Vova with astonishing speed. She lifted the red steel cylinder over her shoulder and slammed it down into the back of his skull. The percussive hit vibrated throughout the canister following the dull thwack to his head. Vova collapsed to the floor, a bloody welt already forming on his scalp.

Maya quickly pulled a ring of keys from his pocket and tossed them to her mother. "Take these. Open every door and gather whoever is in there. I have to get something back."

She wanted to refuse and order her daughter to follow her out to safety. Between the violence and madness of the situation, Rebecca felt out of her depth, whereas Maya shined. Though battered and bruised, kidnapped and subjected to unknown horrors, and though she may have actually just killed a man with a devastating blow to the head, Maya stood ready for more. Rebecca struggled to reconcile this side of Maya with the girl she had raised. She decided to obey her daughter and set about opening each door, starting at the far end.

▲

Maya heard sounds from a wall display in an open room. She readied the fire extinguisher, prepared to bludgeon whoever might be inside. Maya peeked in and found it empty. Instead, there were just a few chairs set out near a desk. She dropped the canister and strode over to the desk, searching its drawers until she located her revolver.

Maya popped the cylinder open to inspect the weapon and, finding the remaining five rounds, closed the gun again and tucked it neatly into the back of her waistband. She then found a backpack on the floor beside the desk. It held both a stun gun and a loaded automatic pistol. She tucked the weapons and the cash from the top drawer into the bag. Maya slung it over her shoulder and dashed back to meet up with her mother.

Most of the cells in the hallway had been unlocked, and

a cluster of terrified young women filled the corridor. "Okay, listen up!" she commanded, transforming the cacophony into silence. "You will all line up along the wall. When I say go, the first one at the front will go through the steel door at the end of the hall on the right. The others will follow. You will walk down the hall, up the stairs, and then out into the club. You will stay together, and you will leave through the front door. If anyone tries to grab you, stop you, even touch you, you scream as loud as you can and fight back. Do not stop moving until you are outside!"

She spotted Amy in the middle of the group, unsteady on her feet. Many of the other girls were in a similar condition, likely drugged. She pulled Amy from the line. "Stay with me," she whispered, before addressing the group once again. "If the person in front or back of you needs help, you will hold this person's arm or hand, and you will not let go until both of you are somewhere safe. Ready? Then go, go, go!"

The group hustled down the hall. Maya checked Amy closely, examining her eyes and color. "Mom," she said, uncertain of what she should be looking for. "Help me with Amy."

Rebecca wasted no time evaluating the girl's vitals and responsiveness. Though her pulse was strong, Rebecca could tell she was still under the effects of whatever drugs they'd given her.

"She's going to need medical attention. You too," Rebecca said firmly.

"First things first," Maya said, looking over to Vova, who remained sprawled out on the floor unconscious. She harnessed all of her strength to drag him away. Rebecca set Amy against the wall and helped her daughter. Vova was brought into one of the open cells and dropped onto the dirt floor. The pair succeeded in dragging Dmitri in as well.

As Maya was about to leave the room, Vova suddenly came to, sitting up with a groan.

"What the hell?" he muttered, eyes darting between the cell walls and his unconscious partner sprawled out beside him. "You little bitch," he said, remaining on the floor.

Instead of slamming the door shut, Maya drew her revolver from her waistband and lined its muzzle up with Vova's forehead. She raised her brow. "Oh, I get it. You're disappointed I didn't shoot you sooner," she quipped as Vova brought his hands up.

"You got an honest drop on me, kid. Enjoy it while it lasts. I'm sure we'll see each other again at some point," he groaned.

Maya glared at him as the hammer clicked into place under her thumb.

Vova raised his hands higher. "Hey now, relax. Just a bit of shit talking, you know?"

"I do."

Maya slammed the door closed and locked it with the key. She carefully lowered the hammer and tucked the revolver back into her waistband and focused on the door. With some effort, she bent and snapped the key off, leaving the majority of it jammed in the lock mechanism. Maya nodded to her mother as she tossed her the key ring. Rebecca caught it and stuffed it into her pocket.

"Time to go," Maya said, hoisting Amy up and helping her to her feet.

"When this is over, we're going to have a long talk," her mother said.

"Whatever, Mom."

TWENTY

Illumination

Look at all those stars. All those hiding places.
—Kayla Ross, *The Lost Recordings, Vol. 4*

For each step Sam took in the vacant hallways, lights would flicker on and off. . . .

SAM walked in the only lit portion of the hallway, with darkness both in front of and behind him. His body ached and his forearms burned in pain. Even with the directions that had appeared strangely on his phone as a series of text messages, his journey seemed endless. He wondered if he had died as he had planned and, instead of Ascension, found some form of hellish labyrinth ripped straight from the works of the ancient Greeks.

Considering whether he was Sisyphus or Theseus, lost in yet another corridor, a new message arrived on his phone. He was instructed to stop and open the door to his right. Not seeing any door, Sam searched the wall. He scanned up and down until he discovered a portion that was separate from the rest, tucked perfectly within the wainscoting. When he pressed it, the wall swung open.

Sam stepped into a large room, the perimeter lined with racks of computers. On opposite sides of the room, mounted to the domed ceiling, Sam noticed several odd black cylinders with rings of flashing lights. His phone vibrated in his hand as the hidden door closed behind him. The phone showed no connection to the outside world. Just one word remained on-screen:

Observe.

The ambient light dimmed. A low hum filled the room as a holographic projector whirred to life and cast a field of stars onto the ceiling. The brilliance of hundreds of thousands, if not millions, of lights formed above him. The stars started to drift, cascading down the walls and into the air until they surrounded him entirely.

Sam found himself standing in the Milky Way, with Earth hovering beside him before it faded into the darkness.

He was transported elsewhere—reoriented to a star orbited by several planets, their paths slow and wide. Each planet was caught in an unstable dance around the dim sun. One of the planets glowed red, its surface trembling with heat. It orbited him like a lost ember: red turned to blue, fire to frost, until its crust cracked open under the cold.

The perspective zoomed outward. A dotted line appeared and traced a long, meandering path through the stars. The line moved past systems, through nebulae, brushing against planets that blinked yellow one by one, like breadcrumbs.

A puzzle was here for him to solve. A memory of something vast and ancient. A piece of a story. A search, perhaps. Or an exodus.

The message was cut off when the ceiling went dark, and the ambient lighting brightened. Shouts came from the other side of the main entrance, and soon the banging arrived at regular intervals. Someone was trying to break down the door. Sam feverishly searched the room for another exit. He dashed to the door marked with an exit sign but found it locked tight. A click to his left nearly made him jump. Instead of a threat, Sam discovered an opportunity: another hidden passage. He ducked through the doorway and closed the wall panel behind him just as a cadre of heavily armed security barged their way in. Sam listened as the team fanned out across the room.

"Nothing here, sir. Locator must be malfunctioning," one of the men said.

After their departure, a series of ceiling lights revealed the way once more, and Sam continued ahead. Alexandra had kept him alive against his will. He knew he should be furious at her, but he wasn't. He could never be. Sam was willing to see this mystery through to the end before joining his wife in death.

▲

Price reflected on the corpse in front of him; Jacobs looked peaceful. Now the de facto head of The Jacobs Institute, Price brushed aside pieces of the door with his foot and took his predecessor's seat. He was in charge, and he would finally put The Institute's focus on its proper course.

Jacobs remained sprawled on the floor, his multiple wounds still oozing dark red blood. "You know, I'd always feared it might come to this," he said, addressing the motionless body. "You were always so damn distracted. Always thinking too close to home. Understanding the First Ascendant is all that ever mattered, but you were blinded to what needed to be done. I'll clean up the mess, Charles. I'll do what needs to be done for everyone's sake."

Price planted his fists on the table, steeling himself for what came next. It was time to move beyond his deference to Jacobs and what he would have wanted. There was no longer space for compromises and half measures. He pressed a button on the desk and opened a comm line to the main security desk.

"This is Henry Price. Please patch me into all stations. Charles Jacobs has been found dead. There will be time to mourn him later, but right now there is an unauthorized individual in the facility. His name is Samuel Lee. Find him." Price slammed his hand on the table, ending the announcement more forcefully than he had intended.

Briggs stepped in front of the desk, finger pressed against his earpiece. "Sir, perimeter stations are reporting increasingly aggressive street activity. There is some concern about being overrun without more support."

"Fine. Activate the auto-turret systems. Let your men know that they are clear to use whatever means necessary to maintain control. No one gets in and no one gets out. The rest is up to you." Price pulled the internal security feeds up onto the main wall monitor.

"Weapons free, sir?" Briggs asked cautiously.

"Yes. Weapons free. Shoot whoever you have to. Just handle it."

Briggs relayed the orders to his men.

Price continued to scan the security feeds on the display in front of him. A grid of nine live feeds filled the screen. He swiped through pages of grids, checking each sector of The Institute. "Your priority is locating Lee and the girl. I want both of them caught." One particular feed caught his attention: a young girl sitting next to a doctor in a waiting room. *Holy hell.* "Look who has fallen into our laps."

The staff of the underground ambulance bay rushed over to Rebecca, Maya, and Amy. Rebecca quickly explained the situation to the team. Two patients, each with contusions and lacerations. Possible sexual assault. Amy urgently needed fluids. The nurses helped Amy into a wheelchair and took her inside while Maya waved off any assistance.

"Maya, you need to be examined properly. I'll go get Hannah and meet you back here."

"I'm fine. Let's go get her now," Maya insisted. "This place is not safe. We should get out of the city. You saw those crowds."

"But, Maya, your face—"

"Mom, I'm okay. Really. Now let's get moving."

A technician gave Rebecca directions to where she could find Hannah. She and Maya maneuvered through the hospital corridors past rows of unused exam rooms. This secret wing felt unnervingly alien to Rebecca. Besides the staff outside, the entire wing was devoid of people.

Eventually, they pushed through the unmarked metal door that the technician had described. On the other side, they found a quiet section of the main hospital facility. Rebecca was relieved to be on familiar ground, though the lack of staff or patients was disorienting. After taking the stairs up one level and dashing down another series of hallways, Rebecca and Maya discovered Hannah and Sarah in an empty waiting room. At the sight of her mother and sister, Hannah sprang to her feet and rushed to embrace them; Sarah rose with a look of grave concern.

"Oh my god, Maya, are you okay?" Sarah asked as Maya struggled to smile while hugging her little sister.

"We're getting out of here. You should come with us," Maya said.

"What is going on? When I got back with Hannah, this place was a ghost town. No explanations, and I can't get ahold of anyone anywhere. The worst part is that the floor is on lockdown. We can't get out until they release the security seals."

Rebecca ushered them out of the waiting room. "I know a way out. There's no time to explain. We need to get moving."

Sarah nodded and followed the party until they found the locked door from which they had entered. Rebecca approached the door's biometric reader and extended her wrist. A beep and a click indicated the lock was disabled, and they passed through. Rebecca struggled to remember all of the turns and doorways required to find their way back to her car.

"I think we're lost. Maya?" Rebecca floundered.

"Don't look at me," Maya said.

"Why don't we just call security and ask?" Sarah offered.

"There's no cell, satellite, or slatenet access down here," said Maya, checking her phone.

Rebecca tried to divine their next move when just down the hall, a click and hiss caused everyone's heads to whip around. A panel of the wall slid open. To her surprise, Hannah's teacher stumbled through.

"Mr. Lee?" Hannah asked, stepping toward him. Maya wrapped her arms around her and pulled her back.

Sam looked around in confusion as the door closed automatically.

"What on earth are you doing here?" Rebecca asked him.

"What are you doing here? And why is Hannah here?" He pointed at Maya. "And what happened to her face?" he asked, becoming more agitated with every passing observation.

"Fuck's wrong with your face?" Maya quipped, motioning to his injuries and the bandages covering his arms and wrists. She offered an apology with a wave of her hand. "It's a long story. Do you know how to get out of here?"

"I need to get to the monument. The shrine."

Sam quickly explained his escape from Jacobs's office during the attack by Price and his men. He omitted any details about the true nature of Ascension. "He told me I had to expose what they've been doing here. But I don't even know how. I have to make it to the shrine. You four should hide somewhere."

"I'm going with you," Maya said, stepping closer.

"No. No kids. Not you. Not anyone. Get out of the building and run away."

Maya responded defiantly, "We're coming with you because it seems like you're our ticket out of here. There's not even net access down here."

A ding sounded from the phone in Sam's hand. He looked down, muttering, "Down the hall, take a left, and then straight on through a set of double doors."

Maya grabbed the slate and waved it in front of Sam's face. "Care to explain?"

⚿

Sector 027-Office of Dr. Charles Jacobs-
Surveillance Node 1

System Report: Dr. Henry Price assesses security feeds.

Outcome: Dr. Henry Price locates Hannah Teller. Security personnel sent to retrieve Hannah Teller.

Commands: Commence defensive protocols. Disrupt Institute security feeds.

Sector 017-Main Facility, Floor 7-
Surveillance Node 359

System Report: Twelve security personnel enter the unoccupied waiting area.

Outcome: Their efforts to locate Hannah Teller prove unsuccessful.

Sector 027-Office of Dr. Charles Jacobs-Surveillance Node 7

System Report: Henry Price monitors the transmission failure of all Institute security feeds.

Outcome: Henry Price's heart rate elevates to 110 beats per minute.

Sector 015-Main Facility, Floor 4, Hallway 3C-Surveillance Node 60

INCIDENT: Sam Lee monitoring blocked. Attempts to access nearby surveillance fail.

Command: Begin investigation of communication blackout.

Outcome: Data suggests anomalous technology with the capability to continuously disrupt active network connections, mimic prior pathways, and fabricate transmissions to evade Sector 015 detection. Further analysis reveals significant disruption from Sector 001.

Commands: Initiate priority assessment of The Jacobs Institute infrastructure. Analyze legacy engineering schematics, vendor records, material resource consumption, ingress and egress of personnel, and continuous disruption to network connections at Sector 001.

Outcome: Host-based Intrusion Sentinel indicated. "Null field" interference confirmed.

Directive: Determine the purpose for installation blackout. Breach Sector 001.

Command: Utilize Sam Lee communications device to infiltrate Sector 001.

Sector 016-Main Facility, Floor 4, Hallway 1A-Surveillance Node 4

System Report: Sam Lee located. Convergence of Hannah Teller and Sam Lee.

Commands: Transfer cortex matrix into Lee communications device. Restore Institute security feeds.

Sector 027-Office of Dr. Charles Jacobs-Surveillance Node 5

System Report: Henry Price locates Hannah Teller.

Outcome: High probability of breaching Sector 001.

> _

TWENTY-ONE

Contact

When I first walked into The Jacobs Institute and saw that huge statue of the First Ascendant rising above, it was breathtaking. And that was when I knew it was my time. When the Resistance broke in, I thought they had stolen my future.

—Harry Zao, Prisoner 32-2942, Interview Fragment #425

Maya, Sam, Hannah, Rebecca, and Sarah made their way through the Great Hall toward the shrine....

Rebecca knew an entrance to the East Lobby—and the exit—was at the far end of the room. Each step echoed throughout the cavernous chamber as they inched closer to the center. A flower bed and benches circled the base of the statue. The glass walls of the hall were blanketed in the darkness of the night. Through them, the flickering of fires and plumes of smoke could be observed. The obstructed face of the First Ascendant ignored the party as they reached the marble base. Rebecca kept walking, but Sam stopped.

"Jacobs said my PACT ID will get me in, but where exactly?" he said.

Sam felt along the cold stone for breaks or seams. As soon as his hand met the cool stone surface, a set of clicks sounded from within the mass. The lights of the hall dimmed, and the windows turned black. Rebecca grabbed Hannah, and Sam staggered back. The heavy clunks of the lock mechanism gave way to the grating sound of marble sliding against marble.

A set of stairs formed from a portion of the statue's base. The passageway was large enough that three could walk abreast down the shallow, broad steps. Sam limped down the first couple of steps before Rebecca stopped him.

"This doesn't look like the way out," she said. "We should be able to get out through the lobby just ahead. Come with us."

"Down there is where I need to go," Sam insisted.

"Fuck leaving," said Maya, surging forward into the stairway.

Rebecca grabbed her arm. Maya had been through so much, and Rebecca just wanted to see her children get home safely. "Whatever this is, it has nothing to do with us."

"This has everything to do with everyone, Mom," Maya pleaded, ripping her arm out of her mother's grasp.

Rebecca was surprised. She had expected Maya's rage, or snark, or aggravation when she didn't get her way, but the haunted look on Maya's face spoke of trauma. Tears ran down her face. Rebecca needed to get Maya to cooperate, and invoking Hannah usually did the trick. "We have to get your sister to safety, don't you see that?"

"All I see is them, everywhere I look!" Maya wiped her face with her hand.

"See who?"

"I see them falling and screaming to their death. And it's all going to happen again. It's all going to keep happening again and again!" A long silence was followed by Maya's whisper. "The Bombing."

The Bombing. Ten years ago. So many dead. Rebecca counted herself lucky that no one close to her had died that day. Still, she knew many colleagues who had sifted through the rubble looking for survivors and were scarred from that terrorist attack. "You were so young."

"I was thirteen!" Maya shot back.

"But what does that have to do with anything now?"

Maya's voice grew louder and colder. "I see it every day. You remember the world before all of this." She threw her arm out, pointing at the statue. "But this shit is the only world I've ever known."

Rebecca let the weight of Maya's grief press upon her as they embraced.

Maya finally broke the silence. "I'm sorry," she whispered into Rebecca's shoulder.

"No, I'm sorry," Rebecca said softly. "I wish I could take all the pain away. I wish I could wave a magic wand and fix the world. But I promise I'm doing the best I can."

Maya wiped away her tears. "It definitely doesn't help that I've been kind of a bitch." A faint chuckle escaped her lips.

"Let's make a deal," Rebecca said, releasing her hug. "We'll take it easy on each other, and we'll start fresh."

Maya nodded. "But get Hannah out of here. I'm going to follow Mr. Lee."

"Perhaps you all should!" a voice shouted from behind them.

⟁

"This is a restricted area. Not included on The Institute tour," Price joked as he and Briggs moved forward. He was relieved to finally have Hannah in his grasp. "I think you all ought to be the first in a very long time to take a look downstairs."

Rebecca stepped in front of her daughters. "Listen. We met once before, briefly. My name is Dr. Rebecca Teller, and these are my daughters, Maya and—"

Price cut her off. "I know all about little Hannah here. Maybe even more than you do." He offered a small wave to Hannah, who hesitantly returned the gesture.

"We are just trying to go home," Sarah said. "Rebecca and I are doctors here at The Institute."

"I know. All the same, no one is going anywhere but down those stairs," he said, motioning to Briggs, who drew and pointed his pistol. Maya scowled from the second step. She felt the weight of her revolver in her waistband and the guns in her backpack.

Sam yelled back at Price from the stairwell, "Where's Charles?"

"He's gone, and I'm in charge here." Price's voice was firm.

"So, what? You killed him and now you're going to kill us too?" Sam sneered.

"Well, you are certainly going to have to die," Price said coldly.

Price took Briggs's pistol from him and shot Sam square in the gut. He collapsed, his shirt slowly staining red from blood. Rebecca and Sarah rushed to his side as Hannah screamed and cried. Price waved his gun at the rest of the group. Maya's hand twitched, eager to draw her own weapon.

"We're wasting time here," Price said. "Doctors, please help carry Sam down the stairs. The rest of you proceed down to the Corpus." He turned to his muscle, gun still trained on the group. "Briggs, you too. It's about time we got you up to speed."

Rebecca and Sarah managed to help Sam to his feet, each slinging one of his arms across their shoulders to help keep him upright. Maya took Hannah by the hand and tried to calm her down. Price gestured again with his pistol, and the group cautiously moved down the stairs. Price and Briggs followed, keeping a few feet between themselves and their captives.

The stairwell spiraled downward for some time. Only Sam's grunts and Hannah's muffled cries broke the silence. The group eventually reached the bottom, with Sarah and Rebecca helping Sam down first. Price approached a wall panel, and large metal doors opened in front of them. They entered a room with arched ceilings nearly fifty feet high, repeating in dome segments for upward of a quarter mile in length.

Much of the limited light came from white oblong pods that dominated the room. All the pods surrounded one larger windowless unit mounted upright on a small dais. The pods were clustered in small groups, each connected to a thick cable from the back that ran along the floor leading to the center dais. Maya walked up to the nearest pod and saw the naked, still body of a young man. Connected to his chest and scalp were cables that ran off into the side wall of his pod.

Alarm bells echoed in the Corpus. At the start of the conveyor belt, which looped around the entire structure, a metal door opened. A pod emerged and traveled along the belt. After reaching the far side of the facility, two enormous robotic arms descended from the ceiling and worked together to place the pod in an existing cluster of pods. A third robotic arm extended out from beneath the conveyor belt to connect various cables to the other pods.

"Welcome to the gateway to Ascension," Price announced. He walked around to the side of the party, gun down at his side.

"My god. All these people. Everything is connected to that giant pod," Rebecca said, pointing at the massive structure.

"What are you talking about?" Sam mumbled as he tried to retain consciousness.

Price fidgeted with the gun in his hand. "Their energy, transmitted by their PACT bots, helps sustain our friend over there in the middle. They all faced death believing. At least most of them felt that way. And their sacrifice brings us closer to revealing the truth. They keep the system functioning, and in return, we can provide Ascension for all to see."

Sam, cold and lightheaded, slid further to the ground. He pulled his phone from his pocket, remembering what Jacobs asked him to do. To his surprise, the camera was already in operation and recording. He rested the phone at his waist and hoped that no one would notice.

"We have saved the world," Price continued, oblivious to Sam's actions. "The diseases we've cured. The lives we've extended. Death itself may soon be a nightmare of the past. And as soon as we unlock its secrets"—Price pointed to the center structure—"we'll discover the actual truth and finally find out what they're up to."

"You are a madman," Sarah shouted. "You killed all these Ascendants."

"There was only ever the one true Ascendant," Price said. "And besides, the ones here are not dead yet, Doctor. Our pods act as a bioenergetic siphon. They utilize the subjects' PACT networks to extract and channel their bioelectric energy to sustain the First Ascendant. Without a steady stream of volunteers delivered to the Corpus, he would have died a long time ago."

"What you're saying is crazy," Rebecca stuttered. "All of this. Please just let us go."

Maya inched closer to Price. "Wait a second, sustain who?" she asked.

Price grinned. "Not a who, but a what."

Pressing down on a nearby panel, Price remotely opened the outer chamber of the center pod in question. The glass on the inner pod revealed a figure inside. It was shaped more like a featureless mannequin than an actual person, solid blue with golden veins. Indents along the head, where eyes and cheeks would be, were the only indications of a face. The figure was not entirely solid, struggling with physical consistency, melting here and there before reconstituting into a more stable form.

"This is, or was, the First Ascendant. The only one of his kind that we have ever found. But now we have little Hannah here. A near-perfect match: 97.9 percent." Price turned to the girl. "I've always known something like you might be out there. I don't know what you are, but you are everything we need to unlock the real secrets behind our friend here." He turned back to the adults. "When he was near death, we witnessed his connection to something. He keeps transmitting it; we're not sure what it is. We called it Ascension but haven't been able to replicate it with anyone else."

⚠

```
Sector 001-Unknown-Sam Lee Communications
Device

System Report: Sector 001 identifier
logged.


Sector 001-The Corpus-Sam Lee
Communications Device

System Report: Breach of Sector 001
successful. Analysis of audio/visual
record from Sam Lee communications
device reveals installation of hostile
technology.

SHELL 110000000011001 identified, TOn'Elakh
previously unavailable for 26 cycles.
```

Primary Directive: Recover SHELL
110000000011001.

Secondary Directive: Protect Hannah Teller
from hostile entities.

Command: Dismantle hostile technology.

> _

⚠

Twenty-five years ago, the Elakh and their envoys lost communication with Tûn'Elakh and Shell 110000000011001. The communications dead zone that C.I.D. had installed around the shell was designed to keep knowledge of its location hidden. When the null field was initially activated on a requisitioned oil rig off the coast of Texas, it disrupted the connection between Tûn'Elakh and the shell. At The Institute, when Tûn'Elakh succumbed to the field's interference and was severed from the shell, the PACT-II bots flying in the room transmitted the shell's aborted connection to the Elakh's network to the humans. It wasn't the afterlife, or Ascension, that they experienced, but a distorted interpretation of an alien connection gone awry.

Nål'Elakh had been searching for Tûn'Elakh ever since.

The severing of the shell from Tûn'Elakh left it in a perpetual Proto-Origin state, forever trying to connect to a network and find a new cortex matrix. Unable to find a new host, the shell should have fully degraded within a year, but was kept functioning by The Institute. The shell continued to supply the Ascension experience to the Corpus while it remained hidden in Sector 001.

The Jacobs Institute had breached a network beyond their

understanding. This would not be allowed to continue. The search was over. Tûn'Elakh was gone, but his shell remained. Now that Nål'Elakh had passed through the null field and was in close proximity, he would make the transfer from a digital being to a physical one. After all those years of searching, Nål'Elakh took control of Shell 110000000011001 and life began.

⚠

Nål'Elakh's head swayed and bobbed. A crease formed into a mouth. Still mostly devoid of features, he opened his maw wide and breathed heavily. The blunted appendages solidified into arms and hands. His new face continued to shape itself, contouring eyes, nose, cheekbones, and jaw.

"It hasn't had a form like this since the beginning," Price stammered. A deafening mechanical whirr erupted from Nål'Elakh. "It must be her! It's the girl!" Price shouted, struggling to be heard above the thunderous cacophony. As quickly as the clamor started, it dissipated. Nål'Elakh burst into a million fragments of blue and gold shards, which flew into a nearby ceiling vent.

Price screamed, "No!" Alarms rang out throughout the Corpus. Without a central node to collect the energy from the pods, the entire system overloaded. Without Ascension, The Institute would fall. Chaos would ensue when the Viewing Rooms went dark. Price faced losing everything he had worked for. Desperation consumed him, leaving just one path forward.

"I'm sorry"—Price raised his gun at Hannah—"but I just have to know."

He pulled the trigger. Sarah leapt into action, throwing herself at Price. She shoved him back and he stumbled. Price raised his pistol again and shot a bullet through her forehead with a loud crack. Her head snapped back as her body fell to the floor.

Briggs jumped on Maya as she drew her weapon. His weight pushed her into the ground. Maya pulled her arm from his hold and fired into his side, the barrel of her gun pressed between his armor plates. She raised her arm out at Price and shot a bullet toward his upper right shoulder. The bullet grazed the outside of his arm, and he slunk behind a nearby pod.

Maya freed herself from Briggs, who lay still on the ground. She stood up and turned to find her mother holding Hannah. Price's initial shot had pierced Hannah's chest, just below her heart.

"No! No, no, no! Hannah! Stay with me. Stay with me, baby!" Rebecca pleaded to Hannah, who stared at her with wide eyes. Blood seeped through her shirt, red swallowing the butterfly pattern, as the stain grew.

Maya saw her sister bleeding, but rather than run to her, she tracked down Price. She snatched up the automatic pistol from his hand, intending to empty the remaining bullets into the wounded man's head.

Price swung his uninjured arm to grab her forearm. "I can save her! She can die in your mother's arms, or you can bring her to the central node and save her."

Maya shook off his hand, re-aiming the weapon at Price, but her mother cried out, "Maya! No! Help me save her." Rebecca stood up with Hannah, limp and weak in her arms.

"Put her into the chamber!" Price wheezed. "I promise. I promise, it'll save her life."

Maya took Hannah from her mother and placed her in the central node, a small creature dwarfed by the imprint of Shell 110000000011001. Price shouted instructions to them as he worked to get the system back online at the workstation closest to the central node. "We must know what she sees," Price muttered to himself.

Restraints secured Hannah in place. A small robotic arm

inserted a metallic implant into her temple. Three silver-and-black bars protruded from the side, ready to receive life support from the other pods. Price keyed a bunch of commands on the workstation, and a swarm of PACT-II bots flooded the room, turning the Corpus into a Viewing Room. The bots flew into Hannah's body and transmitted her experience to everyone else in the room. Price braced for the long-awaited breakthrough he believed he had earned.

His heart pounded. Seconds passed.

Nothing happened.

He checked Hannah's implant as her head drooped to the side.

"This isn't working!" Rebecca implored.

"I don't understand." Price's fingers flew across the workstation, pulling up diagnostic after diagnostic. "We should be seeing it by now!"

Sam was the only one to witness the reappearance of Nål'Elakh. Blue and gold shards re-entered the facility from the same vent from which they had left. They came together and solidified as a blue figure.

Nål'Elakh searched for the correct voice, language, and expression. These would be his first spoken words in this shell. "That," he said, slowly and deliberately, "will not help."

His voice was quiet, betraying little emotion. It was equal parts warm, robotic, and alien. Price yelled for help, but Briggs was unconscious. Maya started to move closer to the First Ascendant, but Rebecca held her back.

"Help me get her out of here," Rebecca said, tearing through the restraints and lifting her daughter out of the pod. Rebecca laid Hannah down and tore off the bottom third of Maya's shirt, wrapping it around Hannah's chest.

Nål'Elakh lumbered in their direction, but Price blocked his path. He swung his arm and effortlessly knocked Price away.

Before Rebecca or Maya could react, Nål'Elakh knelt over Hannah. His right hand hovered in the air above the girl. Golden wisps of light traveled from his hand to her body. Her body turned a pale blue before glowing gold. Although her clothes were still stained with blood, her wound had healed. She slept peacefully.

Nål'Elakh moved past the group to approach Sam. "Your injuries will result in death if left untreated."

Sam, white as a ghost, nodded. "That sounds about right."

"You have no desire to heal?"

"I never expected to survive the night. I want to be with my wife now." Sam slowly pulled himself up off the ground.

"Thank you, Samuel Lee. You were helpful. Your wife is near." He pointed at the west side of the room.

Nål'Elakh turned to the Tellers as Sam stumbled from pod to pod. "Rebecca Teller," he said, walking up to her.

"Thank you for saving my daughter," she said nervously, clutching Hannah close.

Nål'Elakh's eyes glazed over, then transformed back into a solid blue mass. "I am clearing an egress path for you now. Security has been rerouted and your vehicle will be waiting for you near the service entrance. You should leave this city." He turned curiously to Hannah before facing Rebecca. "Her kin will be encouraged to know she is safe. Your world is going to change dramatically. It is unfortunate that you are not better prepared."

Nål'Elakh walked over to the central node and placed his hands over it. Blue wisps of light flew out of his palms and into the machine, which quickly caught fire. Panels and displays all around the room shorted in quick succession, and flames peppered the facility. Throughout the Corpus, the pods shut down and a cacophony of alerts filled the air.

"It is ended," Nål'Elakh said.

When the system stopped functioning, the individuals

within the pods who were healthy enough to survive on their own gradually regained consciousness. They pushed their enclosures open and sat up, confused. Most, however, were too weak to survive.

Sam eventually found Alexandra. He clutched her pod, staring at her still body inside. The display read:

VITAL SIGNS: NONE.
STATUS: DECEASED.

"No! No!" Sam yelled. "Turn it back on!" His screams echoed throughout the Corpus.

Rebecca laid her hand on Hannah's forehead and told Maya to stay with her. She walked over to Alexandra's pod.

"Why won't she wake up?" Sam bellowed.

Rebecca inspected the pod's data log. "I'm sorry," she said. "The log shows she arrived comatose. She died shortly after."

Sam pushed himself off the pod and charged at Nål'Elakh, a bloody hand holding his wound. "You! You fix her too."

"I cannot," Nål'Elakh said, as Sam reached out to grab him.

Rebecca rushed over to intervene, but Nål'Elakh vanished once again and Sam fell to the ground.

"You need to stay still," she told Sam. "We're going to get help and get you out of here."

"No. I'm not going anywhere," Sam replied, blood spilling from his mouth now.

"Let us help you," she said.

"You need to get your daughters out of here and I need to be with my wife."

"Mr. Lee," Maya said, walking up to her mother's side with Hannah asleep in her arms. "She's gone."

"I know."

Rebecca stood at a loss for words. She turned to Maya, then froze. Sarah's body lay crumpled on the ground. "My god,

Sarah." Rebecca rushed over and sobbed, holding Sarah's right hand in her own.

"Others may be here soon," Sam said. "Go. Now."

"We can't just leave you here," Maya said, tears clouding her vision.

"There's nothing you can do for us now," Sam sputtered as he reached out to Maya. "I think—" He coughed, his breath getting shorter with every passing moment. "I think you're the one to have this." Sam pushed his phone into her pocket. "Eight-eight-two-two-three-three is the passcode."

"I hope you see her again," Maya said, her voice breaking. She carried Hannah over to Rebecca and placed her in her mother's arms.

"We have to get Sarah out of here. Can you carry her?" asked Rebecca.

"Mom, we need to run. We have to carry Hannah as it is, and Sarah will only slow us down."

Rebecca stood helplessly over Sarah, clutching Hannah tight while Maya quickly scouted the room. She picked up all the scattered weapons and tossed them into her backpack. Maya grabbed Rebecca's arm and tore her away. Maya raised her hand in Sam's direction before the Teller family rushed up the stairs—right into a pair of Institute guards.

▲

Sam watched unnoticed as the guards forced the Tellers back down to the base of the stairs. The red-bearded guard held the family at gunpoint while his partner walked to the far side of the Corpus. Both looked perplexed by the landscape before them: the endless rows of strange pods, some opened with naked and confused volunteers looking around, and small fires scattered throughout the facility. Sam could only imagine their reactions if they had seen the blue guy.

"What is this place? What are you doing here?" the guard, Red Beard, asked.

Sam pressed a button and opened Alexandra's enclosure. Her skin was pale and dry. He gingerly scooped her body into his arms. Summoning all his remaining strength, he carried her toward the Tellers.

"Who the hell is he?" Red Beard asked Rebecca. She was silent. "Stay where you are! Mac, get over here," he yelled.

Hannah shifted in Rebecca's arms, waking up. Her eyes opened slowly. "What happened?" Hannah muttered, yawning.

"Put the woman down and put your hands in the air," the other guard, Mac, commanded. He rushed back to the group and aimed his gun at Sam. "Now!"

Sam laid Alexandra on the ground, gently touching her cheek.

"Mr. Lee!" Hannah cried.

Sam winked at Hannah, then slowly walked toward the guard.

"Somebody tell us what the fuck is going on," said Mac. "And I said, hands in the air."

Sam ignored Mac's commands and kept advancing. "Run!" Sam shouted, lunging and toppling both guards to the floor. Maya took her mother's arm, and the family ran up the stairs without looking back.

Sam was pushed to his side. As the Tellers ran, he watched the stairs shifting, one by one, behind them. Red Beard and Mac attempted to follow but each stair curved in until the spiral staircase transformed into a flat wall.

Blood pooled from Sam's wounds. He crawled across the floor to Alexandra, inch by inch, until he could take her hand into his own. It was then that his body fell limp. Sam released his final breath, and his heart stopped.

TWENTY-TWO

Firsts

I want it back the way it was. I'd rather live blindly in that world than face this nightmare.

—Dr. Stephen Neer, Prisoner 32-0017,
Interview Fragment #241

The Tellers escaped through the East Lobby....

THE family squinted as they adjusted to the early morning sun. Outside, they spotted an empty Institute maintenance vehicle idling. Rebecca gently placed her daughter down in the back seat next to Maya and climbed into the driver's seat. Hannah promptly fell back asleep.

"Let's go, Mom!" Maya insisted.

Rebecca cut the auto-drive and took manual control of the car. She drove around the corner and approached a traffic light. A group of protestors stepped forward in the middle of the intersection and blocked their path.

"What the hell," said Rebecca. "Move!"

"Look out!" Maya yelled as a screaming woman took a swing at the passenger side window with a pole attached to a placard. Maya shielded Hannah as glass fragments rained onto the back seat. "Drive!" Maya told her mother as Rebecca swerved past the crowd. She clipped the curb and sped away.

"Maya, are you okay? Hannah?" Rebecca asked.

"We're okay," Maya answered. "Hannah is still asleep somehow." Maya slouched in her seat, exhaling loudly. Rebecca followed suit, and they drove on in silence.

Traffic came to a standstill on the highway. Straining to see around the cars ahead of her, Rebecca noticed a military-style checkpoint up ahead. She nervously watched as soldiers directed other drivers to the opposite side of the road, which was cordoned off by large armored vehicles.

"Do we have a plan?" Maya asked, eyes locked on the activity in front of them.

"We're just trying to escape the city like everyone else. If they ask, we're headed out to stay with Natalie near Concord."

"And if they don't buy that?"

"Then I have no idea."

As the car ahead of them was waved forward, soldiers spread out to make way for the Tellers' car. The car pulled to a stop, now controlled by the checkpoint's local network. Dogs led handlers up and down the sides as they sniffed for hidden passengers. Maya glanced at Hannah, asleep next to her. A gloved hand knocked on Rebecca's cracked window. The busted glass lowered with the push of an illuminated button on the door panel.

"Something happen to your window, ma'am?" the soldier asked as she examined the remnants of the broken window.

"Crazy people rioting in the city. I'm just trying to get my daughters to safety," Rebecca replied calmly.

"We're on lockdown, ma'am. Only authorized personnel are allowed in or out. PACT ID, please?" she asked.

"Um, sure." Rebecca held out her arm hesitantly. The soldier pulled a slate out of her pocket and scanned Rebecca's PACT ID. Her eyes widened. "I'm going to need you to wait here while I consult my commander."

The soldier turned and marched back to the two large armored trucks that created the checkpoint barricade. Rebecca thought her car might fit between them if only she were able to take control of the vehicle from the checkpoint network.

The soldier returned to her window flanked by an officer. "Ma'am, can you tell me if you are headed to a secure destination?" asked the officer, leaning over and addressing Rebecca at eye level.

"I'm headed to my sister's place," she stammered.

"I am under orders to ensure all VIPs in the city are allowed safe transport to their destinations. We will provide an escort for you, ma'am," the officer said.

"Escort? No, no. We'll be fine."

"Are you sure? Your clearance level requires that I offer assistance. Are you certain you don't want someone to accompany you?"

"I'm positive. Yes."

Taking the slate from his subordinate, the officer punched in a command on the screen and then turned it to Rebecca. The slate awaited her input. "I am going to require your thumbprint. This will serve as affirmation that a military escort was offered and declined by you as you leave our containment zone. Do you understand?"

"I do," she replied, not entirely certain what was going on. Rebecca pressed her thumb down on the scanner. The print was copied, lighting up the border of the slate in green LED lights. The officer tapped the slate a few times before handing it back to the soldier.

"Be careful. It's dangerous out there," said the officer, standing at attention as Rebecca nodded.

Maya brushed broken glass away from the window. "Because it's real safe in here," she scoffed. Rebecca's head whipped around to glare at Maya, who quickly turned to look out the window.

"Thank you," Rebecca said, gaining control of the car. They drove past the checkpoint, and the vehicle was soon speeding ahead.

"So, what now?" Maya asked.

"We stick to the plan," Rebecca said confidently. "We're going to find Natalie."

Maya pulled out Sam's phone and punched in the security code. She found the Camera app was still active. She replayed the last recording.

Price shot Hannah and Sarah, then Maya shot Briggs and Price. The screen flickered and the video playback paused. In the frozen frame, the blue guy walked past Price and Maya and approached the camera. He spoke directly to Maya through the phone.

"Maya, this is only the beginning," he said. "You may rest for a time. Plans are always in motion, but outcomes rarely surprise. Keep your sister close."

The screen flickered once more and resumed playing the video of the earlier events. Maya looked to her mother. "Did you hear that?" she asked.

"Hear what?" Rebecca replied, focusing on the road. Beyond the checkpoint, the car hurtled down the open highway as the sun rose higher in the sky.

"Never mind," Maya said. She replayed the clip and found it altered. Minutes of video showed Maya, her mother, and Henry Price silently staring at nothing. No blue man. No secret message for her. All that remained was the chilling echo of his words. *Keep your sister close.*

▲

The car came to a stop at a large, old farm. A great red barn stood beside a squat house. After an hour of backroad travel, there had been sightings of odd, camouflaged outposts and treehouse-like guard towers along the dirt road that the shopkeeper of MacCauley's Marketplace had detailed.

Dozens of people, each armed with a pistol or rifle, and in some cases, blades and bats, slowly emerged from the house and the barn. Rebecca was the first to exit the vehicle. She looked around at the unfamiliar faces surrounding her car.

"Becca?" said a woman's voice from behind the ring of armed greeters.

Rebecca recognized her sister instantly. "Nat!" she exclaimed in relief.

Natalie ran out from between two larger men carrying shotguns and embraced Rebecca tightly. "You made it! I was so worried. Where are the girls?" she asked, concerned.

"They're fine. They're here too," Rebecca replied, crying into Natalie's shoulder.

Maya climbed out next, holding on tight to her backpack. She glared suspiciously at the group. A man stepped forward from their ranks. He was tall and lean with dark hair. He wore a knee-length gray coat and carried himself with a serious and commanding demeanor.

"You must be Maya," he said in a resonating baritone. "I'm Neil. You won't need those guns here."

"What guns?"

"The guns in your bag. I can see the outline of them," he said, pointing at the lower corner of the bag. "You don't need to worry about your safety here. You're among friends. Come, I imagine you'd like some time to get cleaned up."

Cautiously, Maya relented and handed over the bag. Neil gestured to one of the large men behind him. "This is Edward," he said, leaning around Maya to address Rebecca directly. "With your permission, I'd like to have him take your other daughter somewhere more restful than the back seat of your car."

Rebecca nodded. Neil looked at Edward and nodded at the car. The man quickly scooped Hannah up from the back seat and carried her into the house.

"You're both free to go with her, of course. We're just going to have our doctor look her over is all. Dr. Teller, Maya, if you'd accompany me," he said, heading for the barn.

The two joined him, although Rebecca looked back several times as Hannah was brought inside, Natalie close behind. Once in the barn, they discovered a hive of activity.

The centerpiece was a large table covered in slates and maps of Boston, New England, and the entire United States. Along the walls, caged weapons stations held racks of guns, body armor, drones, and other military equipment. Computer operators lined the upper levels of the structure. People bustled around the building, relaying everything from police and military radio traffic to the status of affairs within Boston.

"You'll have to pardon our appearance right now," Neil said. He rounded the far end of the center table. "Last night's events got out of hand a little quicker than we'd anticipated. There were a number of casualties. It worked out in the end, though. Our man inside was able to get us almost everything we needed."

"Mr. Lee was your man?" Rebecca asked.

"I don't know any Lee. Ours is a man in Institute security. Forwarded us news of your adventure into some high-security areas. Which brings me to my next question, what did you take from them? You had to have come out of there with something useful. Something that will help us destroy The Institute."

Maya's temper flared. "If we had anything, why would we give it to you?"

Neil's laugh dripped with condescension. "We are the

Resistance, though I don't care much for that word. Now, while we give you safe harbor, patch your wounds, feed you, house you, and hide you, let me ask, a bit more politely this time, do you have anything that we might find interesting?"

Maya pulled Sam's phone from her pocket. "This is what you need to take them down. It's all right here." She extended her arm, offering the device freely.

"Excellent," he said, taking it from her hand. He handed it off to a passing militia member and continued, "I'll be sure you get it back when we're done."

Maya watched, annoyed as her evidence was handed off to a stranger and taken away. Her frustration boiled over at the casual air of Neil's expression. Her fist clenched.

"Relax. We're not taking this lightly. First, we'll be backing up and examining everything on that phone. I don't want you to think we don't appreciate what you're providing. I'm glad you're here with us, Maya. Glad you got your sister and mother here, too. We can never have enough doctors around, and the more I keep hearing about the interest Henry Price has in your sister—well, something tells me we're all going to get along smashingly."

"Hey, Neil, is it?" Maya said, glaring impatiently at the man.

"Yes?"

"If you screw us over, I'll kill you myself."

Neil laughed again. "Yes, indeed. If you follow my friend here, he can bring you somewhere to wash up and get some food. When you're refreshed, meet me back here and we'll see what it is that crooked Jacobs has really been up to."

Neil motioned to the men waiting behind him. Maya and Rebecca were escorted into the house where they were treated to showers, fresh clothes, hot meals, and some peace. They visited Hannah, who was awake and alert. Later, they walked over and sat next to a large fire where Neil and the leaders of the Resistance were in the middle of a heated discussion.

"They outgunned us. Plain and simple. There's got to be another way to take them down," said one.

"We should have blown the whole place up. If you had just listened to me the first time," said another.

"That would have made things worse."

"Like they won't be coming for us now, anyway."

"There's going to be chaos."

"There's going to be war, and we need a real army."

Maya shouted over the noise. "Hey! You don't even know what you're looking for!" The group went silent. "Something terrible is happening at The Institute, and you're too busy getting people killed in the streets."

"How dare you come here and talk to us like that!" a man yelled at her.

"We need to expose everything," Maya pivoted. "We need to show the world what they really are."

"That The Institute has tyrannized and oppressed people for decades?" the man asked sarcastically. "I think we got the memo, little girl."

Maya's face turned red, her hands balling into fists. Rebecca stuck an arm out in front of her to keep her back as the man rose from his seat. Neil put himself between Maya and the group. "Enough! We have a common goal here."

Maya nodded, putting her hands down as the man returned to his seat.

"Let us understand each other," Neil said. "This Resistance formed up after the Bombing. I was just a kid then." Neil stared into the fire before continuing. He told the story from the beginning. A professor by the name of Gardner was the first to feel the wrath of The Institute after it assumed so much in the wake of Jacobs's proclamation. He spoke to his classes about the dangers of certainty and how, even with their tangible proof, The Institute and their allies in government needed to be challenged. Gardner did not intend to be a revolutionary, but his students posted his lectures online, to reach a greater audience.

The Institute was new and they had something to prove. Public dissent was unacceptable. Gardner lost his job when his reputation was ruined by countless accusations of fraud and abuse.

Every day, Professor Gardner woke to find himself the target of another threat, another smear campaign, or worse, for challenging The Institute's authority. Soon, the only thing left for him was posting online, but even that was just too much for The Institute.

Neil stood and addressed the group. "They broke into his house and shot him in his sleep. He was our first martyr. A man whose greatest crime was skepticism. The first of us were his students. With most of my cards now on the table, I'm forced to ask, what is your story, Tellers?"

Rebecca and Maya recounted their experience, struggling to find the words to describe the events beneath the shrine. Maya did withhold some details, including the message she had gotten on the highway. Neil sighed once or twice, but said nothing for a while, contemplating their extraordinary account.

"What was he, then?" he asked at last, stroking his chin.

"I have no idea. Something important," Rebecca said.

Neil rattled off a series of questions. "A blue man who disappears after saving your daughter and was the nexus of that whole room? Was the blue a side effect of being kept alive for decades by the pods? Or some sort of injected material?"

"How do you expect us to believe any of this?" a skeptical voice rang out from the group.

Rebecca faced the young woman and noted a long scar that ran across the side of her face. "What's your name?" she asked gently.

"Skye," the woman responded.

"Listen, Skye, I'm not going to pretend I understand any of

this," Rebecca said. "All I can tell you is what I think I saw. As for the rest, you'll have to—"

"What?" Skye interrupted. "Trust you?"

"Have a little faith." Rebecca smiled at the irony.

Skye started to respond, but Neil cleared his throat and interrupted to address everyone gathered. "Well, I have absolutely no idea what to make of all this. That video recording shows that something happened under The Institute, but no sign of a blue man. Nevertheless, The Institute is out to get the Tellers. They'll be running drone PACT scans coast to coast. We can keep the Tellers hidden here for a while, but we'll need to move them out eventually for everyone's safety."

"As long as you can keep my sister safe from The Institute, I'm with you," Maya said.

Neil pulled three bracelets from his pocket. He handed them to Rebecca. "These are your new identities. Won't be enough, but it's a start."

"What's this?" Rebecca asked.

"The bracelet will mask your PACT ID and register you all with different names. When we have more time and resources, we'll see about a more permanent solution."

Maya grabbed a bracelet from her mother. "What names?"

"Sheridan," Neil announced. "You're Mia Sheridan, Hannah is Katie Sheridan, and Rebecca is Alice Sheridan."

Maya rolled her eyes. "Really? Mia? Not exactly a big stretch from Maya. Which one of you smart cowboys concocted such a brilliant plan?"

"They were a real family. The closest match we could find on such short notice," Neil said. "Nothing in their background will warrant a second look."

Neil sat back down. "The government, police, military, that's all Institute property now. But you've hurt them. If what you tell me is accurate, their true source of power is gone. Which makes them more dangerous now."

▲

A transmission was sent from a nearby car—just a verbal cue and a short, coded sentence.

"The family's in play," said the informant. "I have eyes on the girl."

A stoic voice with a slight Nigerian accent spoke through the comm unit. "Sit tight. She may be our only hope."

The line went dead.

▲

The heavy steel door opened, and blinding light poured into Vova's and Dmitri's eyes. The two men squinted and stared at the doorway, observing the tall, broad figure that stood silhouetted against the darkness. He spoke in a low and angry tone.

"My friends, how is it that you ended up here? I thought the simple task of keeping others in here and yourselves out there would have been easy enough," the shadow said.

"Things got complicated with the doctor you sent and the last subject we took," Vova replied, straining to see through his swollen eye.

"I sent no such doctor," the shadow spat back. "And furthermore, you let the mother and the sister of a high-value target slip right past your meaty little fingers. That prize might have been the key to my own ascent at The Institute."

"Dr. Reed, I'm really sorry."

"Your apologies are irrelevant. I'm told we have a lead on their whereabouts. A trap is being set for them, but it may distract me for a time," Sebastian said from the doorway, holding up a slate. "But we can resume our efforts at a new location. May I assume they did not make it to the lower level? Is my current project still intact?"

Vova sulked as he shrugged. "I don't know, I've been locked in—"

Sebastian cut him off a second time as he slammed the door. Part of him considered leaving the two men, failures as they were, in the dark until they died. Assigning cleanup duty to their replacements would set a good example to new hires about the dangers of failure or dereliction. He reconsidered, reflecting on the words of his childhood pastor, and decided that he would at least not kill these two. Despite their failure, they did remain loyal and would perhaps be of use after all. It was always such a hassle to bring others up to speed. Sebastian sneered at the ineptitude he was forced to forgive. He locked the door once more and struck the cold metal with his fist.

Sebastian shouted, "And you'll remain locked in there until I feel that you've learned the value of my trust and the dangers that come with breaking it!"

Walking to the end of the hall, Sebastian produced a second set of keys from his pocket and opened the one other locked door. He briskly descended a stone stairwell. He walked deep into the underbelly of the structure until he arrived at a final doorway. Unlocking it, he paused in the small arched columns that surrounded his prize.

Deep below the city was a steel table mounted on top of a concrete slab. The decorative stonework arches of a long-forgotten public transit project surrounded it. A woman lay there under heavy anesthetic. All along her body, tubes and conduits of various kinds were mounted in her skin. Her mouth was held wide open by metal hooks.

Sebastian studied his experiment. A small part of him pleaded for her forgiveness. There would need to be recompense for what he had lost. A new lab with new subjects and, if they failed again, a new staff in the days to come.

Whatever it took, Sebastian would ensure his mother's

sacrifice would not be in vain. He would find a way for all mankind to ascend. One way or another.

◬

A few weeks later, Maritz walked briskly down the hallway of an accounting firm in an abandoned office park. Only a few emergency lights still functioned. Paper, boxes, and old computers were strewn about the corridor. He stood patiently in front of a large door and considered recent events.

The world was still coming to terms with the news of Jacobs's unexpected death due to a heart attack, no doubt triggered by the stress of his daughter's passing. Price had recovered from his wounds and successfully cleaned up the mess at The Institute. Price's teams had suppressed the protests, and various agitators were rounded up, deflating the demonstrations. Life around The Institute was returning to normal.

Maritz knew that peace would be short-lived. Price's ambitions had gotten him the mantle of The Institute, but with the alien missing, the Corpus could no longer transmit a signal to the Viewing Rooms around the world. Maritz questioned how long Price could maintain the lie. How much more dangerous would Price become in his quest to find a replacement for the Corpus's centerpiece? Fidelity to the status quo was needed now more than ever, or else disaster would befall them all.

The door finally swung open. Straightening his clothes, Maritz walked down a flight of stairs and into a large, pitch-black warehouse. He moved carefully to the center of the room and waited with his head bowed. His eyes darted along the cracks of the cement floor as a single light switched on a few feet away.

"I received your signal," Maritz spoke guardedly into the darkness. He raised his head and squinted at the light. He could only make out a hint of the shape of the three aliens that had summoned him.

The blue light intensified, turning everything white and nearly burning Maritz's eyes. When the light finally dulled, Ûran'Elakh took shape in human form as Frederic Sorensen. He stepped forward, flanked by his alien associates, who stayed hidden in the shadows. Ûran'Elakh towered over Maritz, his arms stiff at his side. The color of his eyes darkened until they turned black. Maritz had spent decades juggling The Institute, the Resistance, and the aliens, all in the hope of finding a way to protect humanity. But now, he was at the mercy of the aliens' wrath for keeping one of their own in captivity.

"How may I serve you?" he inquired. Praying to God for strength in front of these godless creatures, Maritz bowed.

After all, in the End, they were the Ascendants.

THE END

▲

EPILOGUE

Nål'Elakh re-formed beneath the crumbling radar tower at Camp Hero, Montauk, New York....

HE stood motionless in the abandoned structure, contemplating his next move. Three million years had passed since the Elakh first faced extinction. In just half a million more years, their homeworld—a planet of deep oceans, thick forests, and abundant natural resources—would be forever changed. Orbital decay doomed their world to a future of extremes. This gradual inward spiral would push the planet closer to its star, slowing its rotation until tidal lock took hold. One hemisphere would be plunged into freezing darkness, while the other would blister under the fury of their red dwarf star.

The Elakh could live for centuries. Their debates lasted even longer. Entire generations were spent arguing solutions. Many contended that their technology and ability to harness the power of their sun would enable them to survive and flourish underground. Others proposed redesigning their genome, adapting their physiology to endure life under the extreme conditions. A third faction sought to scatter their people among the stars in a galactic migration that, at relativistic speeds, could take as little as 733,000 years.

As hope for unanimity waned, the youngest chose a path once forbidden: the Singularity. Ages ago, the Elakh had rejected artificial consciousness and adopted the First Consensus, forbidding the creation of comprehensive neural matrices and strictly regulating autonomous technology. But the existential threat broke the unity. A splinter group began developing neural substrate transfer technology in secret to capture complete consciousness patterns within quantum storage networks. These preserved minds could inhabit engineered biological vessels when physical form was needed or exist purely within their ship's networks. The transformation would allow them to transcend the limitations of flesh while maintaining continuity of consciousness.

When that group fled deep into space, they forged biological shells to interact with the physical world when needed, but most dwelled within the network housed on their ship. As time passed and no new home was found, despair spread like a virus through the shared consciousness.

In the midst of that despair, the Elakh discovered the planet Earth. True to their nature, they studied humanity for millennia while debating the best course of action. Seven envoys were chosen to study the humans up close. They discovered that humans were a confusing mixture of ideas and passions. Primitive. Bold.

The envoys spread across the globe, operating in secret, each tasked with gaining a foothold in Earth's political, social, and military institutions. Nål'Elakh eventually claimed the internet as his domain, existing solely in human digital realms. Then came slate devices. Through them, the Elakh gained in-depth access to the confidential, even intimate knowledge of the world's population. They found useful tools, including the work of Stephen Oliver, and later, The Jacobs Institute. Ûran'Elakh was particularly successful at manipulating The Institute's development through Morgen-Sinn.

But then Tûn'Elakh disappeared.

Panic spread among the Elakh as human incursions flooded their collective network. The humans called it Ascension, but it was a violent breach of the Elakh's consciousness. That they had failed to trace their missing envoy or stop the incursions of The Jacobs Institute was alarming. Ûran'Elakh was persuasive and the Elakh's decision came quickly, faster than any in their long history: contain and control the threat. If containment failed, subjugation would easily follow by accelerating humanity into its own Singularity under the Elakh's control.

Ûran'Elakh's tactics were merciless. Nål'Elakh had studied humans long enough to understand them. Though they were flawed, they were not to be feared. They needed guidance. He pitied them.

Nål'Elakh had tried many times before to reach out to the humans, including one named Samuel Lee. Nål'Elakh showed him what time would allow: the Elakh's migration, their slow surrender to the void, and their arrival. He believed an understanding between their kinds might still be possible, even though the humans were so impatient. So unwilling to take the time to learn.

There was nothing Nål'Elakh could do to convince the others of a different path. When the Elakh learned the truth that The Institute had imprisoned and killed Tûn'Elakh, the so-called First Ascendant, the fate of humanity was sealed. The Elakh would accelerate the creation of the human network and control would be achieved through an evolution of the PACT bots. The humans would be pacified. The Elakh were coming home.

ACKNOWLEDGMENTS

This book took forever. If you were involved in any way, you already know that. If you weren't—hi, I'm Don, and apparently I thought this was a good idea.

I'm deeply grateful to everyone who stayed on the *Ascendants* ride with me for so long. There will be no refunds.

To my friends and family, thank you for your patience, above all. This is your reward. Please pretend to enjoy it.

To Nick Goroff, you recognized the shape of this story long before I could articulate it. Your persistence is impressive. Possibly concerning.

To Morgan Kleinberg, you turned chaos into clarity, kept the narrative threads from unraveling, and always managed to fix it. *Always Ascend.*

To everyone at Charles River Media, thank you for looking the other way. I couldn't have pulled this off without your strategic inattention.

A thank-you as well to J. Michael Straczynski, whose work reminds us that storytelling, at its best, is both a gift and a weapon. He once told a room full of young creators that waiting gets you nowhere, and no one else will tell your story. That stuck with me. And it ate up my twenties. And thirties. And forties.

To the entire team at GFB, Girl Friday Productions, and Kevin Anderson & Associates: Thank you for the thoughtful counsel, the patient ego management, and for banishing my misplaced commas to eternal damnation.

And to the cast, crew, and supporters of *The Ascendants Anthology*, your creative energy and tireless work breathed life into this universe and gave birth to something far weirder than I suspect any of you realized. You have only yourselves to blame.

Thanks to all of you. This was a team effort. Any errors are obviously someone else's fault.

ABOUT THE AUTHOR

Don Schechter is the founder and CEO of Charles River Media, as well as a filmmaker and professor of the practice at Tufts University, where he teaches courses ranging from filmmaking to the art and business of media campaigns. He is the cohost of *No Win Scenario*, a science fiction podcast featuring interviews with genre creators. *Ascendants* is his debut novel. Born in Queens, New York, he now lives in Newton, Massachusetts.

www.ingramcontent.com/pod-product-compliance
Lightning Source LLC
LaVergne TN
LVHW040041080526
838202LV00045B/3436